Three Cedar Road

By

Jean DeGarmo

Chapter 1

Jon waited for Mae at his house on Three Cedar Road. He tried to avoid her, but she called earlier that morning and asked if he would meet her. Because he said yes instead of no, he spent the day worrying: *she wants something from me, something I can't deliver.*

He wished he hadn't answered the phone.

He wished he'd never met her.

But he stayed put, wondering what she wanted to talk to him about as he picked out the tools to repair a leak in the kitchen sink. He drank coffee. He put another log in the woodstove.

And he knew, no matter what happened, he could *not* let himself get too close to her. He decided long ago that his father, Elbert, was the only dependable force in his life. Elbert understood Jon wanted to stay single and live alone until the day he died.

Far from dying, Jon had a feeling this *meeting* would turn out to be a waste of time. He would tell her again to keep away from George Coulter; or maybe he wouldn't bother; maybe he'd encourage her to let Coulter mistreat her. Use her. Change her nature from strong to weak.

She probably needs money, he thought.

Or, more than likely, she would ask him to find the people responsible for dumping toxic waste at the Coulter Logging sites. She already told him that George is involved. Jon had worked with George long enough to know he was loud and unpredictable. He was dangerous and deranged.

Jon couldn't understand why Mae would want to be with a man like George anyway. She was either trapped or she was stupid.

Trapped himself since his mid-twenties, Jon's life consisted of cutting down trees during the day and working on his house at night. He had no social desires, and no time for travel or romance. Day after day, he dealt with people like George Coulter, George's brother Reese, and their father, Lucas. He learned long ago to ignore dysfunctional personalities. He focused on his work: the grueling, sweaty, push-it-to the-limit physical labor he had come to expect. Forget the difficult people.

His goal was to finish his two-story house. The house would eventually have five rooms, including the kitchen, a bedroom downstairs, two upstairs, a living room, an attic, and a screened-in front porch. Next, he would build a large pole barn, a two-car garage, and three sheds. The project might go on for the rest of his life. Or he might abandon it entirely.

For now, he focused on the pipes beneath the sink. Where's the leak? *Mae will ask him, where's the leak in the logging crew? The men you work with; who is dumping chemicals from the Conrad Paper Mill?*

The scent of varnish and wood smoke on this chilly September night made him drowsy. He looked around the kitchen, proud of the work he had done so far.

He lived behind Elbert's house in a two-room hunting cabin. The house he was building was on a forty-acre plot of land next door to Elbert's on Three Cedar Road.

He was thirty-eight years old. He had friends, namely Dale Washburn, who was sixty-two, and his father, Elbert, who was seventy-one. He had female companionship as well, but he was always careful to make those encounters brief.

The wood smoke was heady and hot, because he had put too much dead elm into the stove in the living room. Too strong, almost intoxicating…until it was replaced with her cologne: half citrus, half ether.

Who is she to just walk up the front porch and through my kitchen door?

Who was she to invade his life, little by little. She had chosen him, of all people, to confide in? As if he was a *friend.* A brother.

She said, "I'm here."

"And you're late," he pointed out. He noticed the way her pastel-colored clothes accented the drywall behind her like a melting watercolor —a series of purple and yellow lights shimmering off her skin.

He looked at her, still. She was a fever. Slow burning.

She was slightly muscular for a woman; full-figured but only five foot three. She was also flighty. He had never, *ever* in his life liked flighty people. Her movements, from rapid hand gestures to darting eyes, made him wonder if she were high or drunk.

"So?" he said. "What do you want?"

"The chemical dumping." There was a tone of anger in her voice, as if she was tired of repeating herself. "What I told you before. Someone in your crew is dumping excess dioxins from the Conrad Paper Mill."

"I'll tell you one more time," he said. "I'm too busy."

"But you said you'd look around," she insisted. "You and Dale."

She wore blue jeans and a lavender sweater. Her shoulder-length blonde hair was fastened to the back of her head with a silver barrette. She had on red lipstick that he didn't like, and there were too many rings on her fingers.

She said in a softer voice, "You promised me." Then she walked right up to him. "We already know that Coulter Logging's unloading chemicals for the Conrad Mill. And the last time we talked, you said you and Dale would find out who and where."

Jon knelt down to tighten the elbow pipe beneath the sink. Using a wrench to adjust the bolt, he twisted once, twice. He stood up to inspect his work.

He wasn't a plumber by any means; he referred to manuals, three in fact. He wasn't a carpenter, either. It had taken him two years to build the kitchen and living room. He even had help along the way: a friend who owned a building company, and his co-worker, Dale Washburn. Along with Elbert, who before he retired, worked independently in drywall and masonry.

Jon felt the heat of her breath on the back of his neck.

He turned to look into her eyes. He had never seen eyes like hers: specks of blue rushing through oval clouds.

"I work. I get a paycheck," he summed up irritably. "I don't have time to play detective. For *you* or anyone else."

He couldn't believe she scowled at him.

"You're wasting your life," she said. As if she knew his aspirations, his capabilities. "You should take Clara Halverson up on her offer!"

"Who told you about that?"

"Clara herself told me."

He wondered why she was wearing diamond earrings, and did she get the dimples near the corners of her mouth from her mother or her father? He didn't know much about her, other than she was a teller where he did his banking. Her parents were dead; she had been living with George for several months. She had an older sister named Paula who lived on the family farm.

"Back when she was staying with your dad," Mae explained. "They came to the bank so she could set up a checking account. Remember?"

"Why would I remember *that?*"

"I don't know. I thought maybe your dad told you."

He knew Mae worked at the Credit Union in Tennick. She had an associate's degree in business management, another in biology, and she claimed the bank job was temporary. Her interest in biology was a crucial part of her environmental studies.

Jon inspected the turn of the elbow pipe. He had finished the task several minutes ago, but pretended to continue working, hoping she would get the picture and leave.

"She made you the executor of her estate."

"That's crazy," he said. "I told her I didn't want any part of her *estate.*"

Mae shrugged. "She doesn't have any heirs, and she thinks you're an upstanding man. Are you?" she asked, pacing near the refrigerator he had recently installed. She inspected the maple cabinets, the matching table, the counter space, and the brand-new stove and refrigerator, both beige in color. "This is coming along nicely. When are you moving in?"

"Not any time soon," he said.

"Before winter, I hope."

When she mentioned winter, he wanted to tell her where he chose to live was none of her business. Even more than flighty people, he didn't like nosy people. There was something about her he didn't trust, and there was an attraction towards her he couldn't deny.

Ignoring her curiosity, he said, "I have to get up early tomorrow."

She was sitting on a stepladder, her legs stretched out. She wore brown leather boots with heels, he noticed, and her hands were folded together in her lap. Suddenly, she smiled. He wasn't sure what to make of her mood shifts. Or of her, overall.

She said, "Clara's rich, Jon. You could start your own logging company. Do things ethically."

"Oh, really?" He turned to look at her. He was thinking how naive she is; how out of the loop when it came to the timber industry and the dangers of exposing men like Lucas Coulter. Never mind his sons, George and Reese. And never mind their paper mill connections, the EPA, and the local law enforcement, all paid to look the other way.

"I can't help you," he said again.

"Can't or won't?" she asked, standing up and moving through the kitchen. She opened the door to a spray of porch lights, a lamp at both ends of the overhanging roof. "Why is this road named Three Cedar?"

"The three big cedar trees at the beginning of the road," he said. "They were here before the road was built."

"I see," she said, but she didn't. "One more thing. Melanie McMasters. She's Lloyd's wife. I think George is seeing her, using her to blackmail Lloyd at the mill."

"And yet you're living with him." It wasn't a question.

"As soon as I get more information about the chemicals, I'm moving out of his house. I *will* miss his house," she admitted and walked down the front steps.

He knew all about George's three-story log house. It was elaborate, too expensive, and didn't seem suitable for a degenerate like George.

He noticed Mae's blue jeep was parked next to his black pickup truck. He watched her climb into the jeep. She pulled the door shut and rolled down the window. "Go to Marquette and get your money," she told him. "The lawyer said you won't answer his letters or his phone calls."

"You seem to know my business." He could feel the night air turn colder by the minute. He put his hands against the porch railing, leaned there, and watched her.

"You'd be surprised at what I know," she said, and drove away.

CHAPTER 2

An hour after Mae left Three Cedar Road, it started to rain. Jon stayed at the house overnight. He had the woodstove going, and it was cozy and warm. But he didn't have any furniture in the bedrooms, so he slept on the couch in the living room.

He hoped things were all right at his cabin, a mile behind Elbert's house. He kept all of his valuables there. As soon as he finished the upstairs bathroom, he would move more of his belongings— clothes and so on—to his new house. All night long, he listened to the rain tap against the roof of his house. *His* house; something he had saved for and created. He tried to make it unique, with cubby-hole storage closets and shelves, a pantry off the right of the kitchen, and a bedroom to the left.

He jotted down notes on a tablet he kept on the table next to the couch.

He woke up at six thirty the next morning. He had only slept for three hours and was wearing yesterday's clothes. Note: finish the laundry room as soon as possible. That way, he would not have to rely on Elbert's laundry facilities.

After he completed the bedroom, the upstairs bathroom needed attention, and the downstairs bathroom off the bedroom was only framed in. Until one of the bathrooms was finished, he would have to rely on Elbert's shower and toilet.

On the note pad, he wrote: Complete bathroom first. Finish laundry room next. Then buy furniture for the bedrooms. At least for the downstairs bedroom, where he had already decided he would sleep.

He wasn't sure why he needed three bedrooms upstairs other than he could use one for storage, another for a study, and the third as a guest room.

His work gear was packed in his truck. He would wear the same outfit he wore the day before. The same clothes he had slept in: brown workpants, black t-shirt, gray-and-black flannel shirt. He went into the bathroom next to the downstairs bedroom. There was a square mirror on the white-painted area above the vanity sink. He noticed that a lot of gray had blended in with his black hair and the whiskers on his face.

He definitely needed a shave.

But he didn't have time to stop at Elbert's for breakfast, let alone shave, or change his clothes. For the first time in years, he was going to be late for work.

September's chill suggested color changes: the leaves turning yellow and orange. Everything outside was damp, thanks to the rain the night before, leaving a mist hovering over the bushes and in the cedars throughout the yard. It was still sprinkling but far from muggy.

He got into his truck, wanting coffee. Note: Hurry up with the plumbing. Turn on the water. There was definitely no time left to stop at Elbert's. Too bad, because Elbert was a great cook. He learned to cook when Jon was five years old and his mother left them. Elbert cooked. He cleaned. He had worked hard as an independent contractor. One could never tag Elbert as idle.

As Jon drove down Three Cedar Road towards Highway 41, he passed Elbert's yellow house. Elbert's beagle mix, Beau, was sitting near the steps waiting to be let back inside.

"Beau-regard," he said, and saluted.

• • •

Most of the time at work, Jon wore leg chaps over his pants. It was the smart thing to do, and he always wore steel-toed boots. Over the years, he had learned that working in the woods was a struggle against insects, fallen trees, and scattered branches. And, he had learned that weather factors were equally important: the fall rain, spring thaw, mud slides, electrical storms, and of course ice, sleet and hail.

But he knew how to cope. For one thing, he knew when certain environmental infractions were going on around him, it was easier to look the other way.

• • •

Later that afternoon the heat settled against the damp ground bringing about a sluggish barrage of insects. Jon saw a swarm of bugs—a hybrid of orange and black beetle—floating above a cluster of tag alders. They were stuck for several seconds and finally pushed their way through the balsam and cedar branches.

Something stung his kneecap beneath his jeans, probably a bee or a mosquito. The heat, the bug bites. All the sweating. Truthfully, he would rather deal with snow.

He wore a hard hat and adjusted the face guard as the insects clicked around him. He checked the diameter and lean of a birch tree, moved his chainsaw to a precise angle to make the undercut, and removed the quarter-inch wedged piece of the trunk.

He made the cut on the opposite side. The tree fell to the ground with a loud crash. He then de-limbed, measured, and cut the tree into pre-marked lengths. Fighting to stay alert and focused, he considered the terrain and studied the details: the ground conditions, the position of his feet, the size and lean of the tree. He learned as a teenager that particularly when the woods seemed harmonious, there most likely lurked an ambush.

Ambushed. By the late afternoon humidity as the whine of the saws and the clanking of machinery ceased to the echo of a blue jay's squawk. Jon walked up a ridge of rocks and thistles and lowered his saw into the back of his four-wheel-drive truck.

He watched the skidder operator, Dale Washburn, approach. Dale was tall in stature and short on stamina. He swaggered in and out of the pines and along a churned-up road. "Hey," Jon said by way of a greeting. "We're running out of daylight." Meaning, *we're running out of time; am I the only one who sees it?*

"It's hot for late September," Dale said, blinking. He rarely wore eye protection and he was partially deaf in his left ear, making it difficult to absorb certain words. "Maybe I'll move farther north," he added dismally. "Alaska. Canada?"

No doubt he's a bit warm, thought Jon.

Dale had on a light blue T-shirt beneath a gray flannel shirt with the sleeves buttoned at the wrist. He wore the usual work pants, socks, and steel-toed boots. When Jon watched him take off his hard hat and push a bent finger across his forehead, he knew Dale would stare into the midday sun. No eye protection, whatsoever.

"Before you head north," Jon said, "walk back to the river with me and help me figure out where George and Reese are burying the chemicals."

Dale grabbed a handkerchief from his back pocket and wiped his sunburned neck. "You think they're that stupid to bury it at the work sites?" he asked, turning irritable.

Jon already knew the Coulters were dumping excess chemicals. "You say they were nosing around the Whitewater?" Dale prodded. "You heard about it from that woman, I'll bet."

"Her name's Mae," Jon reminded him. "She thinks George is dumping chemicals for Conrad. I told you this days ago. And I think I know where."

Dale slid his tongue over his crooked teeth; he scowled so hard his eyebrows touched. "Now I suppose you want to catch 'em in the act, hey?"

"Not necessarily," Jon said. "Maybe follow them awhile." He brushed a branch aside and walked down the trail, meditating and listening at the same time. When he turned right, down another trail, Dale followed. Jon stopped every few feet to listen. "Someone's around," he said. "Look for tracks."

They walked up a ridge, following bulldozer tracks, and turned on a shortcut down a deer trail to one of the places where he suspected George and Reese were disposing the barrels.

As they stepped through barren raspberry bushes and withered burdocks, Jon thought about the streams and the deplorable act of driving machinery across them.

Anger pounded his chest as he imagined cutting too close to a river, pond, or any body of water. He envisioned pools of dioxins and gasoline and shards of paint, bubbles of grease and oil … all elements contaminating the streams, rivers, and eventually the Great Lakes.

He thought of Lake Superior. And of brook trout and rainbow, crawfish, minnows—aquatic life choked within the bed of the river. He saw human interference in the form of discarded metals, tires, beer cans, scraps of appliances, the wheel of a bike, the muffler off a car. Man-made trash clogging the ecosystem: the air, the ground, the spirits.

Yet he had stood by, knowing Coulter Logging took measures to cut costs. He had known this for years as an employee, but he looked the other way.

Today he could not. Mae came to his house, up his porch steps, and through his kitchen door, forcing him to acknowledge the facts. The unpardonable abuse happening right and left and all around him.

And so, this awareness had taken over his conscience. And somehow stayed there. All thanks to her.

He concentrated, his forefinger stroking his chin. He stopped walking. "Go to the right," he said. "by the old well casing," more to himself than to Dale, who listened with his eyes because his damaged ear would not let him.

The abandoned well casing revealed they were standing on the site of an old homestead, a foundation of brick and rock; evidence of the past. Perhaps a house or office belonging to a company from back in the logging boom of the late 1880s into the 1900s, when most of the timber— primarily white pine—had been cleared off in the Upper Peninsula. The old railroad grade was a sign; the location too close to the Whitewater River, making Jon shudder and wish he had a camera.

Dale stooped over as he followed Jon. He pulled a pair of sunglasses from his shirt pocket and covered his eyes, discreetly, methodically. The morning sun was too bright; apparently, any kind of light, Jon noticed, was too bright for Dale these days.

Jon motioned for Dale to go first on the trail, while he, Jon, went to the right, looking for tracks, both human and mechanical. As he walked onward, he worried that Dale, who had put in nearly thirty years as a skidder and bulldozer operator and could maneuver any machinery equated with the industry, was showing his sixty-two years.

Not only that, but his breathing, snagged in his throat, meant that the heat, and probably the walk itself, stressed him in a way Jon could not identify with.

"They dumped by the river," Dale said to a thicket of brambles. "That's illegal and fucking stupid."

But nothing new, Jon was thinking, although he didn't have to say it. It was enough that Dale agreed with him. This was the second time Jon heard distress in Dale's voice. The first time was when Dale spoke to him about Carolyn Coulter, Lucas's deceased wife.

Jon had met Dale eleven years ago through Elbert. Elbert, Lucas, and Dale went to the same school, but Elbert and Lucas both dropped out after the sixth grade. For several years, Elbert worked for Lucas, but when Lucas's business faltered, Elbert quit to do carpentry and construction work. Dale stayed with Lucas and met Jon when Jon signed on as a piece cutter at the age of twenty-five. Approximately a year and a half later, Lucas's logging company had prospered.

And Jon knew why. Lucas Coulter might not be solely responsible for the unethical tactics of his employees, but he ignored when his sons cut over surveyed boundaries. He closed his eyes when they added pulpwood to the hardwood logs to enlarge the stacks, altered reports, dumped contaminates at logging sites, left trails covered with slash, and tossed remnants of litter behind. Now they were dumping excess chemicals for Conrad Mill, and if Lucas knew about it, he was exceptional at pretending he didn't.

• • •

They continued walking through the woods towards the pounding roar of the river, just as they moved onward from the present year:1993—towards the new millennium. Jon hoped Dale could keep up with modernization. He noticed again that Dale struggled as they followed a set of tire tracks to the river. There was no question that the tracks belonged to George Coulter's three-quarter-ton diesel truck.

Dale pressed a hand against the trunk of a white birch and watched as Jon knelt down for a closer look. Touching the dirt, Jon traced the imprint of trailer wheels; apparently George had pulled a trailer behind the truck to transport the barrels. "Ah, look here," he said. He showed Dale the butt of a mentholated cigarette, the same brand George Coulter smoked.

Jon stood up and walked around a group of popple trees, what was left of their leaves quaking. He pushed the leaves and twigs away from a suspicious-looking circle with the side of his boot. He could tell, just by studying the soil eruption, that George and Reese had dug a couple large holes, shoved the barrels inside, and tossed dirt over the areas.

It was at this exact moment Jon understood he was working for a man who didn't care about the repercussions of his profession. Who didn't care about the desecration of water tables, bird and plant life, altering essential air and land systems, impairing natural regeneration, and tampering with environmental sequences.

Dale said, "Listen." Jon knew if Dale heard something, handicaps included, then it was so. And then Jon heard it also—a subtle beat of sorts, footsteps maybe, but more like robotic limbs supporting human mobility.

"Let's go back to the road," Jon said. "Move slow."

Once they were back on the trail leading to the road where they left their trucks, Jon told Dale he thought they might be followed by the environmental terrorists he had heard about. Dale asked, "Here, in *our* woods?"

"Yes, environmental fanatics," Jon elaborated. He knew Dale didn't watch much television, and he wasn't good at picking up on gossip. Jon attempted to relay the facts. "A group of fanatics is going around blowing up equipment and blocking roads to the mills. Maybe they found out about George and Reese."

As soon as Jon said *Reese*, Coulter's mechanic, Tom Foster, stepped out of nowhere and stood in front of them. "I've been looking for you two," he said from behind a cloud of cigarette smoke. "Lucas said to meet him at his place."

Jon waited for the smoke to clear. He wanted to see Foster for exactly who he was. At least physically. Jon was good at studying facial expressions, eye movements, and hand coordination—to separate fraudulent intention from sincerity. But for the first time ever, he studied Tom's sunken cheeks, and a face speckled with jagged scabs. And he couldn't tell. Exactly what Tom had meant.

Tom had on a yellow shirt, tan overalls, and his boots were patched with leaves. He picked at his shirt and blinked when he added, "Seen you two walk into the woods. What's up?"

"Nothing's *up*," Jon said, falling silent. Tom was a superior mechanic, and could fix all the machinery. But being superior on the job didn't mean he could ask questions. Or stammer. Or pretend to be uninvolved.

"If not for my wife and kids, I'd quit this job in a heartbeat," Tom went on, smoke crouched among the spruce. "You're lucky to be bachelors, living alone."

When Jon smelled whiskey, he snapped, "Sure, we're lucky."

"Maybe Lucas is planning on giving you two a raise," Tom said with false admiration. "All I know is he's mad and wants to talk to you."

Jon watched Tom flick the burning cigarette to the ground—it was not mentholated, he noted—and it landed a couple feet from where they stood. Jon waited for Tom to stomp it out, but he didn't bother. He merely turned and walked towards his truck.

"Nah, what in *the hell* could Lucas want?" asked Dale, taking off the sunglasses and sliding them back into his shirt pocket. "The last thing I want to do is blab with that fat son of a bitch."

"We'll find out," Jon said.

After Jon ground Tom's cigarette out with the heel of his boot, he reached into his pocket for his keys. He gathered up his tools and put his saw in the back of his truck. "I'll drive," he told Dale. "You do the thinking."

"I'm too tired to think!" Dale yelled and sighed to prove it. "You don't even *need* me, dammit!"

"Oh, I need you," Jon said as he climbed into his truck and started it up. "I need you as a witness."

Chapter 3

Jon drove south on Highway 41, two miles past Kiva, and turned left on a road named Dead Springs, where they would find Lucas Coulter's modular home, and hopefully, Lucas himself.

He turned onto a gravel road lined with aspens, sugar maples, and various shapes of green and blue conifers. He saw Lucas's maroon truck parked by a pole barn. He noticed that there was a line of smoke lifting from the stove pipe of the house.

Dale was snoring next to him in the passenger's seat. *Sleeping. Looking old.*

"Wake up!" Jon shouted.

Dale stirred, lunged forward. "What the hell?" he wondered.

"Nap time's over."

Jon shifted his concentration to the woodpile by the pole barn. There were three rows piled high and lined up according to size and species. He also saw the skeletons of two rusted vehicles behind the shed, one compact-sized sedan on blocks and the other a 1978 Blazer. *It's 1993*, thought Jon. *Get rid of the Blazer and other car parts, Lucas. Clean up your act.*

But he knew chronic laziness when he saw it.

Lucas bragged about his mechanical expertise, although no one ever saw a finished product. There were parts scattered around the yard: engines, tires, pieces of metal. Jon was disgusted with the debris, especially when he noticed a discarded freezer near the back of the property line, the chipped appliance oozing contaminants, assaulting his eyesight as well as his composure.

"What a mess," he said, nudging Dale out of his slumber. Jon condemned Lucas's homestead as a hazardous dumpsite after one glance; a stark contrast to the hallucinogenic beauty of the woods encircling it.

He was so enraged he clenched his fingers before turning off the engine.

He had always prided himself on his ability to control his temper, and knew, if he were to let loose, it would happen in front of Lucas Coulter's face, not out here where only tin cans, car parts, decaying vehicles, plastic scraps, and wheel barrels—all defying a purpose—would serve as proof.

At least he has an impressive woodpile, Jon admitted.

Lucas owned over four hundred acres of land, but this sample of wreckage was all Jon needed to see. The color theme of the buildings—including the modular home that was longer than it was wide and the woodshed to the right of the barn and sauna—was tan with dark brown trim, but all the buildings, especially the house, needed a new coating of paint.

Lucas gave off the impression that he was a workaholic dedicated to his timber company, and apparently, the fantasy allowed him to let his house and surroundings fall to ruin. Also, his wife Carolyn died thirty years ago. Thus, the garden and flower beds were strangled by weeds; hostages to time.

It had been at least a year since Jon set foot on Lucas's property. He had delivered updated insurance papers, but he didn't go inside the house. He stood on the porch and handed the papers to Reese, who in turn gave them to Lucas.

Now upon further inspection, Jon noticed there was a room added onto the back of the structure, no doubt a kit; it was obvious the addition had been slapped together by amateurs, yet the material was of the highest quality. "Huh," Jon said, looking for carpentry flaws.

Dale Washburn sat upward in the seat. "I never noticed we worked for such an ignorant slob," he said, his voice scratchy. "And the conversation coming up will get us nowhere. So, make it quick."

"This is what happens when you close your eyes and plod along to earn a living," Jon said.

He opened the truck door and stepped onto the ground. He was so disgusted with Lucas's property—littered, damaged, scarred—he had trouble speaking. The words were so clotted, he almost choked on them. "Oh well," he mumbled.

His temporary relapse of control required a stroll around the yard before a showdown with Lucas began. He reversed his rage, romanced some self-control. He looked over at a dented barrel used to burn trash. He decided it was too close to the long-needled red pines and turned to say, "Let's do it."

Jon climbed the steps and pounded on the door once, two more times. He was about to hit the door a fourth time when it opened, slapping against the wall to reveal Lucas inside a flurry of flannel and cigar smoke: "Get on in here dammit! I've been waitin' for over an hour!"

Jon and Dale moved through the entryway of Lucas's house and down a hallway to the kitchen, where Lucas had been frying burgers inside a cast-iron skillet. Lucas hurried back to the stove, leaning over it, both arms flapping. He spat: "Stubborn *bitch!*" as if the concoction of sizzling meat was expected to cook itself.

He beat the hamburger patty into submission, turned off the burner, and tossed the potholder into the sink. "Je-sus Christ," he said morosely. "Guess I burnt dinner!"

"Why don't you just order out?" Dale asked as he pulled a chair out and slid into it. He crossed his legs and closed his eyes, signaling for Jon to do all the talking.

But Lucas's laughter interrupted. He wheezed into the stale air. Without warning, he pulled down his suspenders to shed his flannel shirt, exposing a muscle shirt, sleeveless and soiled. His flesh was hairy and splotchy. He opened the refrigerator door to search for a beer.

He handed a bottle out to Jon, who told him *no thanks* and one to Dale, but Dale's eyes were still closed. Dale said, "This place stinks to high hell, Boss."

Lucas popped the lid and guzzled half the bottle before speaking again. "Sit down Lo-sure," he said, his tone raw.

Jon stayed put. He leaned against the counter with his arms crossed, waiting still, and thinking fast.

Lucas made it a habit to pronounce Jon's last name "Lo-sure," although he knew it was pronounced "Lewshay."

"What is it?" Jon asked. "Foster said you wanted to talk to us. So, talk."

Dale shifted inside the chair. He was going to put his elbows against the tabletop for support, but there was jam or orange juice or something equally as sticky stuck to the surface. There wasn't much room for leaning on elbows anyway what with dirty dishes and glasses stacked every which way. "Maid quit or what?" Dale shouted, provoking laughter from Jon.

Jon too felt light-headed thanks to the stench of Lucas's kitchen. He zoomed in on the overflowing trash bag propped against the wall near the back door. He noticed there were boot prints across the buckled linoleum, and he thought he saw a rat skitter from under the refrigerator over to a dark place near the counter.

This man lives in squalor, he decided. *Shame on him to allow it.*

"Sit down Lo-sure, *I said!*" Lucas repeated, his eyes three-quarters shut.

Jon studied Lucas. He inspected his stiff trousers and white T-shirt with stains down the front. There were gray whiskers springing from Lucas's nose and forehead, and there was a tattoo of a naked woman high up on Lucas's left arm. *That* he had noticed from day one.

Jon said, "I'll stand."

"Fine; stand there like a fucking moron," said Lucas. "I got a job for you two and you'll do it, hey? And get yourselves a nice bonus."

As Lucas lowered into the chair across the table from Dale, Jon was taken off guard with the name-calling. Although it shouldn't have been a surprise; Lucas had demeaning nicknames for everyone, especially his sons and most of his employees.

Yet, combined with the litter outside Lucas's house and the scent of rotted fish throughout the hallway, this time the name-calling offended him.

Dale whistled after Jon gave Lucas a thumb's up when in fact he felt like punching his big, foul mouth—in trade for the remark.

But Jon was endowed with patience as well as courtesy, particularly in the face of adversity.

"God*dammit*," Dale pleaded, bored with Jon's composure. "What's this job you want done and how much of a bonus? We got better things to do than sit in this shithouse!"

"Lo-sure," Lucas said, apparently wanting only Jon's attention. "I know you've been watching my boys and I think you got things wrong. If not, then maybe just go on following them and report to me what you find out. I'll pay you both for your trouble."

Jon needed more to go on before a reply could be formed. "And," he prompted.

"Jesus Christ!" Lucas pleaded. "My boys! I think they're up to no good! I think they've been working with Lloyd—my sister's only kid, God rest her soul. Carrying chemicals or some such nonsense. They've been skimming dioxin levels and dumping the excess. I want you to find out when and how they do it!"

Lucas pulled the suspenders back over his shoulders. He waited for Jon to speak. Jon said, "McMasters," and peered into Lucas's eyes. "Conrad Mill?"

Lucas clutched his chest with one hand and drained the bottle of beer with the other. He took his time choosing an answer, as if he wanted to say enough to pique Jon's interest and not a syllable more. "I suspect it," he admitted, slamming the bottle down on the table. "Just check on things for me, if you don't mind!"

Dale glanced up at the ceiling, apparently needing Lucas to acknowledge a distant complaint. "*Damn you*, Dale," Lucas said. "I know what you're brooding about!" He nodded at Carolyn's photograph on the file cabinet, encased in glass and framed in silver. She was nineteen years old when the picture had been taken. Her face radiated youth and hope, but her eyes had faded, as if she lost her way and knew she would never find it again.

"I know all about it, you sentimental bastard!" he added. "I don't want to ever hear no more about it!"

"It's raining," Dale told Jon.

Jon too heard the rain snap against the window above the kitchen sink, strumming the metal roof. *Tap … tap …* oily droplets ….hitting Lucas Coulter's slanted house.

Dale shuddered. Jon couldn't help but wonder about Carolyn Coulter. What happened between them and how did Lucas keep her here all those years?

Dale stood up. "Whatever you think," he said to Jon.

Lucas pulled a worn wallet from his hip pocket and selected two fifty-dollar bills for Jon to take. "Here's a start," he said.

Jon wanted to laugh at the offer. "Keep your money," he said. "We're planning on following them anyway."

"No DNR," Lucas yelled, his face turning red. "You hear me, Lo-sure? No law!"

"Maybe." Jon walked past Lucas and the two fifties. He stopped at the front door. "But I've got this to say: I'm not happy with what I know so far."

Dale Washburn sighed; this time, making light of Lucas, his offer, and his lifestyle in general. He nodded towards Carolyn's photo and turned, putting his face close to Lucas's. "We'll talk about *her* another time," he promised. "You can *count* on it."

He grabbed the two fifties from Lucas's bloated hand and stuffed them inside his shirt pocket. He followed Jon to the top step of the porch.

Jon didn't speak. He was gifted that way too: providing quiet when no amount of talk would help. "I want to hang them out to dry," Dale said as they climbed into Jon's truck. "Take me home, dammit!" Dale added, as if sleep was his only pleasure.

All the way back to Trenary, Dale watched the raindrops slide down the glass. Even when they stopped for three deer to cross the road at the turn off from Highway 41—a sight that normally brought on enthusiasm for the up-and-coming hunting season—Dale was silent.

Jon knew then that Dale had been in love with Lucas Coulter's deceased wife. And he wondered … yes, he truly wondered how it all came to be. How she did she die? So young. So tragic.

He didn't know that Lucas sat alone in his cluttered house, listening to the rain pick up speed. Lucas looked at her picture again. He stood up, but every bone and muscle in his body ached, weighing him down, down, and trying to keep him down for good.

He dialed Lloyd's private number at the Conrad Paper Mill. "Lloyd?" he shouted. "What's that? I'll call whenever the hell I want! You get out here tonight, hear me? I got to talk to you! It's important! Fine, then come tomorrow night, but you'd better do it!" He listened into the phone; it wasn't easy to hear Lloyd over the racket of machinery in the background. Lloyd had warned him to never call at the mill, but time was running out. "Folks are onto you," Lucas hissed. "Get out here by tomorrow night or I'm coming after you!"

Without waiting for Lloyd's response, Lucas hung up. He poured a glass of whiskey. He reached inside his pocket for a cigar, hearing Carolyn say, *Please don't smoke in the house.* He looked at her picture and said, "If you was still alive, none of this would be happening!"

Even as he said it, his words were weightless. George was bad news. With or without his mother. He was trouble, he was evil; and Lucas could sit there all night long, brooding over his dead wife's picture, imagining his life had turned out differently, and it wouldn't change a thing. Like his mother, George was as good as dead.

CHAPTER 4

The following night, Jon talked Dale into going to the Conrad Paper Mill to check out the dioxin filtering allegations. They met at Dale's trailer outside of Tennick and used one of Dale's spare trucks—a red 1984 Ford—to remain undetected since people were used to seeing Dale driving his two-toned green Chevy.

Of course, the idea was to inch up towards the gate where they knew Lloyd worked as the foreman and find out exactly where George and Reese were draining the chemicals. Then follow them to find out where they were dumping the load.

Dale dozed on and off while Jon drove, causing Jon to take note of Dale's deterioration. He wanted Dale to see a doctor, find out if something was physically wrong, or maybe he just needed vitamins to energize his system.

Jon decided this business with Lucas Coulter was too much for Dale, especially now that Lucas's dead wife, Carolyn's, name had been thrown onto the table. The conversation had possibly pushed Dale into a deep depression. Jon knew one thing: it would be wise to proceed with caution.

Just as he knew to drive cautiously through the last of the two back gates of the mill, turn off the headlights, coast down the gravel road, and park behind a concrete structure away from the security lights. He would investigate on foot.

The mill was in full swing with the noise blasphemous against the autumn night. The grinding and clanking of machinery and the diesel trucks driving to and from the area was nerve-racking. Even the hissing of water pumps and the belching of hydraulics contributed to the level of noise amplified by the rain that began when they left Lucas Coulter's road the night before.

Now everything was damp again, causing an echo of banging metal and iron; a screeching of tires, blasts of smoke——vibrating against the chain-link fence and the conifers beyond.

Jon left Dale dozing in the truck. He walked towards one of the generators, after noticing a landfill enshrined within another square of chain-link fencing. He wondered about the chemicals filtering through the ground, so close to the river he could hear the flow of the current.

There was a filtering system; but from what Jon knew about the bleaching process necessary to make the paper white, chlorine was the culprit ingredient. The chlorine was to be rinsed out, processed, and only so much of the excess was allowed into the river. Any amount was too much in Jon's thinking, but there you have it: the necessity for rules, regulations, and the EPA.

In this case, Jon knew that Lloyd McMasters, the night foreman, was helping George and Reese siphon the leftover dioxins into the tank. Next, the substance was drained into barrels, maybe at the remote sites; and last but not least, the barrels were buried to save on the cost of filtering and line their pockets. The big shots. *The fat cats,* as Elbert called people in charge.

Lloyd had hired George and Reese to transport the excess toxic waste into the woods and bury it; quite risky, in Jon's opinion, when inspections were conducted at random.

Jon had known something was going on, yet he remained blind and mute. Now he found himself crouched behind a cement structure in the middle of night. He saw a fuel truck, angled outward from a fence, and assumed this was the truck they used to carry the chemicals. It looked like the truck Jon noticed last week near one of the logging sites; the same tanker on a flatbed that Jon thought he saw Reese driving down Highway 41.

Several more minutes went by before he saw George Coulter step out from behind a gray building, connect a hose to the tank, and run it through a gate into a metallic square box attached to the side of the building. The process went on for about a half hour.

George jerked about with the static movements of a man expecting to get caught. But George Coulter, as Jon knew him to be, was jumpy by nature. Patience was not an adjective suitable to describe him; neither was sensibility.

Jon watched, thinking: *It's just too asinine to believe.* Then again, it was the brainstorm of the Coulters, and their cousin, Lloyd, who up until lately had the reputation as one of Conrad's most valued employees. Although Lloyd had a degree in biology, he worked for Conrad as a machine repair technician and graduated to foreman. However, something had happened to make him desperate enough to gamble away his retirement pension, his marriage, and even his health—for this insidious venture.

At first, the noise from the mill blocked out the conversation between George, Reese, and the mystery source who Jon figured to be Lloyd, even though Jon couldn't see him well because he moved in and out of the shadows. They were all three wearing masks and pulled them down to talk.

Jon crouched behind the dim lights outside the main building. To the right was a temporary landfill. Either the airwaves had shifted, or the noise had changed from deafening to tolerable, because Jon was only able to hear pieces of the conversation.

He had trouble decoding the words until he moved to the right and slouched behind two crates.

The mystery man was nearly as tall as George, who was six foot. He wore a dark blue shirt with the sleeves rolled up to the elbows, and gray pants. He had a thin, jagged moustache over his upper lip, and his hair was a dull brown. Jon wished he had a video camera to record this meeting. For now, he would have to rely on his keen memory and impeccable hearing.

The man peered to the left and then to the right. He pulled out an envelope and shoved it into George's hand. "Listen to me," he said. "Dump this batch at a different location and find another place soon. That goddamned group's in the area. You got to be careful."

George thumbed through the contents, boasting, "They get in my way, they'll meet up with a bullet."

"Don't get stupid!" the man warned, his voice low. He moved a hand down his blemished neck. "Melanie said they have a network in the area. They catch you, it's all over!"

"Not likely," George predicted as he pulled a handkerchief out of his back pocket and stuffed the envelope back into it. He paused to wipe his nose; apparently, the chemicals aggravated his sinuses. "I'll kill the son of a bitch who tries to sneak up on me. And I told you before, cousin, you worry too much. Speaking of Melanie, you ought to keep a tighter rein on her."

Now Jon was certain the man was Lloyd McMasters. George called him "cousin," and he already knew Melanie was the name of Lloyd's wife.

Reese, who was a few inches shorter than George although stockier, snickered over George's comment until his eyes watered. He was in worse shape than George. He wore the same black-and-blue checkered shirt and faded jeans for days on end. His boots were caked with mud, his curly hair was plastered to his skull with gel, and his round face was concealed by a wiry beard.

Reese was forty-two and George was forty; however, Reese had always followed George's lead.

After *getting* the insinuation of his wife's indiscretions, Lloyd shoved George. "You don't *know* her!"

"I don't *know* her?" George asked, touching his chest. "You say I don't *know* your wife?" He laughed again, this time too loud.

Jon shook his head, thinking about George's lack of common sense. He also noticed they weren't wearing gloves to protect their hands; *very stupid.*

"Explain that!" Lloyd demanded. "What are you saying?"

"I don't have to *explain* a damn thing to you!" George said. He started to fold up the long hose. "If you don't know what I'm talking about, then it's probably for the best. Now get out of my way."

Lloyd watched George wrap the hose around the clasps on the side of the fuel truck. George started picking at a callus on his left hand with a knife he had pulled out of nowhere. "What do you know about my wife?" Lloyd persisted. "I want you to explain, hear me? Explain!"

George grabbed him by the throat and placed the tip of the knife to an artery. "Don't *ever* touch me again."

"Hey now," Reese broke in. "Calm down!"

George released Lloyd so quickly Lloyd toppled backwards. "Your wife's not very careful," George added, putting the knife away.

He motioned for Reese to head to the fuel truck, but before he climbed into the front seat he reminded Lloyd, "There'd better be an extra five hundred next time, Cousin. I'll let it go for now, but you said it yourself, things are getting dangerous. So, me and Reese need another boost."

As soon as George got inside the truck and started the engine, Lloyd pressed his hands against the door. "You know we can't filter out too much at a time," he said. "What we dump, we save in cost. That's the way it works and that's why you get paid. You're lucky I agreed to this. I could lose my job. And Christopher; we have to pay him for his part at the DNR end. If not for him, we couldn't pull it off at all!"

"You mean, if not for Christopher being a corrupt DNR biologist. Sure, we got *that* part, dumbass. You just do what I say and get us more cash, or you can dump the chemicals yourself."

"I'll see what I can do. But *You* concentrate on Lucas. Somehow, he found out I'm involved, and he wants to talk to me tomorrow." Lloyd grabbed George's arm and squeezed for emphasis. "Do *you* hear *me?*"

"Old Luke won't be a problem much longer," George said, revving up the vehicle. "Like I told you before, *I'll* deal with him."

George put the truck in reverse and backed out of the paved lot. Jon moved from behind the crates and went back to his truck, where he nudged Dale out of a sound sleep. "Wake up," he said. "They're heading out with the chemicals."

It took Dale a few seconds to register where he was and why he was out in the middle of the night with Jon. "Did you see anything?" he asked, his upper lip twitching. "What happened?"

"They used a hose to fill the truck with the chemicals. It was Lloyd McMasters helping them. Like Mae said. Money exchanged hands and they got someone from the DNR in on it."

Dale shook his head. "Get names?" he asked. "Anyone else we know?"

"The biologist's name is Brent Christopher," Jon said. "He probably alters the reports for the EPA. We'll follow them and find out where they are going to hide this batch of chemicals."

"Maybe we should just make a phone call and let the law handle it," Dale said. "We already know they're hauling for Conrad, and Lloyd's involved and someone from the DNR. That's enough evidence."

Instead of arguing, Jon drove forward through the trees. They kept up with the fuel truck and turned onto a winding road, remote and dark. Jon pulled back so they would not be seen; but as a result of slowing down, another vehicle came up behind them.

"Now we're being followed," Dale observed. He twisted his sunburned neck to see beyond the other vehicle's headlights. "Who in the *hell* is *this*? What sort of stupid son of a bitch would drive so fast on this *god*-damn bumpy road?"

Jon wondered the same thing, but he concentrated on keeping the truck on the road. It seemed as if the truck behind them wanted to push them into the abyss of the ditch. The front bumper almost touched the back bumper of Dale's truck. Then it swerved to pass them on the left, sped up, and was lost in the tunnel of trees.

Jon said, "That was Lucas's truck."

Jon was about to turn around, but the truck came back with headlights dimmed. When Lucas stepped out of the driver's side and ran towards them, Jon rolled down his window. But all Lucas could say was, "Never mind following them! Hurry up and get out of here!"

Jon turned the truck around and drove back to the highway. He didn't know what to say, but Dale did. "Lucas is in on the whole thing. I knew it. Let's back off and watch them hang!"

"He was right behind us," Jon said, intrigued. "He was right behind us the whole time."

Jon peered through the windshield to the dirt road, watching another rain shower start out slowly with tiny drops tapping the glass. He turned on the windshield wipers.

"Lucas is in on the whole thing," Dale said again. "The motherfucker."

Jon made a wide turn off the road and drove back to the highway. He was starting to put the pieces together: the part Lucas Coulter played, why Lloyd McMasters was risking his job, and most importantly, now he knew more about Carolyn Coulter's role in Dale's past.

Amazing what one sees when one decides to take a good look around.

Jon knew Dale was beyond conversation, for now, but Jon had one more thing to say after they turned off the highway onto the side road to Dale's trailer where Jon left his truck.

His comment forced him to reevaluate his own ability to observe. "I say we turn them in *after* we get more evidence. But first, I'd like to know why George looks so much like you."

CHAPTER 5

Unlike the similarities between George and Dale, Melanie McMasters would remain a mystery. Without even knowing her, she would try to turn Jon's life upside down.

The morning after Jon and Dale witnessed Lloyd help siphon the chemicals at the paper mill, Melanie had trouble waking him up for work. She knew Lloyd was tired because he had been working day shifts, and some night shifts as well, at the mill. He had always worked hard, but his recent desire to make more money had been Melanie's idea. She was behind the dioxin dumping. She was pushing him to extremes.

She reached over to the night table for her hairbrush and brushed her long brown hair while watching Lloyd sleep. She was sick of him. And he didn't even know it. He appeared to be at peace when he slept, but Melanie knew his conscience was getting the best of him. She knew he had taken her advice and paid Brent Christopher to conceal the actual chemical discharge amount after the bleaching process. The discharge was to be measured within certain percentages, and they paid Brent Christopher to alter the reports by writing down false results. Lloyd also paid Reese and George Coulter to dump the excess; again, Melanie's idea.

She was trying to talk George into taking over his father's company.

And then, Jon Loucher caught her eye. *I have plans for you, too,* she thought.

An hour after Lloyd left for work and the children were at her cousin's house for the day, she was to meet up with George and find out how Lloyd was weathering the ordeal. It was essential for Lloyd to go along with the plan; if he didn't hold up his end, things would fall apart and Melanie would have to leave him sooner than she had planned.

Melanie untied her satin robe and dropped it to the floor. She put on a pair of jeans and a green sweater. Although she didn't like the random rain showers, autumn had been warm, so far, but, the last two mornings had started off with a chill. She would have to tell Lloyd to buy more firewood for the woodstove.

Or she would ask George and he would get all the firewood she needed. He worked in the woods and was handy when it came to such matters. Tom Foster was on her list of conquests, too. He was a necessary addition to her plan of leaving Lloyd.

"Hey, wake up," she said. She looked at the clock; it was almost time for her cousin, Ellen, to pick up the kids. Lloyd was to be at the mill by nine o'clock for a meeting and George was supposed to show up at nine thirty.

Lloyd moaned something about the mill. Melanie knew he was obsessed with working extra hours. He was becoming just like her: sneaking and plotting, looking over his shoulder, day and night. *But he doesn't know why,* she thought. *Not yet.*

Briefly, Melanie felt compassion for him, which brought back memories of loving him, long ago. But loving Lloyd was connected to the year before her first son was born and maybe several weeks after. The past year or so, however, living with him was like being confined to a cold dark cave. He was too predictable and devoted all of his time to his job. She knew he wasn't going to change, and so she decided to take advantage of his quest to make money.

Besides, she was the one who contacted Brent Christopher. She offered him generous payments if he helped alter the measurements after the bleaching process. The results were the dioxins: the chlorine by-products. Melanie knew only a certain amount of the discharge could go into the rivers and the remainder had to be disposed of. Disposing of excess dioxins the proper way was expensive. If Lloyd could make the surplus chemicals disappear, the money saved would turn into additional income. There were clever ways to lower the cost of production, and there were methods in which to dump unwanted chemicals.

That is, with the help of Brent Christopher, a man Lloyd had been good friends with since high school. Lloyd knew that Christopher's greed would outweigh his environmental opinions. Then there was George: George was always looking for a way to make extra money; and through his job, he had access to hiding places in the woods.

Melanie had heard through the grapevine that George was having problems with his girlfriend, Mae Lakarri, the blonde who worked at the Tennick Credit Union. This fact alone made him vulnerable. Melanie heard a rumor that Mae was fed up with George's late-night carousing, which was mostly late-night chemical dumping. These factors were to Melanie's advantage.

George was easy to control, and like most men, he was susceptible to Melanie's manipulative ways. Then Lloyd, she knew how to push him into making money, and if he died in the process, she would collect on a large life insurance policy.

George was necessary to the scheme of dumping the chemicals and keeping Lloyd in line. Tom Foster, Coulter's mechanic, was necessary because he was stupid, had a thing for fire, and she was convinced he would take risks to sabotage Coulter Logging.

But Jon Loucher? He was a potential problem. She could tell.

She had to shake Lloyd again. "Wake up; it's time for work!"

He sat in a daze on the edge of the bed. She wondered if he was hung over. But he wasn't. He was just worn out from the dream he had where they were all turned in for disposing illegal chemicals. "I'm tired of work," he said.

• • •

After Lloyd and the kids left the house, Melanie waited in the kitchen for George. She watched the wind shake the red and orange leaves of the maple trees in the yard. Later, she might rake the leaves into neat piles. She should put the white lawn furniture away in the shed and maybe plant some bulbs for the following spring. But she didn't want to bother with preparations for next spring or any other season in the future; she had a feeling she wouldn't be in this house much longer. A lot was happening around her, and all the interlocking changes depended upon her wit.

At nine thirty-five, George's pickup truck pulled into the yard by the garage. George could care less if Lloyd was home. He took what he wanted, when he wanted it, and a husband was no obstacle.

George let himself in through the kitchen door and leaned against the wooden cabinets. He was wearing a clean shirt. It was a dark shade of green, and he also had on a new pair of jeans. He wore steel-toed boots and an orange hunting vest. He had shaved, and his clean-shaven face enhanced his features: a slim nose and full lips. There was also the scent of a spicy cologne coming from him, and his light-brown hair was trimmed around the ears. He even wore a new watch on his left wrist.

He was appealing when he bothered to clean up. He had expressive hazel-colored eyes, that Melanie thought were his best feature. His face was splotched red by heavy drinking and working long hours outside. But he was attractive, nonetheless. Although he acted like he didn't care: about life, love, or anything to do with human feeling.

He said, "Don't you look nice this morning."

Sleeping with George was awkward, but she had to please him to get him to do what she wanted. He could stir her emotions, whereas Lloyd couldn't even prod them. However, George had a habit of pinching and biting, and she only permitted it because he was necessary to her plan.

When he grinned, tiny indentations appeared near his mouth. "You hear me?" he asked.

Melanie said, "Yes, I hear you. Did you know Mae's been seen with Jon Loucher?"

She had planned on saving the information about Mae Lakarri for last, but due to her jealousy over Mae living with George, she played the card too soon.

He cleared his throat. "It's pronounced Lo-sure. Not Lusher. And anyway, why should I care who she's with?"

Melanie let the comment pass; it was easier than asking him what he had meant. It was smarter, too. "I just wondered if you knew about Mae and Jon, that's all. I've seen her drive out to Three Cedar Road. Jon's building a house next to his dad's property."

"No shit," George said, mocking her. He pushed against the cabinets, making the veneer sigh. "He's just a half-breed. She won't want him."

Melanie knew she had to outmaneuver him. "Lloyd's acting like he wants out. Don't let it happen."

"Lloyd's in too deep to get out." George stepped forward from the cabinets while his eyes scanned her curves. "I'm *ready* for you."

"Only if you keep Lloyd in line," she said. "I need the money he brings in."

"I got money."

"Not like Lloyd."

"How would you know how much I got stashed away?"

"I know he makes ten times what you'll ever make."

George's grin turned into a pinch of malice. His eyes roamed the kitchen; she could tell he hated all the yellow. "So, Tom Foster, that ugly jerk off who trips over his own feet, *is* your type?"

He chuckled. Melanie challenged him with a smile. "Poor Lloyd thinks of you as some kind of queen," he added.

She knew he wanted to push her to the floor and make her taste him.

"You should watch out for that eco-terrorist group, not Lloyd," Melanie countered, knowing she was losing his attention. "And you can leave Tom Foster to me. I need him to throw them off the track. If I were you, I'd keep an eye on everyone in your crew. Even Reese could be one of them."

George touched his shirt pocket for his pack of cigarette. "Reese can't peel a banana without my help."

"Keep it that way. And don't even think about smoking in here. I've got children with healthy lungs."

George lit the cigarette anyway. "That's right, you're the good mother. Our plan might have to end anyway. Lloyd says Lucas knows. We're to meet at his place tonight for a little chat. If Lloyd wants out, I can't do much about it. I can't help it if he's scared of Lucas."

"Are *you* scared of Lucas?"

She had to steer George back into the right direction. If she lost control of him, she would be stuck in this small northern town until the day she died.

She watched him, but he continued to smoke the cigarette, filling the lemon-scented air with vapors of nicotine. She asked with downcast eyes, "If I asked you to shoot Lucas and Lloyd, would you?"

"That depends," George said, smoking and looking at her breasts, then down to her hips, "on what *you'll* do for me."

• • •

Twelve hours later, Lucas ushered Lloyd into his house and slammed the door shut. "What in God's name is going on?" he yelled. "I told you to quit running them chemicals. Are you out of your mind?"

Lloyd straightened his tie. "No!" he said, pushing Lucas away. "Get your hands off me. And keep your voice down!"

"Keep my voice down? What the hell's wrong with you? You got a good job. You don't need more money! You get too greedy the whole thing will blow up in your face!"

"Don't talk to me like I'm some hick. I've been working at the mill for nineteen years. They don't pay me enough!"

"But now you got my boys involved! They get caught, there goes my business. A business I've worked hard to build. Do you think it's easy in the timber game? I want this chemical thing stopped! I know all about Brent Christopher too. He was on suspension a few years back, so don't think the DNR's not watching him close. And on top of that, we got this terrorist outfit—them environmentalists—holding protests and going around tree spiking. I got far too much on my mind to worry about my sons and nephew dumping chemicals!" Lucas sighed and heaved, turning crimson all over. "I'll turn you in myself if it don't end now!"

"Settle down," Lloyd said when Reese's truck pulled into the driveway. "Here they are now. Explain it to them yourself!"

Lloyd sat down in a chair at the table while George and Reese invaded the room. But Lucas wasn't finished with Lloyd. He said viciously, "It's that nutty broad you're married to. That Melanie bitch who thinks she needs to live high and mighty. I say get rid of her. And do it now!" Lucas turned to George, who was standing near the refrigerator, picking at a callous on his palm with a knife.

Lucas slapped the knife out of George's hand; it hit the wall and bounced against the stained linoleum. George stared at Lucas as if he had just punched him.

Lucas shouted into George's inert face. "Dumbass! The chemical thing stops today or I'll turn you in myself!"

"Don't threaten me," George said. "You're too sickly to threaten me now, old man."

Reese shuffled by the door. "Calm down," he told George.

"You've gone too far this time, "Lucas shouted. "You'll get caught!"

"Why would you care? You'd be rid of us both and you could hire your buddy, Loucher, to take over. You think of him as a son anyway. Right... *Daddy*?"

"Never mind him!" Lucas screamed, his voice busting down the hallway. "You're using one of my trucks to do the hauling. I won't let it go on!"

"Why should I listen to you?" George asked, snapping Lucas's suspender. "You old son of a bitch, why *in the hell* should I listen to you now when I could easily deck you, cave in your fat-fucking head?"

Reese yelled, "For God's sake, George!"

"I'm your goddamned father, *that's* why," Lucas said, shrugging off George's threat. "You're a drunken manic mess! You're pathetic!"

"My *father*? I heard different."

"What do you mean?" Reese asked, his voice brittle. He turned to Lucas. "*What's* he talking about?"

Lucas's hand moved up to his white hair. Lloyd simply stared, waiting for the answer as well. There was too much being said for such hard-silence. The only sound was the buzz of a fly in a window. It too hunting for a way out.

Lucas screamed at George, "Just do what I say, and I'll give the business to you and Reese. Screw it up, there won't be nothin' left for nobody!"

"My mother told me Dale Washburn's my father," George said, picking his knife up off the floor. "She said you found out and threatened to kill her if she tried to leave you."

"Stop the illegal dumping!" Lucas yelled. He was now hysterical, with veins and muscles jumping in his forehead and neck. "I'm not messing around here! I'll turn you both in before I let you ruin my reputation!"

George motioned for Reese to follow him. He ignored Lloyd, who was still sitting at the table, looking deflated and useless. "Your *reputation*? That's a joke!" he taunted. "But you know what, I'll think about it. Meanwhile, I suggest you keep your sick, perverted mouth *shut*."

"Where are you going?" Lucas demanded, following George to the front door. "I'm not through here!"

"Well *I* am. And I got a date." George pointed a stained finger at Lucas's nose. "Scream at me ever again, old man, threaten me or bring up the name of my beautiful mother and I'll finish you off for good."

CHAPTER 6

George's "date" was with Mae. After leaving him a week earlier, Mae moved in with her sister Paula. George was a man on the edge, and at first Mae found him to be intriguing, but then soon she decided he drank too much. He was arrogant and rude. And when she found out he was dabbling in illegal activities, she knew it was time to leave him.

She called Jon, and after work, she drove out to his house on Three Cedar Road to talk to him. She didn't tell him, however, that she had left George.

Who else but Jon had the capabilities, not to mention the intelligence, to investigate the criminals? she thought.

The plan was to push him into action.

But her situation changed after she moved out of George's house and into the farmhouse with Paula. Although she told George she needed a break, he turned violent. Her explanation for leaving him didn't work. She knew he believed she loved him and would never leave him.

Especially not to move in with her sister outside of Tennick. Paula had inherited the family farm from their parents who, like 85 percent of the population in the area, were of Finnish descent. Paula was forty-two years old, divorced, and the mother of a twelve-year-old son named Jared. She was a Certified Public Accountant, but most of her work was freelance, and she had a part-time job at a restaurant in Chatham to make ends meet.

Mae worked at the Tennick Credit Union as a cashier and also typed and filed insurance claims part-time for a company in Marquette. She was looking for full-time employment with better pay and benefits and scanned the "Help Wanted" ads every day.

Although she had an associate degree in business, she also studied environmental science. She was thinking of going back to school but, for now, she wanted to be near the investigation.

She spent the morning searching through the "Help Wanted" section of the newspaper before cleaning the downstairs of the house. By the time she finished her chores, morning had passed into afternoon.

She went outside to stand on the porch and smoke a cigarette. She was trying to quit and only smoked four cigarettes a day. To justify her habit, she concluded that after living with George she was suffering from anxiety attacks.

The sky turned gray and the wind picked up, indicating another storm was on the way. Mae walked out to the apple orchard, a large field outlined by hardwoods, mostly cherry and maple. She had a feeling that George was going to show up. When she first left George, he appeared at the farm every evening. Sometimes he would call in the middle of the night and demand to speak with her. Paula would always hang up on him.

Along with the claps of thunder, she heard a truck approach and knew right away it was George. She moved towards the barn. If she went inside, she was trapped, so she walked all the way back to the orchard. Paula was at work and Jared was in school.

"I knew I'd find you here," George said.

She watched him come towards her. "What do you want? I told you to stay away from me."

"I just want to talk." George stopped at the stump of a maple tree. He put his booted foot upon it. He plucked his ball cap off his head, scratched his scalp, only to slap the hat back into place. He paused to light a cigarette, both hands cupped to stave off the breeze. He inhaled slowly and shoved the lighter back into his pocket.

Mae pushed her blonde bangs away from her eyes. She felt the breeze fan out around her. George was drunk, she knew, but he was strangely calm as a result. She had learned from previous experience with him that when it came to his higher levels of drunkenness, it was best to play along.

When she first met him, he drank occasionally, but the past four or five months, she noticed he was drunk more than sober. She thought maybe he was haunted by the death of his mother. He told her once that his mother had wanted to escape from Lucas, but her strength gave out long before she was ready to leave.

"I suspected you've been seeing Jon Loucher," he said, his forefinger trembling. "I saw you drive onto his road the other night." He stared as if scrutinizing the swirl of clouds above her; as if he could see people long since dead.

"Other people saw you too," he added. He smoked, inhaled deeply. "You're making a fool out of me."

"Jon and I are friends," she said. "I went to see his dad, ask him where Clara Halverson is buried. You remember her?"

"No, I don't know a Clara Halverson. And you need to pick people *I* like for your friends."

Mae looked over at the porch of the farmhouse. She wondered which was closer: the porch or her jeep near the barn. It was her nature to fight rather than back away, but she knew George was swift in his depression. Alcohol made him act out what his mind pictured, and there was no self-control past a certain point.

She said, "I'm not interested in your opinion."

"You should be. You lived with me for six months and suddenly decide I'm not worth it? Maybe I can't keep you satisfied? He's such a great lover? Whatever the reason you left me, now you expect me to accept you got someone else?" He asked the trees, the chickens, the sky above.

Mae moved a few steps back. "You're drunk!" she yelled, trying to stun him. "I want you to leave, *right now!*"

But he grabbed her arm before she could take another step. He squeezed her so hard, she leaned forward to keep her balance. He pushed her to the ground and sucked her neck. "I'll kill him," he said into her ear.

She focused on George's breath, fouled with whiskey and nicotine, and she concentrated on the probing of his fingers when his nails cut into her skin under her blouse. She shoved him, but it didn't do any good. He licked her and rubbed her, even slapped her; and she tried to fight him, but it didn't do any good.

* * *

A half hour later, he stumbled back to his truck and drove away. Mae sat in the living room of the house with an icepack pressed against her forehead. It was the bump on her forehead that hurt the most, a punch delivered in the first part of the struggle. She held the icepack against the wound, even though she knew it would still be there, and probably even bigger, when Paula came home. Once Paula was on the scene, she would make Mae call the police.

Unable to move, Mae listened to the tick of the antique clock, thinking of her father, who looked old to her even when she was a child. He never forgot to wind the clock. Just like he never once forgot to buy flowers for her mother, every other Friday. The gesture signified their love: a half-dozen red roses every other week until the day she died.

Soon after Mae's mother died, her father died too, and that was the end of roses in this house.

Thinking of her father giving her mother roses made Mae want to cry.

No one has ever given me roses, she thought.

Mae could not mourn the death of her parents; they had been secretive and stoic the entire time she knew them. They spoke lovingly to each other, but conversations and actions towards their daughters were seemingly forced. They were from the Old Country and Mae often wondered if that meant that they had no room in their hearts for anyone except each other. With her parents gone and no grandparents or aunts, Mae had no one to depend on but Paula. And Paula would insist on action.

Paula is home. Mae heard the whine of hinges as the screen door opened and shut. She heard Paula talking to her son, Jared, asking him to put his book bag on the counter. Jared was the one who found Mae sitting on the couch in the living room—pillows surrounding her—with an icepack held to her swollen eye.

Her hair was tangled and her clothes were stained with grass. Jared stood in the doorway and stared; he was used to Mae looking pretty and tidy. He turned back towards the kitchen to get his mother.

"What *is* it?" Paula asked, rushing to the living room. She was drying her hands off on a towel. When her eyes settled on Mae, she told Jared, "Go upstairs!"

Paula was a robust, stout woman. Her shoulders were wide and her arms muscular as a result of exercise and work. She wore a waitress uniform; the front was spotted with grease, and the tips of her auburn hair were wet. Her hands dropped to her sides when she saw that Mae had a black eye and a red angular cut over her lip.

"George Coulter did this!" Paula yelled without even needing to think about it. She marched from one end of the room to the other. "I'm calling the sheriff. I want the crazy bastard put away!"

Mae sat up among the pillows. The last thing she needed was for Paula to go public over George's antics. "No, George didn't—" she stopped and turned to look at the clock. "He couldn't go through with … that part."

Paula twisted the dishtowel with her hands.

"He was drunk," Mae said, trying to explain her battered appearance. "I don't want cops around here. I told you; we're close to getting the Coulters!"

"Who do you mean by *we*?" Paula wanted to know for the third time in a month. "You keep saying *we*. Is it that man you meet at the bar?"

"His name's Rick Peterson. That's all I can tell you. Just promise me you'll keep quiet about it for now."

"Only if you tell me who this Peterson character is. And why you meet him!"

"I can't tell you right now," Mae said. She wasn't sure how much she could trust Paula, but she had always known that sooner or later, she would have to tell her the facts. This was Paula's house, after all, which put Paula and her son in danger.

Paula's blue eyes narrowed when Mae warned her, "You'll just have to trust me."

"I trust *you*," Paula said. "It's George Coulter I'm worried about! Did he rape you? Tell me the truth!"

Mae decided to go upstairs to her bedroom and take a nap. She wanted to be alone and she wanted to sleep for a few hours so she wouldn't have to think about what to do next. "No," she said. "I'm going upstairs to lay down!"

Paula didn't comment. It would take time to think about what to do, and Mae knew if Paula didn't call Jon tonight, she would call him in the morning.

CHAPTER 7

Jon sensed Mae was in danger and couldn't stop thinking about her. He picked up the pace working on his house so that he could move into it by early winter; if not, his two-room cabin near the back of Elbert's property would do a bit longer. After all, he was a bachelor and had lived in his cabin since he graduated from high school. After high school, he enrolled in a technical school in Marquette part-time and also worked with Elbert part-time; but he still lived in the cabin to maintain his independence.

He needed a place of his own to store his belongings, and the cabin was convenient and private.

His "belongings" consisted of fishing supplies, from fly rods to poles and a dozen tackle boxes. And of course, an extensive gun collection: modern handguns; rifles; shotguns; antique flintlock rifles; hundreds of knives and other hunting paraphernalia; acquired artifacts; thousands of tools and gadgets; deer heads and loose antlers; and obviously, family keepsakes from Elbert.

Jon's cabin was far enough from Three Cedar Road and Elbert's house that the only *noise* came from birds and other natural inhabitants. *There is no need to allow*

Mae, or anyone else, back here, he thought. He usually parked his truck on the road and walked a mile and a half through the woods to get there. The jaunt itself reminded him of the fact that this parcel of land used to belong to Elbert, and Elbert gave it to Jon as a gift when Jon turned eighteen.

But now there was Mae. Again. And several weeks ago, he *did* let her invade his privacy. He had been working on the house up by the road and she stopped in to see him. It was the first time the dioxin dumping subject came up. She told—without even knocking on the door, she simply walked into the kitchen—she *told* him she needed his help investigating Coulter Logging. She was tipsy; he could tell. The topic of illegal chemicals changed into: "*Really? You actually live back in the woods in a cabin? Can I see it?*" Not a good idea, he knew, but she persisted; and then she turned irritatingly friendly and asked for a cup of coffee.

They went to Elbert's for coffee and Elbert's exceptional cooking—spaghetti and garlic rolls—and that's when Mae met Clara Halverson. Clara was visiting Elbert; she and Elbert had known each other since they were kids. One thing led to another. Clara had two glasses of wine and offered Mae a glass (before the coffee) after God knows how much Mae already had before visiting Jon.

Clara told Mae about her plans to leave the bulk of her estate to Jon; she had no family, etcetera, etcetera. *"I want to see your cabin,"* Mae kept insisting. He gave in and drove her back to his two-room cabin. She stayed the night and slept in his arms. He wondered all these weeks if she remembered what happened that night. When he walked her back to his house and to her jeep, she seemed fine. She smiled and kissed him goodbye and that was that.

She was gone.

Until the other night when she came to him again, asking him—no *telling* him—to investigate Coulter Logging.

He had hoped she had forgotten about the night in his cabin, and what they did beneath the heavy patchwork blanket. She either remembered and didn't want to discuss it with him, or she had no memory of it whatsoever.

He *sure* remembered; it marked the day he began to scrutinize his life. He decided that maybe he *was* a hermit and too much of being a hermit was not a good thing. He should ease into the next phase of social interplay. He *did* interact with his fellow employees and he was, in fact, good at communicating with landowners and foresters via his profession. But, as he became older, in midlife—single and childless—he wondered if he should think about making some important changes.

First, he knew that Mae, or any woman like her, would insist on improvements. He sensed she was materialistic as well, which meant he had to build further than his original architectural layout and extend the house into something grand, not basic.

He also knew that in the near future, the life he was accustomed to would end. In two years, he would turn forty and it was time to move his belongings to Three Cedar Road. Still remote and scenic, but closer to civilization.

It was time for adequate plumbing, no more outhouse; time for electricity—he would be done depending solely on generators.

But, why should I care?

Just concentrate on work and paying the bills, not Mae and her opinions.

Just think about eco-terrorists sabotaging logging equipment and harassing local crews. He might tell Lucas he was ready to blow the whistle, and if Lucas fired him because of it, thanks for the favor. He could always find work elsewhere, or take Clara Halverson's offer of roughly a million dollars to start his own business. She died two weeks ago. And her attorney left three messages on his phone.

He rolled off the couch and pulled on his pants. He had been so exhausted the night before, he fell into bed wearing long underwear. He would need to take a shower later at Elbert's house, bringing to mind another reason to complete his house: he could finally use his own shower. No more freezing rivers and no more having to use Elbert's facilities. Plumbing was already listed as number one on the notepad by his bed at the house.

Before leaving his cabin every morning, he made sure the fire in the woodstove was completely out. In the wintertime, he let the coals burn down on their own. He knew this fear had to do with Elbert's kitchen stove catching on fire when Jon was child. Only two months after Jon's mother had abandoned them, Jon experienced bouts of insomnia. One night in January, he awoke to the acrid smell of smoke. Elbert's house had a top floor; it was an attic that expanded across the entire length of the house, and Elbert remodeled the area for Jon to use as a bedroom. Jon walked down the steps to find Elbert slapping a dishrag at flames shooting upward from the stovetop. Finally, with a lid from a cast iron skillet, Elbert smothered the fire. When Elbert saw Jon standing wide-eyed on the steps, he assured him, "Nothing to worry about. Just a potholder caught on fire."

Ever since the potholder incident, Jon checked the burners of the stove to make sure they were set on the off button. A couple of times, he turned Elbert's oven off when Elbert was in the process of using it, baking a cake or a casserole.

Jon never told Elbert he overheard him talking to the police after Jon's mother died in a car wreck with her lover that she had been burned; disfigured and charred.

Jon locked the door of his cabin behind him and walked out onto the porch. The morning air was brisk, and patches of frost made the weeds and brush sparkle, signaling that winter was on the way. The geese overhead converged into their *V*-formations, heading south. Jon heard them honking in the distance, and covering his eyes from the timid morning sun, he saw a long *V* high up in the sky over the tops of some balsams. He watched the geese until they were black specks and disappeared into the haze of the September dawn.

He started the mile and a half walk through the woods to Elbert's house. Elbert owned eight hundred acres of land. The road, marked by three large cedar trees by the entrance off the highway, was still gravel, but mostly dirt, and except for state-owned parcels and a few hundred acres owned by neighbors, most of the land was Loucher property.

Every morning, Elbert served breakfast at seven-thirty-sharp. Jon would usually eat with Elbert, and Dale Washburn. Elbert had taken Dale under his wing years ago out of pity. Dale was a bachelor like Jon, but Dale had proven to be an extreme loner, ten times worse than Jon.

Dale claimed he was too old to adjust his habits for marriage, yet he was the sort who needed *someone* to look after him. *That means*, said Elbert, *Dale needs assistance*. It was a known fact that Dale wouldn't clean his trailer; at least, he didn't put much effort into the task. He might pick up a pile of clothing and move the foul mound from point A to point B, which brought up the fact that he didn't do laundry either; why should he, when Elbert offered to do it for him?

The business of looking after Dale Washburn, thought Jon, seemed like Elbert had acquired another son, not as a father might but as a mother *had* to. Besides, how could Elbert allow Dale to starve?

Cooking was Elbert's favorite hobby. He liked to prepare stuffed guinea hens, sautéed shrimp, homemade pasta with rich spicy sauces. He would experiment with flamboyant four-course meals and also make the "good stuff," such as pies, cookies, bread, rolls, and strudels.

On this chilly morning in September Jon hoped breakfast would be bacon and eggs, something identifiable. The week previously, Elbert had served a three-cheese-onion-sausage soufflé; it was so rich and gut-wrenching, Jon was still popping antacids.

Jon approached Elbert's backyard from the trail that led to the edge of the property line and right away, he saw Dale's two-toned green truck in the driveway. Dale was always on time.

Jon stepped around the few remaining chickens Elbert had left and up to an old beagle-collie mix named Beau. Beau was white-faced and overweight and didn't bother to get up when Jon approached him. Jon reached down to scratch behind Beau's ear. "Hi there, Beauregard," he said, and walked onward.

He came to Elbert's house, yellow with white shutters. Elbert said he would have preferred a log house, but when Jon's mother married him nearly forty years earlier, Elbert decided to take the quickest route and built a three-bedroom, two-story house. There was also a front porch, an attic—Jon's old bedroom—two bathrooms, and a sizeable kitchen and living room.

In the yard, there were three sheds, a barn, a fenced-in area because Elbert used to own four horses, and a garage where he stored a red '64 Chevy pickup truck. He seldom drove the truck. He was more likely to ask Jon to drive him around to do his grocery shopping, banking, doctor and dental appointments, and so on. He enjoyed driving, but explained to Jon that it was more convenient and economically sound to be driven about. Not to mention he couldn't see well, and except for reading, he refused to wear his glasses.

Jon walked up the front steps and into the kitchen without bothering to knock; after all, this was his boyhood home. He knew they would be waiting for him. It wasn't yet seven o'clock. The scent of bacon cooking and biscuits baking in the oven made him hungry right away, and the first person he saw was Dale, who sat at the table with his legs crossed. Dale sucked on a pipe and nodded a greeting to Jon.

Dale looked younger without a hat on; his hair was curled closely to his head, revealing a sunburned forehead. He was freckled in areas and burned easily, probably because he was mostly Irish and fair-skinned. Jon wasn't sure. But he *did* know that Dale had to wear long-sleeved shirts and hats with brims whenever he was outside, or he'd pay the price.

Dale had on a red shirt, blue jeans—clothes that no doubt Elbert had washed for him—and the usual steel-toed boots, which had tracked a fair amount of dirt across Elbert's floor. Nonetheless, Jon couldn't believe that Elbert was letting Dale smoke inside his house. Pipe, cigarette, or cigar, Elbert didn't smoke and told the smokers to "take it outside."

Elbert was standing at the stove turning strips of bacon in a skillet. He said to Jon, "Well, look who's here," and added a grunt of some sort.

Without a doubt, Elbert was the most soft-spoken person Jon had ever known. At times, it was nerve-racking to lean forward in order to hear him. Sometimes what he had to say was petty and not worth the effort. Such as his last remark: *look who's here,* as if Jon's arrival was a big surprise. Other times what he had to say was on the mark.

Elbert was physically striking: significantly handsome, unpretentiously virile. He was six -foot tall, and quite stocky across the chest, making him appear larger than he actually was. At seventy-one, he looked like a man of fifty. His arms and legs were muscular due to all the years he had put in doing carpentry, construction, and working in the woods. His complexion was bronze and weatherworn. His eyes, black as his hair had once been, were piercing one moment and tender the next.

Elbert wore his favorite striped shirt and best corduroy trousers; also, his work boots. He motioned Jon over to the counter while turning the bacon until satisfied with texture. Jon waited. He noticed the counter was shining and spotless. The kitchen smelled of pine-scented disinfectant, quite different from the kitchen of Lucas Coulter.

Elbert said, "That lawyer called again. You better call him back this time."

"I will," Jon said, wishing Elbert would hurry along with the bacon.

Elbert shoved the platter of bacon into Jon's hands. "Take this to the table and tell Dale to lose the pipe."

Jon walked over to the table, put the platter of bacon down, and relayed Elbert's message to Dale, who quickly doused the pipe as if it might blow up. Jon gave Dale a puzzled look: *What gives you the right to smoke inside my father's house?*

Elbert cracked eggs open into a bowl; he slid the eggs into the hot skillet and they sizzled in the bacon grease. He said, "She has a nephew, remember? His name's Neil. She thinks he'll try to contest her wishes. She wanted you to go with her to see her lawyer. Remember she told you about it? Before she got real sick went to the hospital?"

"Didn't know any of that," Jon murmured from his place at the table. He noticed Dale was watching him with interest. Jon rested his elbows against the table top, knowing Elbert wasn't finished.

But Elbert was taking his time flipping eggs in the skillet. He put all six over-easy eggs onto the platter. He moved towards the table with the eggs, and another platter with golden biscuits. "She made it easy for you. The lawyer, what's his name—" He gestured towards the counter. "I wrote his name down. Said all you have to do is pick up a check. Might want to beat the nephew to his office. It's in Marquette. On Front Street."

Jon was busy with the eggs and bacon: arranging plenty on his plate, handing the remainder over to Dale. He nodded, acknowledging Elbert's information. He was busy eating and wanted to finish so he could begin the long day ahead.

Elbert put two mugs down on the table, and proceeded to fill them with fresh coffee. He went to the refrigerator, catty-corner to the stove, found the vanilla creamer, carried it to the table, and placed it near Jon's elbow. "Hmmm," he said. "You probably don't need the money anyway," he added with a lilt of sarcasm in his voice. "You're so well-to-do."

"I told your dad about the chemical thing," Dale interjected. He was busy buttering a biscuit. "That they're hauling for Conrad and their cousin's in on it."

"Turn them in," said Elbert. "Buy them out."

"We want to find out where they are burying the stuff before we say anything," Jon said, thinking of food and coffee, not criminals.

"I see," said Elbert. He was wiping down the cupboards with a rag. He moved on to a cabinet where he stored odds and ends like sugar and flour. "Get your evidence. Makes sense."

Jon knew Elbert had always been an on-the-fence environmentalist; he was pro conservation, protecting wetlands, planting trees, and so forth, but he also understood the importance of supply and demand. *Ethics,* to him, as he told Jon many times, *is about moderation. Put back what you take. Clean up where you have been. Do not contaminate your surroundings.*

Jon knew that Elbert was thinking about Aubrey. Jon knew Elbert had picked up the task of wiping down the countertop to ward off his feelings for her. Aubrey, Jon's mother. When it came to her and only her, Elbert hid heart-twisting sorrow.

The phone rang, startling them all. Even Dale stopped eating, his fork poised.

"Now what?" Elbert wondered out loud as he rushed to the counter to answer the phone. Jon knew Elbert believed that the most impolite thing ever was a phone call before eight in the morning, and at breakfast time no less.

He picked up the receiver, "Yes, hello!" He had always answered a phone that way. "Yes, hello!" Jon thought it was funny, every time. But because of the stern expression on Elbert's face, turning his jowls downward, Jon didn't laugh this time. He waited.

Jon knew Elbert was going to hand him the phone. He dropped the piece of bacon and said into the mouthpiece, "Yes?" He waited for a man's voice but got a woman's.

Paula's said in a piercing pitch. "Jon, I need your help! Mae's locked herself in the bedroom and I can't find the spare key."

Jon envisioned Mae hurt, wounded on the floor, locked up and helpless. "Well," he said. "But, where?"

"At the house! George Coulter attacked her yesterday-"

Jon handed the phone back to Elbert and when he stood up, he accented his anger by slamming the chair against the floor.

"What's going on, son?" Elbert asked, his eyes on Jon's shaking hand.

Dale stood up. "I'd better go help," he said, as he and Elbert watched Jon disappear out the kitchen door with a hardy slap of the screen door behind him.

"No," Elbert said calmly. "Sit back down and eat. Jon will handle it."

CHAPTER 8

Paula went back upstairs to tell Mae she had called Jon and he was on his way, so please unlock the door. But there was no response. Paula pounded on the door.

Mae said, "I'll be down in a minute, I told you *not* to call him!"

"What else could I do?" Paula asked her. "I thought you had passed out, or worse! I knew if I called *him*, you would at least open the door!"

"Go away. I *said* I'll be down in a minute!"

Mae had showered and put on a blue sweatshirt and jeans. She combed her shoulder-length hair and attempted to cover up the bruises and welts near her upper lip with makeup.

She looked around the room, at the antique mahogany four-poster rope bed with a feather tick mattress, large pillows, and a green and pink bedspread with curtains to match. She focused on the vanity dresser with matching oval mirror. The dresser was one hundred years old; the mirror and several other pieces of furniture in the farmhouse had once belonged to Mae's grandmother.

In the tainted glass of the old mirror, Mae's reflection was warped, identical to the way she felt.

She was sick to her stomach and wanted to sleep longer; but because Paula had interfered and called Jon, she had to come up with an explanation to convince him she was fine. She fell back on the bed and stretched out. Her shoulders ached from George shoving her against the ground the day before. She had to collect her thoughts and steel her emotions. She would tell Jon her sister exaggerated without getting all the facts.

When Mae went downstairs to the kitchen, she noticed Paula had put on a fresh pot of coffee and had already finished drying the breakfast dishes. Mae heard the sound of a vehicle come up the driveway. It wasn't the school bus; the bus had already picked up her nephew, Jared, a half hour ago.

Mae peered out the window when she heard Jon's truck approach at a rate of speed that made the gravel fly. *What is the deal with him?* she wondered. *He's just an acquaintance who I spent the night with once, in his cluttered cabin, back in the woods.*

Mae watched Jon park by the barn and step out of his truck. He walked quickly along the cement sidewalk towards the front porch of the house. He was taller than George by an inch at least, and thinner than George by far.

He walked toward the side door of the kitchen, not the front, and so she unlocked and opened it. "Sorry my sister called you," she said. "You didn't need to come."

A sharp breeze followed him into the kitchen. He moved from one appliance to the next. He checked out the bric-a-brac hanging from the wallpapered interior.

His eyes moved to the two shadow boxes and several embroidered scenes of barnyards and pastures.

He scanned the spoon collection enshrined in a rectangular box to the left of the clock on the wall. He studied the china plates and delicate teacups behind the glass of a tall cabinet. He winced as if he suddenly wondered why he was standing in a cold, cluttered kitchen. And said, "Why did you even talk to that son of a bitch?"

Mae turned to him. "What does *that* mean?"

"Nothing!" he admitted, taken aback by his own shouting.

He clenched his right hand into a fist, then flexed his fingers. He paced towards the door he had entered. He wore no jewelry, no rings; only a leather watchband under the cuff of his jacket. And beneath the brown jacket he wore a black flannel shirt. He also had on brown workpants and steel-toed boots, and a black ball cap over short black hair. *A lot of black*, she was thinking, *and the colors of him, as well as his attire, define his mood.*

"I don't understand you at all," she said, shaking her head. "We don't even know each other very well. We—"

"Well enough," he interrupted, unable to take his eyes off the cut above her eye.

She stared back at him. His dark beard matched his eyes; his features shifted to a net of creases near his mouth, and he winced again, and then to her dismay, he trembled, briefly. She knew he could see her completely: that the red welt by her eye had turned black and the jagged cut by her lip purple.

He saw this and couldn't look away.

"Oh, dammit," he whispered.

He moved his hands from his pockets, to ease the tremors that had apparently overwhelmed him. She somehow knew—he was heading beyond self-control. "Oh!" he added and turned as if every muscle in his neck had snapped.

"I can take care of myself!" she said. "I'm getting a protective order against him. You just go about your business and stop thinking about me!"

"He's *done,*" said Jon.

Mae rushed to catch him, but by the time she ran to the side door and out into the chilly yard, he was gone. All she could do was walk back into the kitchen, where she almost ran into Paula.

"Look what you've done!" Mae yelled. "I told you not to call him!"

"George will kill you the next time," Paula said, grabbing Mae's arm. "He's crazy. And you say he didn't hurt you. I don't believe it! Tell me what really happened."

"I don't want to talk about it."

"You tell me what George has on you. Tell me or Jon finds out about the baby!"

Mae sat down in one of the chairs at the table. She didn't have any choice but to tell Paula the truth.

* * *

When Jon arrived at the logging site near Rapid River, George and Reese weren't there, but Lucas was. Jon had the fifteen-minute drive in which to calm down, but calm he wasn't. He was more charged up than ever and knew it wouldn't turn out well if he met up with George now; or even an hour from now.

Sitting in his truck, Jon watched Lucas sip coffee from a Styrofoam cup. As Lucas drank, he walked around the area near the fuel truck, over to the parts truck. He kicked at gravel and appeared indifferent to the sound of chainsaws screeching from all directions.

Lucas glanced around, *pretending to do his job*, Jon was thinking: making sure systems merged smoothly. He looked at the machines; not for safety purposes, but because he had taken out a large loan in order to buy them. He seemed particularly interested in the new forwarder Dale Washburn was operating to the left of the decked logs.

Before Jon got the chance to step out of his truck, Lucas walked over to him. Lucas waited for him to take off his jacket, collect his gloves, and get out of the truck.

Lucas inspected Jon, his bloodshot eyes moved up and down Jon's lanky body. He kept silent while Jon pulled on his gloves, but then he followed Jon to the back of his truck where Jon checked his chainsaw.

"So, where the hell have you been?" Lucas asked, breaking the silence. He rubbed a hand across his withered mouth. "You're forty-five minutes late!"

Jon ignored Lucas's question to ask one of his own. "Where's George?"

Lucas crushed the Styrofoam cup in his hand and tossed it into the weeds. Jon stared at the careless affront of littering. Tossing litter was a habit Jon realized Lucas and people like him did often, without batting an eye.

"I said to leave the chemical thing to me," Lucas sneered, tugging at Jon's shirt sleeve. "I'm going to talk them into ending it. I'll turn them in myself if they don't!"

"I've got something else to discuss with him," Jon said. He checked the chain, made sure the chain break was in place. "This time he's going to answer for it."

"I don't like the sound of that!" said Lucas.

"I don't give a shit what you like, Coulter," said Jon, matter-of-factly.

Lucas put a hand on Jon's shoulder. He leaned sideways and peered into Jon's face, and even though Jon shrugged his hand away, Lucas wouldn't move. "Listen here now," he began. "George's got a screw loose, I know that, but I think I can get him back on track. I want you to wait a while longer; I need more time to pound some sense into him!"

"Why were you following us last night?" Jon asked. "What did you mean by 'they'll shoot us'? Out with it!" He looked at Lucas without mercy. In fact, in all the years that Jon knew Lucas, he sensed Lucas still thought of him as a teenager. A quiet, diligent, hard worker, but a kid, nonetheless.

Lucas cleared his throat. He looked too warm in the flannel shirt, coat, and heavy blue jeans. "Simmer down, for Christ's sake," Lucas said. "It's them eco-terrorists! I decided it's too dangerous for you and Dale to sneak around in the woods. If we see anything, we'll report it to the DNR. We're going to let them handle the fanatics. It's their job anyway!"

"I say we tell them about George dumping chemicals for the mill. Tell them about your nephew, Lloyd McMasters, while we're at it."

Jon knew what Lucas thought of that: stunned by the idea of investigations and drawn-out court hearings, and worse, astronomical fines. Lucas wiped his mouth with his shirtsleeve. "I've done my best with Lloyd," he explained. "He's my sister's kid. But he's also a greedy bloodsucker. I can't do much about that now!" Lucas took a big chance when he poked Jon's chest to make his next point. "I want you to wait," he said again. "Give me three days. I got my sons and a nephew tied up in this crooked fucking deal! Give me three more days before you go to the law. Better yet, we'll go together if they won't listen to reason."

"Do you *know* where George is?" Jon asked again.

Lucas fidgeted. "I have no idea where he is. Or Reese neither. That tells me they're probably hung over. I wouldn't give them the time of day if I was you."

"You're not me," Jon said. To prove it, he pulled his chainsaw from the back of his truck and climbed the ridge to cut his quota and wait.

• • •

Two hours later, George showed up at the logging site. Jon was sitting on a stump, sharpening the chain of his saw. A few minutes later, he could hear George's voice filter through the trees. He heard Reese's grating voice jumbled in with George's, along with the faint whine of another saw.

Jon left his saw and hardhat at the base of a maple tree, but Bryan Kinnenun, another machine operator and a part-time piece cutter, stopped him in the trail.

"What's going on?" Bryan asked, appearing oddly inquisitive. Jon didn't know Bryan very well, even though they had worked together for four years.

Bryan pitched three empty shotgun shells into a patch of decayed elderberry bushes. "Been some shootin' going on around here," he said.

Jon noticed that Bryan's nose was scratched up. His torso was bent; uncommon for a man of twenty-eight. He wore the usual woodsman's garb—the shirt, the jeans, and steel-toed boots. His sandy-brown hair was slicked back and the skin around his eyes was creased. Additionally, he looked as if he had slept in his clothes: his shirt was buttoned wrong and his pants were muddied at the knees. He didn't have on a hard hat, but he wore an orange cap, stuck to his head at an angle.

"I got something for you, Loucher," he said. He shoved a small object into Jon's hand. "A bear claw," he said. "Thought you might want it."

Without another word, Bryan walked away. Jon studied the bear claw before putting it into his shirt pocket. This treasure was enough to distract him from the business at hand, but not enough to make him forget. As George moved closer, Jon started down the trail to meet him. Jon waited while George finished smoking a cigarette. George flung it to the dry ground, twisted it out with the heel of his boot. "Looks like I littered," he said, his eyes glazed. "Oh no. The woods might catch on fire."

George's eyes bore vindictively into Jon's and then he made the mistake of grinning. "You are one brazen son of a—" he started to say and backed up. But not quick enough to avoid Jon's fist.

Jon wasn't about to waste anymore time. He had waited long enough, and not one fraction of his rage had subsided. He was sick and tired of George's voice, his attempts at humor, his outrageous threats and impulsive behavior.

He had punched George without saying a word. He saw blood spray far and wide from George's mouth. George backed up, looking disoriented, with nothing more to say and nowhere to run.

Jon wanted him to react. *Take your best shot,* he thought. But after George wiped his lips off with his palm, he turned for help.

Only Dale Washburn was nearby, although he was operating the forwarder, sealed in the cab with the heater on high. He couldn't hear what was said, but he saw what had happened. He maneuvered the large machine, lifted the logs, and hauled them to the road. A few minutes later, he stopped the engine and climbed out of the cage.

Jon knew by the look on George's face that he was going to call him a son of a bitch, and "son of a bitch flipped around inside Jon's head, along with "bastard" and "idiot;" and he couldn't leave out "brazen."

Clearly unable to let it go, Jon lunged forward, and this time, he grabbed George by both shoulders. He ripped George's skin along with his shirt. He pushed George backwards, into the jagged bark of a red pine, and the tree itself shuddered as George choked on blood.

George bent over, a coughing convulsion tearing his throat lining. He gasped for air. He held his throat as if Jon had slit it with a skinning knife. "God*damn* you," he muttered with a hand over his nose, his eyes wild. "You're a dead man now!"

But he could only stare as blood ruptured from his lips and dripped down his shirt. He slid a trembling hand beneath the flap of his jacket. He attempted to pull out the holstered .357 pistol. *Such an unbelievably asinine move to make,* thought Jon. And consequently, Jon shook George even harder. He held George's head within the vice of his hands and rammed his knee into George's nose. George cried out for help, but when Lucas and Reese and Tom Foster finally appeared, George was flat on the ground, moaning.

"Dear God!" Reese yelled, his eyes darting to the tree line. "You almost killed him, Loucher!" Reese bent down to get a better look. He tried to revive George by moving his head from side to side. "He's down and out!" Reese told the others.

Jon said, "He better be."

Lucas had a different reaction. When Jon walked past Reese and turned to collect his equipment at the maple tree, Lucas grabbed him. His strength was as powerful as his demonic expression. "I told you to let it alone, Loucher!" he seethed through yellow teeth. "Now you've gone and broke his nose. This is assault dammit; attempted murder!"

Jon pushed past him, Tom Foster, and even Dale, whom Jon looked at accusingly, as if to say, *This is your son. Your problem.*

"Throw a bucket of water in his face and wake the fucker up!" Lucas ordered to no one in particular. He walked over to his truck and came back with a thermos. He opened the thermos and poured the contents into George's ashen face. "Get up!" he screamed. "Don't you got the backbone to go after the man who just beat the crap out of you?"

Lucas turned to Dale. "You'd think a man would want his son to be able to defend hisself," he said, loud enough for everyone to hear. "Isn't that right, Washburn?"

George opened his swollen eyes and cried, "I'll kill him. I'll kill the son of a bitch!"

Dale Washburn put his hands into his pockets and shook his head. He heard Tom Foster laugh, but George kept insisting, "I'll kill that son of a bitch! I swear to God, *I'll kill him!*" even though Lucas and Reese had to carry him all the way back to the road.

Chapter 9

Melanie hadn't seen George for over a week. She knew something was wrong. The night before last, she dreamed that she poisoned Lloyd and attempted to run away with Jon Loucher. But George intervened; he cut Jon up with a knife. There was so much blood, it was inside her house and outside in her yard.

Something bad has happened to George.

Before she picked her boys up at her cousin's house, she went to the bank to make another deposit of five hundred dollars. She deposited the same amount every week; it was the extra money Lloyd gave her now that he was dumping the chemicals. Part of Lloyd's regular job consisted of taking care of the payroll. He deleted the extra money in cash, so it couldn't be traced.

Melanie didn't know how much Brent Christopher made or how much George and Reese made, but she was careful to keep a close tab on Lloyd's share. She was supposed to deposit the money in their joint savings account, but instead, she deposited it all in her personal account. Lloyd never caught on. Or if he did, he never questioned her about it.

Melanie picked up her sons, ages three and a half and two, from her cousin's house in Chatham and stopped at the grocery store on the way home. Lloyd would be at the mill until two in the morning. He was working double shifts.

When she got home, she fed the boys and put them to bed. They were always exhausted after staying with her cousin, Ellen. It crossed her mind to call Ellen, who was single and didn't have children of her own, to come over and stay with them so she could go find George. She had to make sure George was okay, because it was important that he keep Lloyd on track.

As the foreman, Lloyd had access to all the buildings; he had worked at the mill long enough, that no one would suspect him of wrongdoing. Not only that, but Lloyd was the only one who could siphon the dioxins after the bleaching process. He had all the keys and he could go in and out of the buildings unnoticed to make sure the proper surplus amount was separated into the holding pools. He waited in the shadows for George and Reese, cleared the way for them to filter the chemicals from the holding pools into their truck, and finally, leave through the back gates.

Most importantly, Lloyd kept the other workers and supervisors at bay. Only Lloyd could manage this complex part of the siphoning. As a high-ranking shift supervisor, no one questioned him. He was also the only person allowed to oversee Brent Christopher's reports for the Environmental Protection Agency.

But recently, Melanie worried Lloyd wanted to back out, especially now that Lucas Coulter knew about the scheme. Lloyd wanted to make the extra money, primarily to keep Melanie happy, but she knew he was taking a big risk: deleting the money from company profits and keeping track of George and Reese's comings and goings with the truck, helping Christopher change the figures on the reports, slipping envelopes of cash to George. In short, lying to his supervisors. All extremely risky, not to mention illegal.

If Lloyd quit the process, there would be no more five hundred dollars a week to put into her personal account. She was up to thirty thousand dollars; another ten thousand dollars and she could talk Tom Foster into leaving town with her. He would leave his wife and three children to be with her. Once they were settled, she would write to Lloyd and tell him she wanted a separation, and eventually, a divorce. During the divorce proceedings, she would sue him for even more money. Lloyd earned a substantial salary at the mill, part of which he insisted on putting into stock, and she would get half of everything in the divorce settlement. She would insist Lloyd sell the house and the land. All she wanted was enough money to leave the area and start over. She would take the children, of course, and take Tom Foster, only because he would do what she told him to do. In time, she would get rid of him, too.

Melanie wasn't about to spend the rest of her life with a boring old man. She was only thirty-one. Lloyd was forty-five. She wasn't willing to waste any more time on him.

While she was thinking about Lloyd, Tom Foster called. He told her he was coming over. He said something happened at work that she might want to know about. Melanie turned on the porch light and went outside to wait for him. Knowing Tom, it could be a while. He always had to dream up an elaborate lie to tell his wife before he left the house at night. Melanie had met Tom's wife once, and once was enough. She was physically and mentally repulsive, in Melanie's opinion, and taking Tom from her would be easy.

Sitting on the front porch wearing a heavy jacket due to the shift in temperature—it was thirty-two degrees and had started to snow—she wondered what Tom wanted to tell her. She wondered why Tom would even think she might care. After all, Tom didn't know about the dumping scam between Lloyd, George, and Reese; at least, he hadn't heard it from her. All Tom knew was that Melanie was building up her savings, and in the future, she wanted him to relocate with her.

Finally, around nine o'clock, Tom's truck eased to a stop next to the garage. Melanie and Lloyd lived ten miles outside of Trenary. Their only neighbor was a mile south. She wouldn't even attempt these meetings with Tom and George if not for the seclusion of their property.

She watched Tom climb out of his four-wheel drive truck. As he approached her, she could see him clearly beneath the porch lights. He was skinny— pale-looking, except for red scabs splotching his neck and arms. He was always covered with oil and grease.

Whenever he smiled, as he was doing now, his four remaining teeth were mismatched with spots of rot. His clothes hung on him, and his boots were one size too large for his feet. His moustache was a darker blonde than the wispy hair on his head, and she couldn't help but think, *How do I let him touch me?*

Tom collapsed beside her on the step. He tried to put an arm around her, but she pushed him away. "Aren't you glad to see me?" he asked, dejectedly. "I came all the way out here to see *you.* I told my wife I got some work to do for Lucas. And this is how you treat me? How 'bout a kiss?"

"Out with it first," Melanie said. She stood up so he wouldn't try to grab her hand. "What's this about George?"

Tom stood up too and leaned against the railing. "Jon Loucher beat him up today at work. Seems George was stupid enough to hurt Mae. She's that pretty blonde who used to live with him. I guess she left George some time ago. Do you even know who I'm talking about?"

"I know who she is!" Melanie said sharply. "Is George in the hospital? Is he dead? Tell me!"

"He's not in the hospital. Far as I know, he's not dead, either." Tom chuckled at the idea of George being dead. He pulled at his stringy beard. "He's not dead but close enough."

The more he picked and laughed, the angrier Melanie became. "Is he home? I need to know!"

"I think Reese took him to the hospital to get him patched up, but yeah, he should be home by now. He's got a broke nose, and probably two black eyes. You should have seen him. Jon beat him up good. But if you ask me, George got what he deserved."

Melanie didn't like it when people criticized George. George was having a run of bad luck and Melanie felt sorry for him. She was repulsed by the way Tom laughed, practically choking on his slobber.

He rubbed his nose and asked her, "You screwin' around with him or what?"

"That's none of your business," she said. "I'm just concerned about him. He's Lloyd's cousin, you know."

"You just seem a little *too* concerned. I see now what I expected to see. You're sleeping with him."

"Never mind! You get your share. Just concentrate on the money I'm saving from Lloyd's paychecks. When the time's right, we're out of here. Then you can have me all to yourself. Won't that be nice?"

"Sure," said Tom, trying to grope her. She pulled away from him again. It was the visual of his decayed teeth more than his body odor that made her cringe. "Come on, honey," he urged. "I know your kids are in bed and Lloyd's not due back for hours."

"First I need you to do something. I need you to watch the boys for about an hour." Melanie checked her watch under the porch light; she checked her pockets to make sure she had her car keys and wallet. "I'm going to the store to pick up some cold medicine for Jake." Jake was her two year old. "You stay here until I get back."

"This time of night?" Tom whined, looking to the trees for an explanation. "Can't you get it in the morning?"

"I'll only be about an hour. Leave the yard light on."

She ran down the porch steps to the trail of the woodshed where she parked her station wagon. She planned to see George now that Tom had tipped her off. She had to check on George's condition. "Make sure you don't answer the phone," she told him as she got into her car, "in case Lloyd calls."

Tom shook his head. Melanie had tricked him again.

• • •

Melanie parked behind a stand of pines near the graveled driveway where she watched Lucas leave George's house. Lucas was the last person she had expected to see this time of night.

Lucas had never been polite to her, much less civil, and if he saw her at George's, he would probably call the sheriff. Why he despised her so much, she didn't know. But it upset her how the old sot didn't bother to get to know her; yet he made harsh judgments about her, mostly that she was a hindrance to his *dear nephew.*

She knew Lucas had tried to help Lloyd after his mother died. Lloyd was only sixteen at the time of her death. His mother was Lucas's only sibling: a sister, two years younger, but as ruthless as Lucas himself. Due to a blood bond, apparently Lucas felt compelled to help his deceased sister's only child. All fine and good, decided Melanie, but Lucas thought he had her figured out when, in fact, he could barely describe what she looked like.

After Lucas's pickup truck went by, she drove up to George's house. She was impressed with the layout. It was a three-story house with an attic. The exterior was wood sided—probably pine— rustic brown with dark green shutters. There was a long porch stretching from one end of the front to the other, several potted plants hanging from the roof, trimmed bushes in the yard, and rocks lining the path from the driveway up to the front steps.

Knowing that George had a drinking problem, Melanie was surprised to find his property and house so well taken care of. There wasn't any trash or discarded car parts visible in the yard, not even in the back. Maybe Mae had been the one to take care of his house and property, but now that she was gone, Melanie wondered if the property would fall to ruin— like Lucas's.

The porch light was on. George's truck was the only vehicle parked in the driveway. Melanie didn't think anyone was with him, but after she parked and walked to the front door, she heard Reese's voice. He was talking about Lloyd. "Lloyd's right. We got to quit now that Lucas knows."

Melanie leaned forward to hear George's reply. "I got to take care of Loucher now," he said in a weak voice. "Loucher's a dead man."

"You shouldn't have bothered Mae. What's wrong with you?"

"You idiot," George mumbled, his voice raspy. "It's no one's business what I do with Mae. Someone, probably her sister, told Loucher. He attacked me in front of people. I'll kill him!"

"Stop it! You're going to rip them stitches! You don't know what you're saying!"

"The hell I don't. Wait 'till I get him alone in the woods. He's gonna have an accident with his saw!"

"I think I'd better take you back to the hospital. You don't look good and you're sounding nuts. I hope it's just all them painkillers talking."

"This is the last time I'm gonna tell you. No hospital! I just need to take out Loucher."

"What'll we do about Lloyd and Dad?"

"They're next on my list."

"No way am I going to let you hurt our dad, much less our only cousin!"

"You dick. Weren't you paying attention the other day? He's *not* my father. Dale Washburn's my father. Our mother told me before she died. She had a fling with him. Lucas found out, and threatened to kill her if she left him." There was a long pause, and then Melanie heard a sniffle; next a coughing spasm from George that was so drawn-out and bone-chilling, Melanie thought he was dying on the spot.

Reese offered to help George sit up to catch his breath.

When George settled down, Reese said, "I don't believe you. You don't even look like Washburn, except maybe the curly hair."

"I look like our mother," George insisted, trying to speak coherently. "Quit arguing with me! My head hurts and my nose is busted. I tell you, he's a fucking dead man!"

"Why hasn't Washburn talked about you being his son, if it's true?" Reese asked, fear jolting his voice. "I don't remember Washburn hanging around the house to see Mom. I think we would have suspected something if it was true."

"Who knows, maybe Washburn doesn't care. Or maybe he doesn't know for sure. Just keep it to yourself. I'll take Lucas up on running the business when he croaks, and if he don't play his cards right, that day might come soon."

"I'm not letting you hurt Lucas!" Reese yelled.

"Shut up and get me another drink!"

Melanie waited quietly as Reese approached. The kitchen was near the front of the house and Reese would have to pass the door to get there. She knocked on the screen door seconds before Reese saw her. He seemed startled and couldn't register who she was beneath the glow of the porch light. She helped him out. "It's Melanie McMasters. Lloyd's wife. Lloyd heard George got hurt at work today and wanted me to come by and see how he's doing."

"He's resting right now," Reese said in a suspicious tone. "He'll be okay. He doesn't want to see you."

"Well, I'd like to see *him*."

Reese disappeared back into the house. The thumping of his footsteps echoed along the hallway and she heard whispers. In a few minutes, he returned to tell her, "He said you can come on in."

George was lying on his back on the couch, a palm over his forehead and the other pressed against his chest. His legs were stretched out and his boots were propped up against the arm of the couch. When she touched him, he opened his eyes and looked at her. "Didn't I tell you to go get me another drink?" he told Reese, who was standing in the doorway.

Reese left them alone. Melanie sat down on the coffee table next to the couch and rubbed George's arm. She saw him wince; there was a bulge of purple flesh protruding from his upper lip and both of his eyes, particularly the left eye. "Jon Loucher did this to you?" she asked, disturbed by the bloated contours of his face.

"He broke my nose," George said. "I never had that happen. I've never had anybody even knock me down before!"

Melanie studied his nose: bruised and bent, fractured in two places. She said, "You should see a doctor."

"For what? A broke nose is a broke nose. Besides, I was in the ER earlier today; they gave me pain pills. Get 'em for me, hey? Over there by the TV."

Melanie got the bottle of Vicodin tablets, shook one out, and propped George up so he could swallow. "Forget about him," she coaxed, sensing anger build up inside him despite the medication she knew he had already abused by taking more than prescribed. "And forget about Mae. We have to keep Lloyd in line. You've got to figure out a way to keep Lucas quiet."

"I *know* a way to keep him quiet."

"Don't do anything you'll regret," she said, glancing towards the kitchen.

"Lucas's health isn't good, and it's going to get worse."

"I don't like it. But he's your dad and you know him better than I do."

She waited for George to say something about Washburn being his father. She wanted to see if he would confide in her, but he picked at his shirt with dirty fingers and looked over her shoulder. "Mae left me," he said. He made it sound like she had left him that morning, not weeks ago. The tone of his voice implied that the hurt was raw. "She's gone," he said.

Melanie bristled at the mention of her name. How dare Mae hurt George, the ruthless bitch. How dare she. But Melanie knew she had to get George focused on the chemicals. They had to coddle Lucas, or the whole scheme would blow up in their faces. Melanie, in her own time and way, would deal with Mae Lakarri.

She leaned close to George, "What about Lucas?"

"He won't be a problem much longer," George said. "It's Lloyd I'm not sure about." George reached for Melanie's hand. She had never seen him this way. His eyes were bloodshot, his eyelids puffed, and he looked like he might have a break down any second.

But he said, "Lloyd will double-cross us."

"If he does, I'll side with you," she promised.

George was worn out with talk. "He could be a problem is all I'm saying. It'll be him or Brent Christopher who turns us in."

"The DNR biologist?"

"If they catch him, we're all done. Especially Lloyd."

"If you hear anything, just tell Lloyd and pull out."

George gripped her hand, hard, which was surprising, due to his debilitated condition. "Mae's left me for good. She left me for that Loucher bastard!"

Melanie brushed the curls away from his eyes. She kissed the side of his face. "Forget about her," she said. "I'll take care of you now. Let's try to keep Lloyd going for another few weeks."

George relaxed as she stroked him, but as soon as she left, he would tell Reese to bring him another drink and more pills. She knew pain was something George couldn't deal with sober; pain was not to be taken straight on. "Stay here," he said. "Don't leave me."

"I have to get on home. I left the boys with a friend and I need to get back."

As she stood up to leave, George pulled her down again. He kissed her on the forehead, his lips rough. "Come back soon. Please come back."

"I'll try. You get some rest."

Melanie pulled away. As she walked down the hallway and passed the kitchen, Reese came into view, holding two bottles of beer. "Want a drink?" he asked. He stared straight into her eyes, making her nervous. "A cold beer?"

"Another time," she said, and walked out the door to escape Reese's waxy eyes, his head tipped as he stared. Very deliberately, at her.

He knows everything she thought. *He's smarter than people think.*

CHAPTER 10

Melanie didn't know why she was drawn to George Coulter, but after she left him, she couldn't get him off her mind. She thought about him all the way back to the house.

Why would she want George over Lloyd? Lloyd was a hard worker; he was clean-cut, and responsible. She met him in Wisconsin when he was studying at the University of Madison to become a biologist and she was in her first year of nursing school. She dropped out after a year, but Lloyd ended up with a degree in biology.

After he graduated, he wanted to work for the Fisheries Department in Marquette or Munising, but he couldn't secure placement and ended up taking a job with Conrad Paper Mill. He was driven, but to Melanie, it seemed whenever he came up against inadequate pay or a difficult coworker, he would take the easy way out. All she had to do was suggest siphoning of dioxins and the names of people who would help—his cousins George and Reese—and Lloyd started researching the possibilities.

Although Lloyd was quite a bit older than Melanie, she married him to escape her life in Wisconsin. She had been adopted as an infant and never felt accepted by her adoptive parents. After she and Lloyd dated for a year and a half, they married and moved to Upper Michigan. She didn't hesitate to make the move; in fact, she had been to the area to visit her cousin, Ellen, the daughter of her adoptive mother's sister.

In short, she was fond of Lloyd, maybe loved him at first, but only married him to build a new life. Unfortunately, life with Lloyd turned out to be horribly dull. Now she wanted to go back to Wisconsin, but she would wait until she had most of Lloyd's money first and file for a divorce.

Her plan was to use Tom Foster to get where she wanted to go.

Tom Foster himself, her human ticket out of this dreary hellhole, was sitting on the porch like a simpleton, waiting for her to return. He didn't *walk* down the steps; he jumped over them and ran towards her as soon as she stepped out of the station wagon. "Where have you been?" he asked, worked up into a frenzy. "It's after midnight!"

Melanie showed him the paper bag. "I had to drive around to find a store that was open," she said. "I wasn't gone that long. You worry too much."

"The phone's been r-r-ringing off the ho-ok," Tom stuttered as he followed her to the porch. "I think it might be Lloyd. And since he got no answer for over an hour, he's p-p-probably on his way home. He could've found me here!"

"You worry too much," she told him again. "Just calm down!"

"That's the last time I do *you* a favor," Tom shouted, unable to control his fear over Lloyd

McMasters driving up to the house, jumping out of his car, and beating him with a briefcase; or worse, shooting him. After all, if he, Tom, caught another man in his house with his wife while his kids slept, he would lose his mind and kill not only the man but his wife, too. Looking startled he said, "My wife doesn't need to know about you until after we're gone!"

"Everything will be fine," Melanie insisted, rolling her eyes. Nonetheless, as soon as the words left her mouth, Lloyd's vehicle turned the corner from the highway and sped up the driveway. "I'll handle this," she said, and hoisted the grocery bag up to her hip to get a better grip on it. "You be quiet and pay attention; follow what I say."

They watched Lloyd walk towards the porch, carrying his briefcase. He swung the case with one hand and unbuttoned the top button of his shirt with the other. "Why didn't you answer the phone?" he asked Melanie. "I've been trying to get you for over an hour!"

"Relax, dear, I didn't hear the phone." Poor Lloyd, she thought, *he's going to have a heart attack one of these days.*

She turned to Tom with a grandiose gesturing of her free hand. "Thank God Ellen's boyfriend, Ben, was able to go to the store for me. Jake's got a cold. I couldn't leave him here alone to get medicine."

But if Lloyd wasn't suspicious upon his arrival, he sure was now. "How could you call Ellen if the phone's down?" he asked, his eyes heading for Tom Foster's anemic-looking face. Melanie knew he didn't think Tom—or rather "Ben"—looked like the sort of man Ellen would date. He looked like some derelict that had wandered in off the highway.

"Ben was nice enough to run to the store for me," Melanie said; she showed Lloyd the bag. She even opened it so he could look inside. "I'd better go in and give some of this to Jake."

Melanie could tell Lloyd didn't recognize Tom as one of his uncle's employees. Lucky for her, Lloyd had never been to one of Lucas's logging sites. He claimed he didn't want to associate with Lucas at all, not even in passing.

She could rest assured that Lloyd had no idea who Tom was or what, if any, role he might play in their lives. Lloyd looked at Tom again. He said, "Thanks for helping out," but his tone was skeptical.

"Any time," Tom said. Melanie could tell he didn't know what to say or do when he nodded and walked to his truck. He glanced back in time to see Melanie take Lloyd's arm and walk into the house—where she could satisfy him, no doubt.

Satisfying Lloyd went on for most of night and didn't end until eight thirty the next morning when there was a pounding on the front door. Lloyd merely turned beneath the sheets, but the knocking startled Melanie. She slipped out of bed, pulled on a robe, and ran to the door before it was beaten down entirely.

She couldn't believe Lucas Coulter was at the door. He shoved his bloated body past her and settled a hand against the table. "Get Lloyd!" he demanded. "Get him *right now*!"

Melanie ran back to the bedroom. Lloyd was still under the blankets, "It's Lucas," she whispered, her heart thumping so hard she thought she was going to faint. "Get up and deal with him!"

But Lloyd only stirred beneath the covers, seemingly unconvinced that Lucas Coulter would appear at their door at all, never mind this early in the morning. "What does he want?" Lloyd asked her.

"I don't know, but he's mad. It must have something to do with the chemicals. Hurry up and get dressed!" She yanked the sheets off him. He couldn't find his underwear, so she picked them up off the floor and threw them at him. "Hurry up. I'm not going to deal with *that* crazy asshole!"

"Get him out of here," she yelled as Lloyd attempted to dress. "And don't let him push you around!"

"He must have news about Christopher."

"What does that mean? What's going on with Christopher?" When Lloyd didn't answer, she nudged him. "Tell me what's going on!"

"Shut up!" Lloyd said. "And stay here!"

Lucas shouted from the living room, "Get your ass in here! We don't got all day!"

Melanie knew that something life-altering was about to happen. She put a hand to his chest when he said, "If they've got Christopher, I'm next. There's eight thousand dollars under the mattress."

"What do you mean?"

But Lloyd zipped up his pants and headed for the kitchen. Melanie leaned into the wall to hear the conversation. Lucas was so upset he could hardly speak. Finally, he bellowed, "Christopher's been arrested. You got to hide for a while!"

"Hide where?" Lloyd asked in a broken voice. "It's over now, Lucas. There's no point in running!"

"You'll hide, goddammit, and you'll do it now! Go tell that wife of yours to keep her yap shut. She doesn't know where you are or who you're with, understand me? I don't want no one to know about this until I talk with my lawyer and warn George and Reese. No doubt that Christopher bastard will spill the beans. I don't want no one suspecting Coulter Logging!"

When Lloyd rushed back to the bedroom, he bumped into Melanie, still standing in the doorway. He took her hands. "Lucas is going to talk to his lawyer and straighten everything out," he explained. "Don't worry. Take care of the boys. And if anyone asks, you don't know a thing."

"But how will I get in touch with you if I need you?"

"Contact Lucas. He'll know." Lloyd kissed her on the forehead. He pulled out his wallet and gave her all but one of his credit cards. "Don't forget about the money under the mattress," he reminded her.

Without saying another word, Lloyd and Lucas ran out the door just as the telephone rang. Melanie hesitated, but forced herself to answer it. "Hello?"

"Lloyd McMasters," said a male voice.

"He's not here; he's on an errand."

She hung up quickly and checked to see which credit cards Lloyd had given her. She had to focus. She went back to the bedroom to count the money under the mattress.

* * *

When Mae found out about the fight between Jon and George at the logging site, she knew George would stop at nothing for revenge. He would drink until he blacked out, and then he would go after Jon.

It was difficult to tell exactly what George was capable of and how far he would go. She knew he was motivated by bitterness, and Jon beating him up in front of the crew didn't help.

She had to convince Jon to stay away from George. So, she decided to drive out to Three Cedar Road and talk to him.

Of course, she found him working on his house. He had paid for a well and a septic system to be put in, yet there was still a lot to do, and it was almost November. The temperature was forty-two degrees. There was a dusting of snow on the ground.

When she walked up the front steps and into the kitchen, she was surprised to find he had finished the interior of the kitchen and had started on the laundry room. He mentioned to her before that the wiring system was the most difficult part for him. He wasn't much of an electrician. She remembered he also told her he was going to hire a contractor in Munising to help with the main wiring, and a plumber would come next to inspect the bathrooms, laundry room, and kitchen hookups.

She heard him working a sander and watched him move around the wooden frame door of the laundry room. He didn't seem surprised to see her standing by the stove. She said, "I'm worried about you."

He gave up on the sanding. The frame was dented and scratched. He selected a different piece of wood, this one not as inferior, and reached down to the coffee can filled with different sizes of nails. He looked at her. "You feeling better?" he asked.

"I'm fine."

"I couldn't let it go," Jon said with a nail between his teeth. "What he did to you."

"I know him," she yelled. "He'll try to kill you!"

She was stunned when Jon laughed. He had taken the nail from his mouth and beat it, hard, into the wall with the hammer.

Mae sat down on a foldout chair he kept inside the doorway. She could feel the heat from the woodstove coming from the living room and unzipped her coat, pulled at the collar of her blouse. She said, "Don't laugh. I'd press charges against him for assault like Paula wants me to, but I've heard that the DNR is close to getting him. And everyone else too."

Jon stopped pounding on the middle shelf and started with the lower. He measured the area first; the metal measuring tape snapped apart, clicked back together. "I'd sure like to know where you're getting your information," he said.

"An enforcement officer with the DNR," Mae said. "That's all I can tell you."

"Is this officer investigating the Coulters or the fanatics?"

"He thinks the group targeted the Coulters because of the chemical dumping."

"How do you know him?"

"I can't tell you right now. I've been giving him information and that's why I can't press charges against George. Just please be careful."

"You give him way too much credit," Jon said. "What do you know about this environmental group?"

"Just that there's been tree-spiking north of Marquette. A piece cutter got hurt and the group's been protesting, blocking routes to the paper mills. The man I know says he thinks someone in Coulter's crew is in on it."

Jon stopped beating on nails and leaned against the door frame.

"I'm worried this time," she said. "*Really* worried."

He was looking at the cut above her eye, which hadn't healed. She had put concealer on by her eyes and the sides of her mouth. "You can move in here," he said. "If you're worried."

"It's not me I'm worried about, Jon. He'll come after *you!*"

She didn't like it when he laughed again. *He's making fun of me,* she thought. So, she turned for the kitchen door and left him alone with his damned precious house.

Chapter 11

Jon heard a rumor that Brent Christopher, the DNR biologist working at the Conrad Paper Mill, had been arrested for tampering of test results. Lucas Coulter didn't have a contract with Conrad Paper Mill; he mostly sold stumpage to sawmills near Rapid River and Munising. And he bought stumpage from private landowners too, and rarely would he try to out bid other loggers to cut on state land. But knowing Lucas's nephew, Lloyd McMasters, worked at Conrad, and that Christopher had been assigned to measure the bleach by-products and alter the percentages, Jon put two and two together when Lucas didn't show up at the logging site.

It was the second week of November; firearm deer season started on the fifteenth. Lucas's crew worked through most of deer season, depending on the job. Deer season meant wearing hunter orange. It also meant weapons would be at hand.

The deer were moving through the woods, on roads and highways, pushed this way and that by hunters. Jon and Dale usually took one week off, but not this year with eco-terrorists lurking about and George Coulter throwing temper tantrums.

But George hadn't returned to work, either. Maybe he was still nursing his wounds, Jon decided, or maybe, as Mae had warned, he was plotting a fatal attempt on Jon's life. Lucas finally showed up; however, for only about twenty minutes. He mentioned that George was taking some time off. He said George was trying to clean up his act.

Reese was the only one of the Coulters who continued with his work schedule. He plunged right in with his piece-cutting duties. He cut his usual quota and even drove one of the bulldozers to clear out brush and make new roads.

Reese could be a positive asset to the company, thought Jon, if only people would give him a chance. Without George telling him what to do, Reese kept to himself, but when consulted on business matters, he was cordial and resourceful.

The morning of the opening day of deer season, Lucas appeared at the logging site. He rubbed his hands together to warm them against the chill. He looked twice his normal size, dressed in a heavy orange coat, red vest, orange cap, and thick overalls.

He walked up to Jon, who was filing the chain of his saw.

"George'll be back to work today," he said. "You keep an eye on him."

Jon looked at Lucas through a swirl of snowflakes. "I'd better not see him at all," he said, spitting a wad of chewing tobacco to the icy ground, where it sizzled. He looked away with nothing more to add.

"Now you listen here, George is next!" Lucas snapped. He bent down so close to Jon's face, Jon smelled his gamy coffee breath accented with cigar. "That's right," continued Lucas, all worked up. "They're about to nail him! The DNR's got an eye on Christopher, and it's just a matter of time before they get George and Reese. I've got to run some errands today, and tomorrow I'm going to see my lawyer in Escanaba. I want you to keep tabs on things around here. Reese is no problem, but I don't trust George."

"That's a shame," Jon said, bored with the conversation. "Your own son." He clicked his tongue against his teeth, loud enough to make his point. "A damn shame."

"My son, well ..." Lucas waved off further comment. Jon had suspected George's true paternity for years now, but Lucas didn't know that. "Never mind," Lucas said with a sardonic edge to his voice. "I'm counting on you to steer the ship while I'm gone. Where's Washburn?"

"Working at the other site."

Jon thought it peculiar that Lucas had forgotten what jobs he had assigned and where. Jon was to work the Rapid River location with Bryan Kinnenun, Reese, and the new skidder operator Lucas hired two weeks before. And Dale was assigned to the Autrain Lake site with Tom Foster and George.

Lucas tugged at his mop of whiskers. "I can't remember nothin' these days," he confided wearily. "Try not to get George stirred up. I'm hopin' to talk him into leaving the area."

"A great idea," Jon said, putting his saw aside and standing up. He faced Lucas and poked Lucas's chest with his finger. "Get *George* riled up?" he asked, angry all over again. "Do you know what he did to Mae Lakarri?"

"Yes." Lucas pushed Jon's hand away. "I heard about it. I'll admit he's a drunk with a short fuse, but no woman's worth a broke nose!"

"I'll break his neck if he touches her again. Never mind his fucking nose."

"I never heard you sound so reckless!" Lucas said, not caring who overheard them now. He slapped his palm across his thigh. And said, "The thing's this: I gave George some extra responsibility, which means he won't be standing around picking his nose anymore. He'll be foreman of this crew. And that one over there." He indicated the new skidder operator. "Name's Savola; I hired him to help out."

"And *I'm* reckless?" Jon chided, ignoring the Savola comment. "Is that because George can run this operation into the ground faster than you can?"

"Don't underestimate my sons, Lo-sure!" Lucas shot back. He shivered from the cold, and Jon saw that his coat was patched at one elbow, and there was a rip near the knee of his left pant leg. "Reese, for one, is smarter than you think," Lucas insisted, spitting. "I'll be back later tonight," he said.

Jon asked, "Any idea who in the crew is working with the terrorists?"

"Where'd you hear a thing like that?" Lucas asked, looking crazed. "Who told you that?"

"I heard. And I'm waiting."

Lucas scoffed at Jon's comment and walked towards Tom Foster, who had called out to him. But before Lucas stumbled up a ridge, he pointed a finger at Jon. "Remember what I said, goddamn you!" Jon watched Lucas stagger away, favoring his right leg. It was unusual for him to limp and even more unusual for him to wheeze, but he was doing both lately.

Suddenly, Lucas turned and walked back to Jon. He put a gloved hand on Jon's shoulder and leaned in again, the stench of rank coffee overbearing. "How 'bout I give you and Dale twenty-five bucks an hour?" he asked. "You might consider getting paid by the hour now instead of the piece."

"I can live with that," Jon said, although he was soon to live without the entire company. He decided to go see Clara's lawyer, check out her terms.

"Keep an eye on George," Lucas said, issuing his final order. "I'm off. Got to see what Foster wants, then talk with the new skidder operator. You meet him yet?"

"No."

"He came to me outta nowhere, lookin' for work. Life can be funny, hey?"

Funny's not the word, thought Jon. *More like insidious.*

Jon adjusted his hard hat, pulled down the ear guards, and went back to work.

• • •

The snow fell all morning and into the afternoon, the temperature dipping to thirty degrees. Even though loggers worked throughout the winter months, it was profitable to get a large part of the work out of the way before winter weather became ruthless. November brought snow and sleet, but the serious storms and below zero temperatures didn't come into play until January.

Lucas didn't specify just how close the investigators were to arresting George and Reese, or if they were to be next in line after Brent Christopher. Just because Brent Christopher was within sight of the law didn't mean they were anywhere near arresting Lucas's sons. It seemed to Jon that Lucas knew the right people; therefore, he had the ability *and* the power to keep certain indiscretions hidden.

I'll be gone soon anyway, Jon thought, *and the sooner the better.* In retrospect, Clara Halverson had worn him down. Piece by piece, hour by hour, breakfast by breakfast, she had managed to talk him into accepting her offer. *It's my final desire on this earth,* she told him the morning before Elbert took her to a nursing facility per her request, *to know that you are operating an ethical, environmentally sound logging company. Logging is necessary, and if done properly, everyone is happy.* And she kept on and on about the fools, criminals if you will, that Jon was working with, which in effect made Jon just as guilty because *he worked for them and knew their ways,* yet he wouldn't seek employment elsewhere. Clara added that her only surviving relative, that no-good upstart nephew of hers named Neil, had always hated her. Told her he hated her to her face no less, and not only that, three years ago he insisted she give him several thousands of dollars. *It will never happen* Clara said, looking at Jon, her bottom lip stiff. *Neil has been nothing but a disappointment to me, his father, and probably even God!* Neil was desperate, she ranted, because he married some buxom slut who tried to bleed him for all his money and he worked himself into a frazzle, for her, a woman who slept around behind his back! Now in the end, Neil was divorced and in the process of being sued for this and that, which prompted him to beg and even threaten Clara to give him money, *more money*. But she wouldn't do it, and she couldn't forget his parting words to her three years ago: *You selfish, dried-up old hag!*

As Jon thought about Clara Halverson's request and contemplated his future prospects— remembering her telling him she had sold stocks and bonds and property and instructed her attorney to write Jon a check— George appeared from the mist.

It was as if he had lifted out of a patch of burdocks, was born from a gnarled elm. George stood on a ridge six or seven yards away. He was smoking with a hand on his hip, hard hat tipped back. He wore hunter orange from the waist up. His jeans and boots were wet from the snow.

He yelled, "Loucher! You head on over to that ridge north of here. Lucas put me in charge, and now we're gonna find out what you're made of."

Jon looked at him, puzzled. He couldn't believe George expected him to jump to his command. Did he forget who had put that deformity to his nose, the cut above his brow, and the welt—still not healed—at the side of his mouth?

Jon spat chewing tobacco to the ground, which was a vice he would partake in when he was alone, back at his cabin or in the woods. He started to walk towards the ridge with his saw. He walked right up to George and steadied his boot against a stump and said, "We are, hey?"

It was George's turn to spit, into the cold air, just missing Jon's arm. He pulled on his right glove, then his left, and said, "Yes, we are damn you! If all the trees within a mile aren't down by noon tomorrow, you'll just have to keep on cuttin'. Say 'til, oh I don't know, next spring?"

"If you still want a job, that is," he added, then pressed his lips together.

He watched Jon's hands.

He turned and disappeared back into the brush.

Jon reflected on the matter before he realized that Rick Savola, the new skidder operator, was nearby, sitting in the cage of the skidder. Savola said, "Seems this George character has some sort of brain disorder."

Jon considered Savola's round probing eyes. Savola looked to be in his late-forties; he was thin and warped, due to the weight of his occupation. He had circular indents on his chin, a white scar on his forehead. He had shoulder-length, blond-gray hair and wore a headband to keep the wispy strands from his eyes. He wore green work pants, a red hunting vest, black boots, and an orange hard hat. He chewed on a weed stuck to the corner of his lips.

When he leaned out of the cage, he propped his left hand against one knee, showing that only three fingers and a thumb were attached. He advised Jon in a harsh voice, "I'd watch that bastard if I was you."

He revved up the skidder, that coughed out murky fumes as it climbed a hill, leaving behind grooves in the damp earth.

Jon watched Savola maneuver the yellow and black machine, and then walked over to a spot on the north ridge. After checking his saw over, Jon stood upon the slushy ground and maintained a steady pace while cutting.

But as the afternoon wore on, the snow accumulated. Jon paused and held his saw, the bar behind him idling. Something told him to shut it off.

He turned after he heard, "Stand still but look around," in a woman's voice.

Then there was silence, except for the swish of a cedar bough.

He calculated the time of day by the position of the sun: three o'clock in the afternoon. The wind picked up speed, forcing leaves not yet buried under snow to bounce along the ground.

Jon knew the beauty could turn ugly; his life over in an instant. There were different ways to die in the woods, tragic accidents he had heard of and even witnessed. The widow maker: a branch hung up in a tree, falling; the barber chair—a spinning branch—falling; faulty equipment; slipping on ice; slippery rocks; slushy snow.

Jon put a hand over his eyes. He looked up to the fog settling among the branches; gauzy ribbons of clouds slipping over patches of purple and gray. He knew the snow would fall in delicate shafts for the rest of the afternoon, and by nightfall, the first blizzard of the season would hit.

He also knew that most of the crew was gone for the day. He started up the chainsaw, pulled three times to get it going, because, despite his thin gloves, his fingertips were numb. He sliced into the base of a tree, one fourth of the way, careful not to pinch the blade.

He made the under-cut notch on the other side of the base and the tree fell over with a crash. He stepped backwards to get his bearings on the measurements. He would cut six inches extra on these eight-foot lengths to compensate for skidder damage. He kept cutting, thinking he would quit after this tree. One more tree.

The air was brittle against his skin and pins of ice clung to his beard. He stepped backwards to cut another limb. He knew he should leave, but the motion itself relaxed him, not to mention the fresh air and the exercise. Both he needed.

He knew the storm had picked up speed, and it wasn't a good idea to be operating a chainsaw alone out in the woods. He would leave; but first, he would wander the area to see if there was evidence of George and Reese using this area to bury more barrels of contaminants.

He slowed his saw. He saw an eagle glide from one birch tree to another, squirrels running about. He heard the strong breeze rock the limbs of the conifers, and he also heard birds—blue jays and chickadees—as they announced the change of weather. *Winter is coming.*

He squinted against the snowflakes and leaned over to cut one more limb, the saw full throttle. Why he elected to crank up his saw one last time he did not know, but just as he was thinking about turning it off for good and packing up for the day, there was a blast from somewhere among the bare aspens. And then silence.

In the blink of an eye, his left leg snapped as he slipped down the ridge, feeling suspended, stuck, before falling the rest of the way. There was no pain at first and only a jolt with the impact of landing. But he knew to toss the chainsaw; if he had held onto it, his leg would have been severed. She said *Drop it Jon, drop it*— and he heard it crash among the frozen weeds somewhere to the right of him.

He lay inert, trying to focus the gray sky, listening to the warning of chickadees and the hoot of an owl. Probably a great horned.

He smelled chainsaw oil blended with decayed ferns. His leg pulsated as if a knife was stuck into the bone below his knee. Beyond that, he couldn't feel anything, and he touched his chest to try to grab the knife. But there wasn't a knife. He had fallen among the trees, gliding, the wind carrying him, although he was flat against the ground, remembering his mother's voice as darkness quickly took him.

• • •

Rick Peterson heard a rifle shot; he figured a .30-.30. Rick was the only crew member, other than George, who had stayed behind at the logging site. He parked the skidder a mile from where Jon had been shot and ran through the woods to the north ridge, slipping several times on the icy ground.

He stopped to look for signs of blood, or anything to determine what had happened. The shot had revealed a sinister ending to a long, dark day. He listened to the sound of a pickup truck starting up and driving away. He yelled, "Hey," cupping his hands against the wind that tried to knock him off his feet. "Anyone out there?"

It was impossible to hear a voice over the calamity of branches popping like gunshots. He kept on walking, stepping over deadfall, following the trail. He came to the area where Jon had been cutting; he followed the boot prints to the edge of the ridge where he found blood.

Jon was lying flat on the ground. Peterson slid down the ridge, not realizing a branch had sliced his face. There was so much blood around Jon, it appeared that a main artery had been severed. Upon closer inspection, Peterson could see that the material of Jon's clothing was ripped, indicating he landed on his shoulder, fracturing bones. There was also a circle of blood near Jon's lower left leg, evidently where the bullet had hit. The tibia bone of that leg was clearly broken and more than likely the nerves were severed. It would take surgery and a long time thereafter to heal. If ever.

Peterson sat next to Jon, pulled Jon's hard hat off, and held his head. Jon was in shock; ghost white without sweating. Peterson had already called for help, even before he left his surveillance post to find out where the gunshot had been fired. Peterson leaned in close to Jon's lips when Jon murmured something about a woman.

Jon could see his mother, although he was only five years old when she died. His memory of her was vague and he had to fill in her features like drawing them into a partially blank face. He could see her long blond hair. Yes, he remembered her hair, and the silver ring on her finger with the yellow sparkling jewel in the center of it.

He could see her slightly crooked front tooth and he asked her: *Why did you? Leave Elbert for another man?*

Jon opened his eyes to a face that looked like Savola's, the character with all the hair and only three fingers on one hand. The same guy who told him to watch his back.

"Where's Elbert?" Jon asked him.

Elbert will come; he has to come.

"It's okay," Peterson said. "You just hold on."

But when Peterson tried to lift him, the pain was so severe, Jon believed his spirit was leaving his body.

After all, his mother was telling him to follow her. And not only that, Elbert said, *You can go with her, for just a day or two. But you can't stay.*

CHAPTER 12

Jon was unconscious for the first two days in the hospital but he knew when hands were turning him. He was heavily sedated most of the time, and in a week, the gash in his shoulder was almost healed.

An hour after the ambulance transported him to the emergency room, the doctors tried to suture the severed nerves in his lower left leg where he was shot. The bullet had gone through the flesh and grazed the tibia bone, but the shooter was far enough away, the surgeon said, that the injury wasn't as extensive as it could have been. Any closer and his leg would have been shot off. But his wounds, internal and external, were severe enough to expect permanent damage.

His shoulder was dislocated; it happened when he was shot and fell down the steep ridge. The medical team repositioned the bones. The wound in his leg required stitches after an irrigation flushing with antibiotics. Infection was the crucial issue from the onset, but soon after surgery, other complications surfaced. The area became infected despite the irrigation and antibiotic IV, and the wound had to be opened up again, flushed, and re-sutured.

The break in his shoulder would heal, but his wrist had been sprained when he hit the ground and his left arm was shattered near the shoulder. He had to wear a brace on his wrist and a cast and sling for his arm.

As he lay in a semi-conscious state, he imagined George Coulter's haggard face looming over him. In between visions of George, Jon heard Elbert's voice. Several times, he felt Elbert's rough palm against his hand.

Even though Jon knew Elbert despised hospitals, he made an appearance to be sure Jon was going to pull through. He stayed in the waiting room during the surgery and afterwards, and when Jon was in recovery, he stood beside Jon's bed and watched him sleep. Occasionally, he leaned over and put an ear to Jon's mouth to make sure he was breathing.

Dale came to visit him every day, too. Jon remembered one visit in particular when he managed enough strength to clamp his fingers around Dale's arm. He knew Dale had something important to say.

Through a fog of codeine, he recognized the outline of Dale's face: the angular chin and pointed cheekbones. Not only that, but Dale smelled of pipe smoke and diesel fumes.

Jon waited for Dale to say something. "Tell me," he whispered.

"Brent Christopher was arrested," Dale said, unable to suppress the information any longer. "And Lloyd McMasters disappeared."

"W-ho?" The word stuck in his throat. *Where's the nurse with the chipped ice?* he was thinking as he tried to keep Dale's face in focus.

"I don't know. That environmentalist group is poking around. You'd better snap to and help me figure out a plan."

In fact, during the past few weeks, as Jon lay dormant in the antiseptic-smelling hospital room, he couldn't get Savola off his mind. He knew he would have died if Savola hadn't been nearby.

Jon licked his lips. "Sa-vola?" Then, with more force, "Was there."

"He jumped down the ridge and hauled you back up. He dragged you to the road, where he called for help on the radio. But, I guess you aren't supposed to move an injured body. Now they think you have more tissue damage in the leg because of it. You know, because of him moving you."

Jon frowned. He wanted to say, *He did the right thing. I hated the cold ground against my back and legs more than anything; more than the pain itself.* "Like hell," Jon said.

Dale looked puzzled by Jon's "like hell," although with all the pain medication Jon was on, it was possible Jon couldn't hear Dale clearly. "Savola said Kinnenun was sitting in his truck when he got you to the road."

Jon wiped the saliva from his mouth with a shaking finger. "Oh," he said.

"Savola's odd," Dale said. "He heard the shot, but claims he saw nothing. Good thing he knows first aid; he wrapped your leg and stopped the bleeding in your shoulder."

"Mae?" Jon asked.

"She's at her sister's. She thinks George shot you."

"Yes," Jon said and drifted off. "Deer season."

He was thinking, *Deer season is a good excuse. People get shot during deer season, accidental or otherwise. And this is what I get for getting involved.*

"That's what they think, but they're investigating," Dale went on, his voice fragmented. "All the commotion with deer season. If you ask me, it's unlikely you were mistaken for a deer. They found a .30-30 shell casing."

Jon couldn't stay awake. He drifted and dreamed. He dreamed about going home and about working on his house. *Would he finish it?* On and off in his sleep, he heard Mae's voice. *Don't worry, we'll see each other again.*

As the days went by, he had difficulty pronouncing certain words. He couldn't lift the volume of his voice and blamed the medication.

He told the nurses to cut down on the Demerol or codeine or whatever; alternate in small doses. His leg hurt more than the shoulder, and yet the shoulder had been dislocated by the impact of the fall.

The physical therapist, named Annette, forced him to walk every day. But the worst part was standing upright; it made his head spin. *It's the drugs*, he kept thinking. Over and over again, he asked his doctor to decrease the dosage.

And this routine went on until he was discharged from the hospital on the thirteenth of December. He lived with Elbert from then until February. His major injuries, particularly his arm, weren't quite healed and he had to use a cane instead of crutches. His doctor prescribed three different drugs: drugs to sleep, to build up his strength, and of course, to numb the pain in his leg and the searing jolt in his shoulder. He didn't want to take drugs, but it was necessary for mobility.

Within a week, he became confused on how much he had taken and when. The fracture in his chest and shoulder had healed for the most part, but his breathing was stressed, and his lungs ached from the pressure. The shattered bones of the tibia area below his knee caused such excruciating pain, he increased the Valium intake.

Therefore, Elbert hid them. "You can't be drugged up on pills this long," Elbert pointed out. "You'll get hooked!"

"Getting hooked" was a phrase Elbert had used often throughout Jon's lifetime, particularly during Jon's adolescence. "Getting hooked" was a state of mind Elbert vowed would never happen to his only son—not in the form of alcohol or drugs.

But for the first time ever, Jon wasn't interested in Elbert's opinion.

He was too busy trying to function within a fog of pain. And since it was obvious he wasn't going to be able to go back to work for two or three more months, or even work on his house, the idea of recuperating under Elbert's keen eye was almost more than he could stand.

Yet at least while living at Elbert's, he was *in* the woods. He could look out the window and find snow and trees and watch the woodpeckers and chickadees. He could poke the .22 out the door and pick off red squirrels (single-handedly), if he felt like it.

Staying at Elbert's was better than lying in a hospital bed where he couldn't see a single tree. *Trees*, he thought, in a drug-induced delirium. *Trees are my reason for living. Cedars, particularly: the healing tree.*

But, again and again, the drugs forced him to take convalescence to extremes. He was unable to exert himself past blurs and echoes; visions swirling; time blending, tricking him. All he cared about was playing solitaire, watching movies, and lounging around for two more days until he finally attempted to walk with the crutches. He agreed to physical therapy, where he learned how to use the crutches for support while building up strength for the cane. The doctor said it would be impossible to predict a long-term prognosis, but one thing was certain. If Jon didn't start walking around to regain his muscle strength, he would become crippled.

Using the crutches proved to be such grueling work, it didn't take him long to give up on the process and settle for the couch. On the couch he could read, watch television, eat, drink, stare, and brood—all without leaving the living room.

• • •

During the holidays, Elbert tried to cheer Jon up. He decorated the house with tiny white lights and green wreaths for Christmas, but the only thing Jon cared about was the card Mae sent him. He kept the card with him at all times, tucked between the cushions of the couch. He would read it occasionally, look at the picture of the pines, birds, and snow, and touch the red letters: *Merry Christmas … have a blessed New Year.* There were sparkles on the picture, representing snow he assumed, and in her looping handwriting she wrote: "Jon, take care of yourself and recover. I will visit you soon. Love Mae."

Love Mae. He read the words over and over again. He heard her say, *Love Mae, Love Mae,* despite the reverberations of his drug-induced thoughts.

Elbert said she had called twice. Both times Jon was asleep, yet she didn't bother to visit him. He supposed it was for the best; his physical and mental deterioration would disgust her. He still had sunken black eyes and bruises on his arms, neck, and legs; and he had lost ten pounds. Add all of that to the fact that he couldn't focus on faces or hear half of what people were saying. The drugs. He knew it was the power of the drugs making him hallucinate, but taking them was better than the pain.

December came and went with Christmas dinner, and Dale Washburn as their only guest. The Christmas tree and red and white lights went up, then down again.

Jon didn't notice.

Time, in general, went by unnoticed; days and nights blending together. Lake effect snowstorms, snow squalls, ice and bitter cold. The only certainty was that he was in pain and at one point, he realized he couldn't stand being sober. He couldn't handle the exercises in physical therapy either and refused to go to the hospital for further sessions.

Nonetheless he knew that when the drugs ran out he would have to go in for a checkup to get refills. But by mid-January, he was addicted to the couch as much as the pain pills. He didn't care about getting better. He was convinced that he would never be able to do the things he enjoyed: working in the woods, building his house, hunting and fishing.

And, of course, there was the fear that Mae wouldn't want to be with an invalid, so he kept himself sedated and defeated and eventually, his only form of activity was shuffling to and from the bathroom, the cane an extension of his body.

The only food that appealed to him was Elbert's homemade pizza. His tongue was so anesthetized by the drugs, he couldn't taste anything but pepperoni, garlic, and green peppers. Bryan Kinnenun, of all people, was supplying him with alcohol. *Interesting,* thought Jon, *that only Bryan can manage this feat behind Elbert's back.*

By the end of February, he started to smoke heavily. Before the shooting incident, he would smoke cigarettes occasionally or maybe chew tobacco, but now he chain-smoked cigars and cigarettes both.

He stretched out on the couch with his maimed leg propped up on pillows, his arm swinging outward to tap the ashes of the cigar off into an ashtray on the floor. His life consisted of one movie after another; empty bottles scattered about, and cigarette butts and cigar stubs stinking up Elbert's house.

Elbert had to take-action. "What do you think you're doing?" he asked Jon one afternoon, while collecting empty bottles and cigarette packages. "Since when do you lay around and waste your life?"

Jon didn't have an answer to that, but he was certain of one thing: if Elbert shut the VCR off like he did the other day, there would be trouble. Although Jon had seen this particular movie three times during the past week, he enjoyed reciting the dialogue. The film was about putting the ruthless cattle rancher out of commission, a story that had been told many times, but the characters and overall setting were enhanced tenfold because Jon was drugged and drunk.

He put up a hand and yelled, "Wait!" when he thought Elbert was going to shut the television off. "I like this part."

"You *like* being a drunkard," Elbert corrected while jerking the vacuum right and left. "Something I never thought you'd turn into. *You* of all people!"

He stared at Jon, not believing the transformation: Jon a bum; his only son a smoking, lazy, skinny invalid with shaggy hair and a thick beard.

Jon shifted upon the couch.

Elbert proceeded, "I thought you knew better than to mix drugs with booze. I got better things to do than watch you rot!"

"Then go do it!"

"Why don't you get off that damn couch and go take a shower!"

"Take a shower? What the *hell* for?" Jon looked at Elbert with watery eyes. He took another puff off the cigar, dramatizing the effort by crow's feet collecting around his eyes.

Elbert yelled, "You look older than me!"

Jon pointed a finger at Elbert. "If I wanted someone to bitch at me all day long, I'd get married!"

"Put that bottle down," Elbert shouted. There was no mistaking his irritation now. Smoke distorting his vision or not, Jon could see that Elbert had had enough.

Jon put the glass of whiskey down on the floor next to the ashtray and dropped the cigar inside it. He had thumped the bottom of the glass, signifying that he too had had enough. He rubbed his forehead, thinking that Elbert hadn't yelled at him since he was twelve years old and lied about skipping school. The shock, the very sound of Elbert shouting, rattled him.

He said in a steady voice people used to know, "I guess it's a bad idea to stay here. I think I'll go back to my cabin."

"And how will you get there?" Elbert asked. "Tell me. Are you trying to kill yourself, son?"

"No, I—"

"Are you trying to get *hooked*?" Elbert leaned in so close, Jon's eyes burned from the proximity of his bronze skin. "Hey?"

"No, not really. I—" Jon said, flexing his fingers.

Elbert cut him off. "Kill yourself someplace else. I won't watch!"

Because Jon couldn't think of anything more to say, he grabbed the remote and clicked the volume to high. He had missed the confrontation with the overbearing cattle rancher, but he liked the part where the rustlers ride off on their paint horses.

Elbert said over the clatter of hoof beats crossing the prairie, "Take a shower, god-dammit!"

After Elbert left the living room, Jon went back to the movie. He listened for the sound of the screen door shutting, knowing Elbert was off to feed the chickens.

• • •

Jon soon stopped taking care of himself all together. His black hair, normally cut short, was matted to his head. He slouched and slurred his speech. He didn't just lie propped up on the couch anymore; he sprawled outward upon it with his head at one end and his feet at the other. He wore ripped long underwear and a permanent scowl.

Elbert summoned Dale Washburn. He asked Dale to find out who was slipping Jon the booze behind his back. Consequently, Dale began to make house calls every night after work.

Dale had been plowing for Elbert all winter anyway, and he was the one supplying the videos, but Elbert warned him about that too: videos and liquor were dangerous vices, enabling Jon to remain in a vegetative state.

Dale began the conversation with: "The DNR got rid of Christopher, as you know. They're pressing charges against him."

The news about Christopher compelled Jon to rise up onto an elbow. He rubbed his beard absently and asked, "What about Lloyd? They find him too?"

"No. His wife doesn't even know where he is. We found a spike in a tree at one of the work sites."

"Globe One."

"Yeah, but no one got hurt."

Jon said, "Huh," but he was smoking a cigar and had to move it from his mouth to speak. "That's interesting. Did you bring my movies?"

"I didn't have time to get to the store," Dale said. *That's a lie*, thought Jon. *Elbert probably threatened not to do his laundry if he brought more movies.*

Jon knew he looked like a derelict; his long underwear was riddled with holes and there were stains under the armpits. The cast and sling were gone, but he still had trouble gathering the energy to sit up.

"Listen here," Dale said after clearing his throat. "Are you planning on laying around forever or are you going to help me find Lloyd? You know what?" He leaned forward, the smoke from Jon's fat cigar making his voice crack. "I think George knows what happened. Lloyd's been missing for four months. No trace of him anywhere. There's a statewide search to find him."

Dale made a clicking sound with his partial dentures. "You need to help me find out what happened. I think Lloyd heard about Christopher's arrest and either killed himself, or George did it for him."

Jon opened his mouth to say something, but Dale wasn't finished. "Could be Lloyd's hiding out in that camp behind the railroad grade near Trenary."

"For four months?" Jon mumbled, taking a pull on the foul cigar. "I doubt it."

Jon was more interested in the dialogue of the movie; he mouthed the exact words spoken by the actors. So, Dale waited a minute before saying, "You got to get up and move around! This isn't like you, and Elbert's worried!"

Jon said, "Worried?"

"Come back tomorrow and help me find Lloyd. What do you say?" Dale glanced around the room. Jon knew he was scrutinizing the trash. And the smell was overwhelming, particularly from the cigar; a brand that Dale himself would probably pass on.

Dale said loudly now," I got to get George to turn himself in. I know he shot you. So, murdering someone's probably next!"

Jon's looked at Dale and nodded; then he looked away, acknowledging that after thinking about it all these months, he agreed. Who else could it have been but George, Dale's son?

Dale stood up and tugged at the bottom of his jacket. He slapped his blue cap back onto his head. "It's time you get moving again," he said, obviously irritated now. "I expect to see you back to work real soon!"

Jon heard Dale's heavy steel-toed boots thump against the hardwood floor all the way through the kitchen and out the side door. Jon shut the VCR off via the remote and forced himself to sit up. He ground the cigar butt into the ashtray, close by at all times and filled to the rim with soggy stubs and smoldering gray ashes.

Sluggishly, he got to his feet—or rather onto his good foot—picked up his cane, struggled over to the window, and cranked it open.

The air was bitter-cold. He heard night birds chirping, a coyote yelp, and suddenly he realized he had missed the very sound of them.

He staggered back to the couch and sat down, contemplating everything that Dale had just said. Beau was curled up near the woodstove; Jon could hear him snore. Beau had stayed with him throughout most of his recuperation, steadfast and without criticism. Jon laughed under his breath at Beau. The dog had more vigor than he did.

Jon thought about Dale Washburn for the rest of the night—what he had said, and the frustration in his voice. Jon knew Dale needed him.

Jon's plans before the shooting came back to him so intensely, he forgot to take his evening round of drugs. He was still thinking about Dale and George the next morning when he shaved, showered, and wandered into Elbert's kitchen with the help of his cane.

"What's going on?" Elbert asked from the stove. "Is it my birthday?" He glanced at the calendar hanging near the refrigerator. "No, my birthday's in August."

Jon stumbled to the table, the cane tapping against the floor. He said, "I'll have coffee, if you got any."

Elbert studied him. Clean-shaven and dressed in new clothes: a blue long-sleeved shirt and gray pants instead of the ragged jeans or tattered long johns. He had also trimmed his hair.

Elbert went to the refrigerator to get the carton of French vanilla creamer. Jon looked out the window, watching birds peck at seeds that had fallen from the feeders onto the snowy ground below.

"What sparked you off your couch?" Elbert asked, looking out the window over Jon's shoulder.

"I feel like moving around today. Whatever you're cooking, I'll take some."

Elbert wasn't cooking anything; why cook for just himself? "I can whip up a batch of pancakes," he said, and went in search of the pans and the mix. "You sit down and drink your coffee."

Jon pulled the curtains to the sides of the window frame to get a better view. He watched a pileated woodpecker quake inside a gust of wind and snowflakes sparkle against the early-morning sunlight.

Elbert said, "And I got bacon. You want bacon?"

"Yes," Jon said, stunned by the sheer beauty of the sunny winter morning. "I also want the keys to my truck. I got an appointment with Dale."

CHAPTER 13

George knew Melanie was trying to find out from Lucas where Lloyd was hiding, but Lucas wouldn't tell her. So, she tracked George down at his house where he was alone and drunk.

"Your father knows where Lloyd is," she said, trying to get him to listen to her instead of moving his hands around under her blouse. "Find out where he's hiding," she insisted, pushing him away. "He hasn't called me since December. Now it's March! I have to find him!"

"You don't need Lloyd," George said, trying to suck on her neck. "It's best he's out of the way. You're just worried you might have to get a job."

"Make Lucas tell you where he is. The DNR won't leave me alone, and the sheriff's been at my house almost every day."

"Sure, I'll talk to him," George promised, pulling her further into bed and covering her with the sheet while trying to take the rest of her clothes off. "Lloyd won't be a problem much longer."

George knew she wanted him to explain his last comment, but when he was this drunk, he would babble and not make any sense. For all she knew, he thought she was talking about Reese or Tom Foster. She gave up on the subject of Lloyd and concentrated on breathing beneath the weight of George's body. He knew she wanted him to be done with her, and then she would try to trick him into telling her where Lloyd was hiding.

* * *

"The law's been questioning Lloyd's wife about his whereabouts," George told Lucas later that night. "No one can find him. She claims she doesn't know where he is."

George put both elbows against the table. He had been drinking since early afternoon. He didn't remember his recent encounter with Melanie, but he did remember a phone call. She called him—yes that was it—she called to ask if he knew where Lloyd was. She claimed she hadn't heard from him in months.

George had on the same jeans and flannel shirt for two days in a row. His words were slurred, and yet, he was able to remain calm.

He still had scratches, welts, and faded bruises on his face from the fight with Jon. His ribcage and shoulder ached. His right eye burned.

He said, "Melanie thinks you know where Lloyd is," and drummed his fingers against the tabletop, causing Lucas to glare at him. "And you *do* know, don't you? You went to his house and got him the day he disappeared. Where is he?"

"Never mind that," Lucas said. He spat into a handkerchief and rubbed his bulbous nose with the palm of his hand. "You just never mind!"

George pounded the table. "Tell me!"

"Don't sit there and pound my table, you ignorant punk!"

"You're calling *me* ignorant?" George asked, his face illuminated. "Talk about calling the kettle black!"

"Shut up," Lucas demanded, "and *listen* to me. Last I knew Lloyd was here in my house; standing by the stove. I told him to stay put for a day or two, but he didn't listen. He had cash with him and a couple of credit cards. For all I know he skipped town, which believe me, will cause a big *goddamned* shit-stir!" Lucas shifted inside his chair, took the handkerchief out of his trouser pocket again, and pat his sweating brow.

Even the armpits of his brown-and-white checked shirt were spotted wet, yet he added, "That goddamned Melanie broad. She don't love Lloyd, never did! I know she'll turn him in!"

"She just wants to know he's all right," George said, feigning concern for her and patience for Lucas. He glanced around at all the trash in Lucas's kitchen. "What the hell's wrong with *that*?"

"He's worth more to her dead."

"What do you mean?" George asked, interested in Lloyd's financial holdings. Lucas had been close to Lloyd's mother—his sister—and apparently knew her monetary value.

"I'm talking about a six-hundred-thousand-dollar life insurance policy on Lloyd," Lucas confided, his voice low as if people were listening. "Lloyd told me about it. He said he didn't have to worry about Melanie and the kids because she'd have that to live off of. Plus, with the money he had saved, she won't hurt for nothing."

George contemplated the insurance policy before asking, "Why hasn't Christopher snitched about Lloyd?"

"I think Lloyd paid him off."

"Do you think Lloyd will tell about me and Reese if he's caught?" George asked.

"Probably, why should he take all the blame? Lucky for you, Christopher don't know names other than Lloyd's. Lloyd told me he never brought you and Reese into the conversation. And for that, you should be grateful."

"I'm grateful, sure. But I got to find Lloyd."

"I'd stay clear of him if I was you."

"I have to shut him up before he decides to talk."

"He won't," Lucas said and smacked the tabletop for emphasis. "I *told* you. No one knows you did the transporting. So, leave it be!"

"I know he'll talk if it comes down to saving himself. He's got a family, and what do I got? A half-wit brother. Or should I say half-brother?"

George shook his head before settling his eyes upon Lucas, who said in an even voice, "Don't start that song and dance again!"

"Tell me the truth about Dale Washburn and my mother," George insisted.

"They was friends, I guess."

"Good friends?" George asked, his voice low enough to make Lucas shiver. "Like good enough for her to run to him every time you slapped her around?"

Lucas wiped his brow again and even dabbed at his cleft chin. He had to get George off the subject of Carolyn. If George started talking about her now, there was no telling what might happen.

But George was silent as he studied Lucas.

Lucas had on suspenders, and wrapped the fingers of both hands around the straps. He stroked the tea cup with a forefinger. His gray shirt was buttoned halfway and revealed white chest hairs and the tattoo of a naked woman on the upside of his left arm.

Lucas shouted, "You don't know what you're talking about. You was too young to understand what was going on!"

"I wasn't too young to hear her scream when you beat her, you pathetic fucker."

"Don't start this again! You couldn't possibly know what all went on between her and me. She was a whore!"

"A whore?" George asked incredulously, both eyes shut. "You're talking about *my* mother!"

"Yeah, that's right: your mother the whore."

"My God," George said to the ceiling. Then to Lucas: "You sit there and call my mother names right to my face. I *can't* get over you."

"Well, *get* over me. And while you're at it, get on back to work! I'll be damned if I'm going to pay you for standing around the sites or for sitting here pestering me neither. I made you a foreman to make it look like you're a hard-working man. So why don't you try to *act* like one."

"What's that?" George asked, cupping his ear. "A hardworking—what was that again?"

"You heard me, damn you. If the cops come nosing around the logging sites, I want them to see you and Reese looking like workin' men. Not a couple of idiots with something to hide. Do you have any idea how much they'll fine you if you get caught? Not to mention I could lose the business because of you bastards. Goddammit!" Lucas stirred more sugar into his tea and lifted the cup to take a sip. "Goddammit!" he said again, shaking his head in dismay.

George leaned on one elbow and looked around the room as if he were in the wrong house, wrong town. He just couldn't get over Lucas insulting Carolyn.

"Why don't you look me in the eye and call me an idiot, hey?" he asked Lucas with an audacious squint.

Lucas didn't hesitate. He looked right at George and lifted both hands to emphasize. "Idiot, dumbass, moron," he said, a smirk bending his upper lip.

"You're unbelievable!"

"And I'm sure you've been called worse," Lucas said.

Lucas pushed his ketchup-stained plate aside. He had just eaten fried eggs and bacon, but George hadn't touched a bite. They were supposed to have a productive breakfast meeting and discuss buying some new logging equipment.

Lucas changed the subject. "I'll talk Jon into coming back to work. He's the best piece cutter I got."

George was so perplexed by Lucas's last comment, he couldn't think straight. "You mean Loucher's coming back?"

"You'd better hope to God," Lucas said, wiping his mouth with a napkin. "If it came to choosing between you and Jon, I'd pick him in a blink."

"This conversation's going downhill fast. What makes you think he can even stand up? Last I heard, he's limping around with a cane. How much work do you think he can do with a limp?"

"More than you without one!"

George whistled and leaned back into the chair. "I hate that half-breed," he vowed.

"He's not a half-breed," Lucas corrected. "His father's only a fourth Ojibwa or some such. Get it straight before you go around talking like some fool bigot. Let me remind you that your mother was from Finland and most of my folks was from Ireland."

"And my father?"

"I just said Ireland. Are you deaf too for God's sake?"

"I mean my *real* father, Dale Washburn."

Lucas tapped a finger again; this time against the sticky table, giving himself time to consider Washburn's ancestry. "Washburn," he muttered and stroked his chin. "Couldn't say. He's probably Irish, maybe German."

When George didn't respond, Lucas proceeded to pick his teeth with a sliver of wood. "Hot in here, ain't it?" he said.

"Yep, it's a bit warm," George agreed, moving a hand across his forehead as the alcohol clamped harder against his brain, forcing him to think about his mother. And Mae.

"Here's the thing," Lucas said, shifting inside his chair. "Jon's coming back to work and believe me, if you bother him, if you even look at him cross-eyed, I'll come after you. You and that damned rifle! The next time someone gets shot and falls of a ridge, it'll be you. That's a promise!"

Lucas scratched the table with the sliver of wood and said, "I know what happened out there, you coward, and I'm not about to forget."

"You'd side with Loucher over me?" George asked, fighting to keep down the bile rising up his throat. "You sure shift priorities!"

"I won't jeopardize my company for you. It's people like you who give loggers a bad name. It's underhanded crap like dumping poisonous waste that attracts terrorists and environmentalists. I'm sure you're aware we got them folks sneaking around. Someone could get killed!"

"Yes, someone *could* get killed," George said with a shrug. "What makes you think I shot Jon? Could've been one of the fanatics."

"Because I know *you.*"

George laughed, trying to keep down the vomit. "You *don't* know me. But I've got a few more minutes to talk and here's what we're going to talk about. We're going to talk about cowards and good men. We're going to discuss how you mistreated my mother. I saw you beat her once until she couldn't stand up."

"Does it sound familiar? Somewhat like the way you beat that Mae Lakarri broad around a while back? Don't sit there and lecture me about mistreating women when you're guilty of doing the same thing.

I ought to kick your ass for it. But why bother? Lo-sure did it for me."

George felt sick. He was still thinking about his mother, Carolyn. He could see her face, once unmarred and porcelain, and how over the years, it turned gaunt and gray. How he sensed, even as a child, that her eyes were windows to a terror Lucas Coulter put her through; a living hell, as she became weak and broken, and because George was only a boy, he couldn't help her.

Many times, he tried to intervene, but Lucas came after him, fists swinging.

He remembered Lucas throwing Reese against the wall, Reese crying and begging, and Lucas slamming their frail mother against the floor. He could still see Lucas's hysteria, vivid even now, and he remembered how more than once, Lucas threatened to shoot them all.

"I'll never forgive you for hurting my mother," George said at last, speaking to the audience of mankind.

Lucas placed both palms to his chest and laughed. "Am I asking for your forgiveness? Wake up, son!"

"I'm *not* your son. And I don't blame her for turning to Washburn. If I'd been older, you wouldn't be sitting here now. You'd be six feet under."

Lucas bent forward, laughing and wheezing until his stomach cramped. "I think you're too drunk for this conversation," he said, wiping his eyes with the damp handkerchief. "You was such a skinny runt, I don't think you could've lifted a gun, much less held it steady to aim and pull the trigger."

George pulled the .357 Magnum pistol out from its holster beneath his jacket and pointed it at Lucas's chest. "You mean like this?"

Lucas's smile faded as quickly as the walls and appliances disappeared from George's vision. Lucas curved both hands around the rungs on the back of his chair. "Put that away," he said.

"Looks like I can hold a gun steady now."

"What does it prove?"

"It proves I couldn't shoot you to defend my mother when I was a kid, but I can shoot you now."

"Your mother and me had problems, who don't? But we worked it all out after you was born. She said you was Washburn's kid and I believe it. But she came back to me anyway, and I treated you as if you was my own son."

"That's right, you did," George said, his expression showing he recalled all too well. "You beat me just as much as you beat Reese. Probably more."

"You two boys was rascals," Lucas reminisced in a jagged voice. "I had to rough you up some to teach you right from wrong."

"Teach us right from wrong? We could be arrested any time now and here I am, pointing a gun at your chest. You taught us really good."

"Christ," Lucas said. "Have a cup of coffee and sober up! Put the gun down before you shoot your foot off, or maybe a nut."

George didn't move. He held the gun steady, directed at Lucas.

"She had a restless nature," Lucas attempted to explain. "I didn't know what to do with her. After Reese was born, she got bored with me, with us. She could've left if she wanted to. She said she had nowhere else to go!"

"That's not what she told me. She said you threatened to kill her if she tried to leave."

Lucas did his best to divert his eyes from the barrel of the gun. "Washburn didn't want her. Go point that pistol at him! He's the one who turned on her, not me! We didn't have many heart-to-heart talks, but I never abused her. Not the way you say. I'm sorry if you think I did."

"I don't think it. I *know* it."

"Then shoot me," Lucas said, and laughed again, apparently desperate enough to make light of his predicament. "Just do it!"

"Before I do, I want you to know that I saw you rape her. I was about seven years old."

"That's interesting news. I never raped her. Smacked her around maybe, but I never had to take it."

"I saw you rape her. You shoved her down to the floor and beat the hell out of her and raped her, and it happened more than once. You're the reason she got sick with cancer. You tortured her when she was medicated and dying of cancer. A drunken slob, spitting on her and wiping your filth on her. Pinning her to the floor, you worthless scum. I wanted you dead then. And I want you dead here today."

Lucas held up a trembling hand. "Settle down now," he said. "You got to settle down! You want to go to prison? You hate me so much, you're willing to go to prison over killing me?"

"Admit it! Admit you raped her!"

"Goddammit, sure!" Lucas shouted, his hands clutching the edge of the table. "I raped her! So, what, you stupid kid! She went out on me all the time; said she loved Washburn and all that pitiful bullshit! What was I supposed to do? Let her screw everyone in town but me? She was my *wife*!"

"Shut up, you old son-of-a-bitch motherfucker. Sit back in your chair and don't say another word. Don't even breathe!"

George waited for Lucas to settle back into the chair; he watched Lucas pick up his teacup and put it back into the saucer. Then Lucas hung his hands together in front of his chin, and it was at that precise moment George focused on the beads of sweat forming near Lucas's white hairline.

He could see the age spots at the sides of Lucas's face, identify the beating of his heart. "Put the gun down," Lucas said. When he opened his eyes again, his vision blurred with tears. "Please put it down," he said. "We'll work it all out."

George clicked the safety off. "I can still hear my mother say, 'Please don't do it. I won't leave you, we'll work it out.' I hear her as if it happened yesterday. You say I shot Jon, maybe I did. And maybe the next time I'll aim for his heart and not his leg. You say I hurt Mae; well, I hope so. She *broke* my heart, dammit. I hope she's pregnant and the kid's mine; I nailed her real good. Isn't that how we both do things? Just take it?"

"Dear Jesus Christ!" Lucas said. "*Don't* do it."

"I'll take your life like you took my mother's. She was frail and sick and *she* begged *you* to leave her alone.

Tell me one more thing. Where's Lloyd? I need to tell his wife."

"You're screwing that Melanie trash," Lucas said, rubbing his forehead with shaking fingers. "I knew it!"

"Tell me where to find Lloyd!"

"He went to Canada. Now he's at the hunting camp by the railroad grade."

"That's good," George said. "The waiting's almost over."

"I want to make things right," Lucas stuttered, unable to breathe. "Give me another chance."

The blast tore through the air and through Lucas's chest, covering the wall behind him with fragments of bone, flesh, and blood. "I've had it with you," George said for the last time. "You can't make nothin' right now."

George put the gun down on the table and lit a cigarette before cleaning up the mess. He thought of her; yes, he could see her clearly. If nothing else in his lifetime, he believed he did one thing right: he avenged the death of his mother. He couldn't help her back then, but he made Lucas Coulter pay for her death now, and next he'd get Dale Washburn.

Chapter 14

"Where's Dad?" Reese asked George the next morning at one of the logging sites. "I thought you two were going to talk over buying more equipment. What's going on?"

"He had to make a trip to Lansing," George said. He stepped through the icy muck, trying to ward off the chill. It was starting to look like spring, but they were only having a brief thaw; the snowdrifts were still high and the air frigid. The best thing to do in weather this cold and damp was to keep moving.

George could tell Reese didn't believe Lucas would leave the area without telling him. In fact, George overheard Lucas asking Reese if he wanted to go along on the equipment spending spree. "Lansing," Reese said. "He didn't tell me he was going now. He said maybe in a couple days."

"Well, he decided to go last night. I'll be in charge until he gets back."

"When will that be? When will he get back?"

George shivered inside his jacket. He smoked a cigarette and stomped his boots against the frozen ground. "He didn't say!" George yelled. "I'm taking off. You handle Casey!"

"What do you mean, handle Casey?"

"Tell him we don't need him anymore."

"We don't need Casey?" Reese was astonished by the thought. "What are you saying?"

"We're buying our own rig and hauling the timber ourselves," George said, smoking and surveying. "No more Casey. I heard he has heart problems anyway."

Reese looked confused. "But Dad likes him," he insisted.

"Casey's too slow," George said. "We need to speed things up before the spring thaw. I want the trees cut quick and the logs hauled out *now*."

"Spring break-up isn't for another three or four weeks."

George stomped one boot and then the other to support his weight. He turned to leave. "We'll do this my way, starting now. If Loucher comes back, send him to me. I want him out of the picture."

Reese rubbed his chin and pulled his cap further over his pale forehead. "What happened to Lucas!" he yelled after George.

But George ignored him.

• • •

Jon and Dale had arranged to meet at Jon's new house. Dale seemed impressed with Jon's progress. The kitchen was almost finished except for the selecting and purchasing of rugs and drapes, and the living room area had been paneled with knotty pine. There was a woodstove, but also a fireplace, trimmed in stone. There was green carpeting throughout the downstairs but most of all, Dale told Jon, he liked the cathedral ceiling.

Jon said, "We should check out that old hunting cabin."

"Yes, they probably all hunt there together. And it's remote."

Jon added, "Mae called me this morning; she said Lucas is out of town."

"I didn't know he left. Who told her that?"

"She won't give me a name."

"I'll go to the work site and meet you at the tavern parking lot in Chatham in about an hour. I think I know an easy way to get to their cabin."

It was a good thing Jon's left leg was injured and not the right. He could still drive. He could use his right foot to work the gas pedal and brakes. But there was a stabbing pain in his chest if he moved too quickly and, because the chainsaw nicked a lung, his breathing was stressed.

While he waited for Dale to show up in Chatham, he thought about the pills he had taken earlier. Once in a while he still needed them, but he had cut the dose in half. To deal with the pain, he tried to concentrate on other subjects—George Coulter's whereabouts for one, the environmentalists for another—but his chest muscles contracted each time he took a breath.

Finally, Dale drove his truck up to Jon's and said out the open window, "Follow me. I know where the cabin is. And I found out Lucas went to Lansing to buy some equipment."

Jon followed behind Dale's green and white truck, past farmland, watery fields, and pastures, all the way out of Chatham and ten miles beyond Trenary. Then they took Highway 41 for two miles and turned left just before Kiva.

They drove a half a mile down an abandoned logging trail, pines and cedars along both sides of the road. Finally, they took another left turn down a railroad grade. Jon pulled up behind a rusty well pump and waited for Dale, while looking at a field covered with patches of snow and ice.

He noticed a hawk glide overhead; searching for mice, no doubt. The processes of early spring were in motion, large or small. Survival is key.

He noted that Dale wore a gray cap, a jacket over a long underwear shirt, corduroy pants, and boots. Even so, his face and neck were red from the wind and cold, and probably by the exertion of walking to the window of Jon's truck.

Dale said, "We'll walk on back from here. Can you make it?"

Jon stepped out of the truck without answering. He was dressed appropriately also, but wore a jacket—a navy blue down-filled jacket—a blue cap, jeans, and a light pair of boots because walking was difficult enough. He still used the cane, although in the past couple of weeks he went from dragging his leg to a limp.

Even so, the effort it took to move at all cost him twice the energy as before the accident. But he didn't complain. He needed fresh air. He wanted exercise. He had to see the trees, the stark branches of maples and elm and the green boughs of spruce.

He did his best to keep up with Dale as Dale broke the trail. Not too long ago, Jon was in the lead; now *he* was following Dale. There were certain areas packed with snow; other areas were slippery with icy nonconformity.

Jon stopped several times before they reached a clearing, patterned here and there with spruce and apple trees. They noticed tire tracks coming from a road to the right of the field, and also boot tracks.

"There must be two roads into this place," Dale said, pushing onward to pack the higher levels of snow down with his boots. "I was here a long time ago in deer season. That's when me and Lucas were drinking buddies."

Jon had heard this before. Dale and Lucas at one time were drinking companions; no doubt that's how Dale met Lucas's wife. "It was a long time ago," Dale said. "I knew Carolyn before she met Lucas. Lucas and me would hunt together, but then I found out how bad he treated her. I should have helped her. But I didn't."

Dale closed the door on the subject of Carolyn Coulter. It was clear he didn't want to revisit his regrets, not even with Jon.

They walked to the front steps of the hunting cabin. The cabin had been built out of cedar logs with tarpaper nailed over the chipboard roof. There were windows on all four sides, the largest window in the front. The windows were covered with shutters, except for the small one in the back.

Dale tried the doorknob, but the door was locked, so he stepped back and kicked it open. There was no doubt the cabin had been used recently; there was a strong cedar woodsmoke smell combined with mold. There was also the aroma of cooked food, and there was musty bedding on one of the cots. Most telling, there were hot cinders in the woodstove.

Jon touched the coffeepot on the stove. "Coffee's still warm," he said.

"Someone's been staying here." Dale walked over to the table. "And someone's been playing a game of solitaire," he added, touching a deck of cards.

Jon poked at a duffel bag with the tip of his cane. "Check this," he said.

Dale opened the bag. "Clothes," he murmured. "And look." He pulled out a bankbook and wasted no time opening it. "Lloyd McMasters."

They studied the one-room cabin, but all they found were dirty dishes in the sink and clothes piled in the back room.

"We probably just missed him," Dale said. "I'd turn myself in if I was him. He'll lose his job, so what. But to go through the stress of having the law after him? He's crazier than George."

Jon used the cabinet, along with the cane, for support. "I say George has him. I'm going outside to check the tire tracks. I'll bet they're George's."

Once they were back outside, Jon discovered that not only were George's tire tracks visible in the maze of tracks near the unplowed road, so were Lucas's.

Jon struggled to stand back up. When he searched the area, his eyes narrowed against the hazy sunlight. He pushed the tip of the cane into the snow to steady himself. "See the boot tracks?" he asked. "There are three sets."

Jon was ready to head back for the trail leading to their vehicles when he noticed the fake fuel truck behind some balsams. "Look at that," he said as he headed towards the location of this evidence. "Has to be the truck they hauled the chemicals in. How convenient they left samples behind for us to give to the DNR."

• • •

By ten o'clock that morning, Melanie was hysterical. "Find out what happened to Lloyd," she screamed at Tom Foster. "I can't find Lucas and he's supposed to be the only one who knows where he's hiding! I can't find George, either. You work with these people, find out where they are!"

"Settle down," Tom said. "Reese told me Lucas went to Lansing on business. George is running both sites."

"Tell him I need to talk to him about Lloyd."

"Everyone knows that Lloyd's missing and the cops are looking for him."

Melanie lit a cigarette and smoked half of it while she mulled the situation over. The boys were at her cousin's house and she smoked whenever they weren't around. She was also thinking about having another drink. She was dressed in a short-sleeved blouse and jeans, no shoes, only socks. "I can't believe things have gone this far. Tell George I have to talk to him. Find him and tell him!"

"George and Bryan Kinnenun got into a brawl the other day. Just like Lucas did with Kinnenun's father years ago."

"What's that got to do with Lloyd?"

"Lucas fired Kinnenun's old man because of a work-related dispute. You see, old Kinnenun worked for Lucas, and Lucas wanted to cut past the boundary markers into a wetland area. They got into a big fight over it. Lucas told him if he didn't like his methods, he could leave. So, he did. I think Bryan holds a grudge against the Coulters over it. His dad never did find another job because Lucas trashed his name to everybody in the business." Tom paused to glare at Melanie. "I think Bryan's in with them fanatics. He's sure got motive."

"This is getting more complicated as we go," Melanie admitted. She smoked slower now and crossed her arms in front of her chest. "We could burn a skidder or something. They'd blame it on the environmentalists."

"What would that prove?"

"I'll tell you, if Lloyd shows up dead, I'm going to blame the whole bunch: The Coulters and everyone associated with them! After all, Lloyd *is* the father of my children. I told George to rough him up, not kill him!"

"I don't know what you mean."

"I know you don't. So, just help me and I'll tell you the whole story later. When I say so, we'll leave Michigan—with enough cash to live on comfortably."

"I like the sound of that."

"Good. Then you'll stay for a glass of wine?" Melanie went to the refrigerator to get the bottle before Tom had the opportunity to answer her. She needed a drink. Her nerves were shot, and she was sweating heavily. "The kids aren't here, and *my husband* isn't either, of course."

"I guess so," Tom said, checking out the premises with a jerking nod. "I told the wife I was going to the dentist."

"Haven't you used the dentist excuse several times this month?" Melanie asked. Tom nodded the affirmative. "And yet your teeth are a disgusting mess. She must be dumber than I thought."

"She's not too intelligent," he admitted sadly.

And neither are you, thought Melanie. *That's why I keep you around.*

CHAPTER 15

"I know George shot Jon last fall," Mae told the DNR undercover investigator she had been in contact with for the past several months. "He told me he was going to kill him."

They always met in a secluded place and spoke for only a few minutes at a time. They would usually connect at a pool table or the bar and leave fifteen minutes apart. This time they met at the Tennick Tavern. Mae studied the brands of cigarettes in the machine. Although she didn't smoke anymore and hardly ever drank, she pretended to do both. But the strong smells in the bar were making her sick. Cigarettes, cigars, beer, greasy meat, fried potatoes, and onion rings.

She was having trouble with the pregnancy, yet she had been to her doctor three times now and knew what to do and what not to do. Standing in hot cigarette-smoke filled bars was one of the things she shouldn't do, but she was determined to help this man collect evidence against the Coulters. She wanted to help intercept the small group of environmental fanatics who had infiltrated the area as well. The group hoping to put the loggers out of commission. According to him, the western states like Oregon and Washington were bombarded with the antics of environmental terrorists on a large scale, and it was his job to find groups in Upper Michigan. It made sense: logging and mining were the two top industries in the area.

Mae whispered," You've got to find George. He's on a drunken rampage."

"Yes," the man said. "Tell me what you know about Lucas Coulter."

"Only that he's missing. George claims he went downstate to buy equipment, but I found the records of the places they buy out of, and I called around and no one's seen Lucas. He supposedly left yesterday afternoon. But he didn't withdraw any money from his bank accounts. I used to work in the Credit Union and I know a girl who still works there. She handles the Coulters' business accounts."

"When did George tell you this?"

"I called him this morning. I already had a hunch something happened to Lucas when George told me he went to Lansing."

"Lucas has to be in the area," said the investigator.

"Well, I went to his house, but George's truck was there. I thought I'd wait until he goes to work to look around."

"Stay away from Lucas's. Now I have a personal question to ask you."

"Hope it's not *too* personal," she said, although she knew what he was about to ask her. She was seven months along in the pregnancy. She wore large sweaters and skirts, and her face was fuller. There was no way to hide the fact now, which was precisely why she avoided

Jon. She didn't want to add more stress to his life, and she certainly didn't want him to want her due to a sense of obligation.

She might never tell him. He didn't have to know about the child. He didn't have to know anything about her.

The man glanced at her waist and inferred the question without asking it. She said, "The baby's not George Coulter's."

"I'm not sure what to say. Except good luck."

"I'm going to try and get inside George's house today," Mae insisted. "I still have a spare key. Maybe there's some evidence in his house that would help."

"I don't want you doing this anymore," he said adamantly. "It wasn't a good idea to begin with, but now that you're in this condition ..."

Mae wasn't surprised by his decision to ban her from the investigation, but it annoyed her to hear him say it. "Have you found more evidence of Globe One at the logging sites?" she asked, interrupting him. "I know they're watching the Coulters."

"There's been another report of tree-spiking. If I can get the person—or people—doing it, that's enough to put them away. Congress passed a law that makes tree-spiking or tampering with equipment in any way a felony. Anyone gets hurt or maimed while running a saw into a spiked tree for instance, it's attempted murder. If there's a death, it's murder. Plain and simple."

"I think you should go to Lucas's place. You know where it is? It's about three miles outside of Kiva. There must be some reason why George was there. I'm sure he wasn't watering the plants."

"I'll go tonight," he promised her.

"And please, keep an eye on Jon," Mae said, feeling dizzy from the smell of beer and cigarette smoke. "I've tried to contact him at his dad's, but he's never around. He and Dale are still doing detective work."

"I'll have to put an end to *that*," the man said in a voice close to a shout. "Or the next thing you know, we won't be able to tell the law from the loggers. Guess I'll have to tell Jon who I really am."

"Don't worry, he'll cooperate. He's the only person I trust."

"I've already assigned another full-time investigator working out of Rapid River. He's posing as a cop, with the cooperation of the Rapid River Sheriff's Department."

"What's his name?"

"Ron Evans. He'll say he's a cop, but he's FBI. We'll catch them one way or the other."

Mae leaned against the machine for support and pressed her hand against his arm; if she recalled correctly, the night of conception had been last summer. The only time she had seen Jon's cabin back in the woods; probably the *last* time she would see it, too.

"You've got to find George," she repeated. She couldn't help but think George shot Jon. She knew George turned crazy when he drank too much and he blamed Jon for Mae leaving him. Especially now that she was pregnant. Mae reflected on the fact that she had met the investigator three years ago when she was twenty-five and worked in Ann Arbor. She was taking biology courses at the university. She met him through a special program designed to train students in timber management; specifically, an in-depth study regarding ethical practices in the logging industry. Therefore, she was able to pick up on George's misconduct, and obviously, his foolish behavior made it all the easier.

Coincidentally, the eco-terrorist situation started to escalate in the area and two weeks ago, she noticed the investigator in the Tennick grocery store. He was in disguise, but she recognized him by the tall stature and the space between his teeth. And most notably, he only had three fingers on the left hand.

When she saw him in the grocery store, Mae knew he was in the area to investigate the environmentalists. She had read about the threats in the paper and heard about their destructive techniques through George. The investigation was geared towards watching Brent Christopher for the DNR, but after Mae and the investigator compared notes, it seemed logical for her to supply information about George and the Conrad Paper Mill. And, as she suspected, it didn't take long for the terrorist group to discover what George, Reese, and Lloyd were up to. The investigator had been following them, and surveillance was set in motion.

Mae's contribution to the investigation was to remain off the record, primarily because it was against the undercover detective's—Rick Peterson was his real name—better judgement. He could be suspended and fined for enlisting the help of a civilian, but Mae knew he couldn't pass up the information she was able to supply, especially now that Jon had been shot.

Peterson stood up and tipped his hat in parting. Mae nodded and waited a few minutes; and even though he had told her to stay out of the investigation, she drove out to George's house for one last look.

By the time she went back to her sister's farm, changed clothes, and headed for George's house, it was almost noon. She chose the back route—a remote stretch of road, flat and barren, except for various pastures and abandoned homesteads, which skirted around the perimeters of Trenary.

It didn't take long for her to find out that the decision to go to George's house for more evidence was a mistake. Right after she turned the curve past the country store, she saw George's truck behind her. There was no one behind him on the road, and no one in front of her.

He followed her for nearly a mile and then sped up and swerved wide to pass her. As she pulled over to the side of the road, she locked the doors and waited for him to step out of his truck.

He motioned for her to roll down the window. "Headed out to my place?" he asked, chewing on a match stick.

"No, I'm going to Chatham."

"What's in Chatham?"

"A friend."

"I used to be a friend," he said, his expression creasing the skin around his jaw.

Mae rubbed the steering wheel with an index finger. "Is that what you ran me off the road to tell me, George? Move your hand!"

George grabbed a hold of the window and wrapped his fingers around the top of it so hard, his knuckles turned red. He said, "I was out to your sister's. Can't get over how big her kid is. His name's Jared, right?"

"Are you threatening my nephew?"

"I didn't do nothing to him … *yet.*"

"Get your hand off the window!"

"Come on now," said George. "Come back to me. You don't really want that son of a bitch Lo-sure. I know it."

"I *said* let go and move aside," Mae warned him again, revving the engine.

George shook the window. "I'll cut that kid up and your sister too if you don't do what I say!"

"Get away, George! You need to face facts!"

But he retaliated without empathy. "Drive to my place and no one gets hurt."

Mae tried to buy time, hoping that a car would pass by, but George uncovered the pistol beneath his jacket. "We got to have a private talk. Today."

"We can talk right here," Mae said.

He lifted the flap of his jacket to show her the weapon. "Do what I tell you."

"I'm pregnant. You'd risk hurting your child?"

"Drive to my place and do as I say and the kid lives. Your sister and Jared live. Jon lives."

Mae knew George would use the gun if he had to. She sensed that murdering her would be nothing to him. "Okay," she said. "We'll talk, but Paula's expecting me home in an hour. If I'm not back by then, she'll call the police."

George laughed, but his hand shook; his jaw line and chin contracted, bloodless. "That law's after me anyway, darlin'. Who do you think shot Lucas stone-cold dead?"

When they got to his house, George told Mae to park the jeep behind the garage. There was a grove of pine trees at the side of his house near the backyard, and he knew the trees would conceal her jeep from the road. He told her to walk in front of him, all the way to the house. If not for the gun, she would have tried to escape back at the highway.

It was clear to her that the house had been abandoned for at least two weeks. She knew George was probably living in Lucas's modular home, or maybe with Reese. This house, that she used to live in herself, was far from lived in now.

As they walked towards the house from the garage, she noticed the driveway was packed with three or four inches of snow. Although it was late March, it had snowed recently, and there was enough accumulation to require shoveling. The cold air made her pull her coat around her waist. She felt the baby kick, making her worry over her predicament.

George nudged her into the kitchen. "What would you like to talk about?" she asked. "The baby is yours, you know."

He stared at her with lightless eyes. "That can't be. Because I remember it was a chilly fall day out at the farm. Right out in the weeds by the barn. And I remember that same damn thing happened; I couldn't get it up."

She was at least relieved he wasn't going to pretend the episode at Paula's didn't happened. He could call it whatever he liked. She knew the truth and planned to use it against him. "Right, but that's when it happened. You don't remember?" she said, pretending to be happy about a possible future with him.

George held up a hand and counted off his fingers. "Let's see now, you're how many months along? Almost eight? One, two, and this is the month of March? But our little encounter happened late August or early September. So, it doesn't add up. Even if we did *it*, the kid can't be mine."

He grabbed her wrist with one hand and held the blade to her throat with the other. "We're going upstairs and I'm going to tie you to the bed. That way you won't run away when I leave on business."

"What kind of business? Who are you after now? You tried to kill Jon last fall and you murdered Lucas. Who's left?"

"I got something important to do," was his answer. "You don't need to know everything."

Mae pushed forward to the hallway, away from his grasp, and she knew she was going to faint seconds before she did.

• • •

George knew the truth of another encounter and it wasn't a dream; it wasn't an alcohol-induced fantasy, either. After only ten weeks, Lloyd returned from Canada and Lucas instructed him to stay at the hunting camp near the railroad grade. Lucas kept him in supplies for a week while updating him on the situation. But one day Lucas didn't show up, and that same night, George did.

Lloyd hid behind the camp among the cedar trees. The next morning, George knew for a fact that he hid from Jon and Dale as well, and this was his critical mistake.

George predicted that Lloyd was tired of running. He couldn't hide one more day, or even another hour. He would turn himself in. He left the hunting camp with some of his clothes, probably thinking that at least he would be able to see his wife and sons again. He would be warm, and if detained in jail, he would be fed and able to sleep. He took off on foot towards the highway, but George had been waiting for him. George stepped out from the tree line, out of a vision of smoke and pine and balsam needles. He took aim and fired, and he dragged Lloyd's body all the way back to the hunting camp, in the mist of a moonlit night.

CHAPTER 16

Jon and Dale decided to split up in their search for Lloyd McMasters. Dale went home to his trailer in Kiva and changed clothes before heading to Lucas Coulter's place. Jon drove to Mae's sister's farm to see how Mae was doing, and then he planned to check George's house. Between the two of them, Lloyd would be found. One way or another, dead or alive.

Jon pulled over at a gas station and called Elbert but the line was busy. He stepped into the cold night air and went into the store section to buy a soda. The store was empty except for one other customer, so it didn't take Jon long to buy the soda and go back outside.

The next time he tried Elbert's number, Elbert answered on the second ring.

"Yes, hello!" Elbert said in his usual manner of answering the phone.

"It's me," Jon said, feeling drowsy thanks to the cold. "I wanted to check in with you."

"Where have you been?" Elbert sounded agitated.

Although Jon knew Elbert was healthy for his age, he worried over Elbert's nervous tone. Elbert ate right, didn't smoke, and kept his stressing to a minimum. Nonetheless, Jon could tell that something major had happened.

"The phone's been ringing all afternoon," Elbert said. "Clara's lawyer called and said her estate's about wrapped up. The lawyer wants you to come and get your check." Elbert paused at this point and rightly so. Jon had never heard him pack that many words into one sentence before.

He listened as Elbert continued: "Her nephew, that Neil Halverson fella, called too. Remember Clara talking about him?"

"The nephew who never visited her," Jon said, veering into the obvious.

"That's the one," Elbert confirmed. "He didn't visit *her*, but he's about to visit her lawyer now that she's dead. He claims he's on his way from Ohio. His lawyer says he has grounds to contest the will. But that's all he said and hung up."

"I can't worry about him right now," Jon said, grimacing. It felt like there was an electrical current moving through the bones of his injured leg. "I'll go see the lawyer after this Lloyd McMasters thing is over."

Jon continued, "I'm going to check on Mae first, then head on out to George's place. If I'm not back by morning, stall him."

"I saw on the news the police traced Lloyd to Ontario," Elbert added, speaking fast because he knew Jon had to go. "They're looking for him there."

"Dale and I are looking for him *here*."

"Talk to you later."

Jon hung up and proceeded to drive past Trenary towards Paula's farm. The weather was peculiar to say the least: a pelting of sleet, then drizzle, and yet there was hardly any wind.

Jon thought about spring break-up, that was currently in process and would last through April into mid-May. Every year, it meant road restrictions for logging trucks. It meant no hauling timber on certain back roads, until the muddy roads were passable again. One could cut but couldn't haul, unless one was greedy and reckless, like Lucas Coulter.

Jon wanted to get the inheritance matter settled before spring weather came. Maybe by the end of May, he could start his own company—with Dale's help—and maybe he could talk Mae into keeping the books.

He was thinking about Mae when he pulled into the entrance road to the farm. He wondered why she hadn't contacted him after their discussion earlier, despite the messages that he left on her answering machine to call him back. Why avoid him now?

All the lights were on in the farm house. Jon knew something was wrong, especially when Paula came out onto the porch, wearing a big canvas coat over her robe. Apparently, she had seen the headlights of Jon's truck come up the driveway and rushed down the front steps of the porch to meet him.

"Mae was supposed to be home hours ago," she said. She wore no makeup, and there was a spot of lotion on the right side of her face. "Do you have any idea where she is?"

Jon knew Paula had worked herself into a frenzied state over Mae's absence. There was fear in her eyes and hysteria in her voice. "I talked to her this morning," he said. "She told me about Lucas Coulter."

"That he's missing, yes," Paula said. She had heard the news too.

"And he's supposed to be in Lansing."

"I'm really worried about her this time!" Paula said, fidgeting with her hands. "Her condition, you know. And she's been meeting with an investigator working on the Coulter chemical-dumping case."

Jon stepped forward out of the sleet. "Slow down," he said. "What do you mean *her condition*?"

"You know, the pregnancy," Paula said, irritably. "Didn't she tell you?"

"What about this investigator?" Jon asked, thinking how Mae's "condition" made sense to him now: that way she was avoiding him.

"He works with the DNR. She was supposed to meet him today, but she promised she'd come right home."

Jon searched the yard by the garage to see if Mae had taken the jeep; it was pitch-dark outside and there was only one yard light on, the porch light, illuminating the area in the front yard and driveway.

"Please find her," Paula said, starting to cry. "I have a feeling she's hurt!"

Jon left Paula standing on the porch.

He drove out to George Coulter's house, as planned. He wanted to eliminate the possibility that George kidnapped her and had taken her there. Then he could go to the next place on the list: Lucas's house in Kiva.

At George's house, there were no lights on except for the flicker of a flashlight shining from one window to the next, but suddenly, the light faded.

Jon walked down the driveway behind the garage, where not only did he find Mae's jeep, he also found

Reese's truck. His first thought was that George was inside the house too, with Reese, but why would he be walking around his own house with a flashlight? Maybe Reese was doing the same thing he was: trying to locate Lloyd. Or could be that Reese was trying to stop George from disposing of Lloyd.

Mae's jeep was hidden, which told Jon she was there against her will. The idea of Mae inside the house, unconscious or dead, was enough to make him reach for the twenty gauge shotgun he kept behind the seat. Leaving the cane behind, he hobbled all the way to the back of the house.

He tried to see through one of the windows but couldn't quite locate the beam of the flashlight. He did notice that there was a night-light on in the kitchen.

The side door was unlocked, indicating that Reese, or whoever was inside, had entered through this door. He stepped into the laundry room and listened for movement, but the house was silent. He waited for footsteps, the crunch on linoleum, and yet there was no sound whatsoever except for the slow drip of a faucet.

Listening to the drip, Jon kept his back against the wall, holding the shotgun downward. He would react quickly if he had to. After all, guns he knew well; women with secrets, he didn't.

Again, he heard the sound of boots sliding from somewhere inside the living room, or maybe from the room next to the laundry room.

He peered around the corner, but no one was there. He left the laundry room to investigate the hallway. Even though his leg shook with pain and his hip was turning numb, he made it all the way down the hallway and stopped beneath the arched entrance into the living room. When he saw the beam of the flashlight wobble to and fro in the dining room, he backed up.

The beam shifted from one end of the living room to another, even up towards the ceiling and down to the braided rug on the floor. There was more shuffling of boots, now coming closer as the beam flowed over the contents of the house. Jon could tell that this person knew the layout of the house. He could see the outline of a heavily clothed body—a man, broad of shoulders.

Reese Coulter.

Jon lifted the shotgun. "Don't move," he warned. "And turn around."

Reese turned to study Jon with his light. "Loucher?" he asked, shaking several sprigs of hair from his eyes. "What're you doing here?"

Jon cradled the shotgun with his right arm. "Flip the light on," he said.

Reese went to the wall and punched a button. They were bathed in yellow light. Reese narrowed his eyes to study Jon's boots, his gray and blue clothing, and his black cap. "What're you doing here?" he asked again.

Jon noticed that Reese wore the same ratty outfit as always. He stank of unwashed clothing, and his beard was thickly spiraled. Jon knew he had to determine Reese's role in the disappearance of Lucas and Lloyd before he could trust him with vital information.

He pulled a deep breath. "Mae Lakarri's jeep's outside."

Reese said, "I seen it." He put the flashlight down on an oak table. "Wonder where she is."

"That's what I'm going to find out. Why are you walking around in the dark?"

Reese fiddled with the buttons on his shirt. "I'm looking for George," he said. "I got to find him."

"You think George is dangerous?" Jon asked, cautiously. Reese nodded yes. "Do you know where Lucas and Lloyd are right now?"

"I think George shot my dad."

Reese's eyelids quivered. "Do you have proof he shot Lucas?" Jon asked, again cautiously. He could see that Reese was functioning with little or no sleep.

"There was blood in the kitchen at Dad's house. I went there looking for him, but he wasn't home," Reese said. "Blood was splattered on the table. I could tell someone cleaned up most of it, probably George. George told me a long time ago he wanted Dad dead, ever since our mother died. Did you know Washburn's George's father?"

Jon shifted the shotgun to his other arm. "Yes," he said. "I heard about it."

"George told me and Dad last fall when Dad caught onto—" Reese stopped talking and glanced towards a window.

"The chemical dumping," Jon finished. "You think he might have shot Lucas over that? Or over your mother?"

"Maybe both; I've never seen George this messed up. I don't think he knows what he's doing anymore. I got to find him."

Jon pulled a chair over and slouched into it, propping the shotgun against his leg. Suddenly the room started to spin. But he knew it was imperative to keep Reese talking. "Where do you think George is right now?"

"He's probably at Lucas's covering his tracks. I think Lucas is outside in one of the sheds. The snow and ice keep a corpse from rotting, you know."

"What about Lloyd? We heard he was in Canada."

"I've thought a lot about Lloyd," Reese admitted. "I was just out at the hunting camp. I seen blood on George's chainsaw."

"Go ahead," Jon coaxed. "The DNR already knows you helped dump the chemicals. So far, that's all you're guilty of. Tell them where the chemicals are buried and everything else you know."

"Or tell them everything I know and end up in prison. I'll kill myself first!"

Jon pondered both possibilities. He knew Reese might do time for the crimes, but he doubted he would kill himself. "What do you suspect about Lloyd?"

"I think George cut him up with the saw. He's been upset about Lloyd. Lloyd wanted to quit the disposing, especially after Dad caught on. He said it was too risky. He ran when they caught Christopher."

"And what was Christopher's part exactly?"

"He measured the dioxin levels, the chlorine wastes; something to do with the Clean Water Act. He altered reports that went to the labs. It was our job to get rid of the extra. You know, he'd write down a level amount, but it would be less than what it really was, and then we'd dump what was left, drain it all into barrels in different places in the woods. Lloyd'd collect the money saved on the filtering."

Too much for Reese to comprehend, Jon thought. No need to tell him he'll do hard time for tampering with illegal chemicals, and also pay outrageous fines, as he also was responsible for soil and water contamination.

Jon realized that if hundreds of criminals like George and Reese dumped excess wastes, it was no wonder carcinogens were in the water and food supply. Jon knew enough about dioxins to understand that it couldn't break down, and therefore, gravitated to algae and other plant life in the rivers and into the fatty tissues of fish and animals who live in and use the water supplies: again, rivers, lakes, and wells.

He could tell Reese had drifted off, just by the expression creasing his moon-shaped face. He pulled Reese back to the subject of the hunting camp. "I was there this morning and the stove was hot. If the stove was hot, someone was there before us."

"Maybe George's staying there."

"Or Lloyd?"

"No, I think Lloyd's dead. Me and George thought Dad sent him to Canada after Christopher was caught. Dad wanted to give our lawyer a chance to build a defense. But like you said, he probably came back. If Lloyd's clothes and money was at the camp, he probably stayed a while. Then George found out and killed him. Like I said, I seen blood on his chainsaw about an hour ago."

Reese wasn't finished. "He probably cut up the body and stuffed it into that fuel truck we hid out back."

"I noticed the truck," Jon recalled all too well. "It's the truck you transported the chemicals in; plenty of solution for a good sample. If George cut up Lloyd and put the pieces in the tank, there's not much left of him now."

Jon attempted to stand up. "I've got to look for Mae."

Unfortunately, he was forced to stop every few steps to catch his breath. He leaned against items: a chair, the corner of a table, and so on, to keep his balance, especially while carrying the shotgun. He decided to leave the shotgun laying across the table.

Reese said, "I don't know what all happened the day you was shot at, but it was probably George. The cops need to look for a .357 bullet. That's what George packs with him."

"No, it was a rifle, a .30-30," Jon said. Yet he remembered the pistol the day of the fight when he confronted George. "They found the bullet."

Jon climbed the steps, but paused to take in long breaths. Reese ran on ahead, and by the time Jon reached the top step, Reese had inspected all the rooms and was coming out of the last bedroom. "She's in here," he said. "She's okay!"

Jon walked into the bedroom in time to see Reese help Mae sit up on the edge of the bed. She attempted to focus her surroundings. Her blond hair was messy, and her clothing was disheveled. "He tied me up!" she shouted, blowing bangs out of her eyes. She rubbed her wrists. After Reese untied her, she flung pieces of rope across the room, where they slapped against the pink and white wallpaper before falling to the floor, coiled and limp.

Jon pulled her to him and held her against his chest, careful of her extended stomach, and in turn, she felt his hands against the back of her neck. She had fainted at the onset of being tied to the bed and had slept through most of the evening. But now that she was awake, although still delirious from the ordeal, she almost told Jon that she loved him.

The words *I love you* were there and ready to move through her lips, but she said to him instead, "You'd better hurry on over to Lucas's. I think George is there."

CHAPTER 17

George searched Lucas's house. He organized the business records; put ledgers, insurance papers, invoices and machinery maintenance lists into separate boxes. He looked for more pictures of his mother, but other than the framed photograph on the file cabinet, he only found two faded snapshots. He noted that she wasn't smiling in either picture, and he tried to remember how old she was when she died. Was she in her mid-thirties, or late thirties? In both photographs she looked quite young. Her hair, long and dark brown, was pulled back in one picture, and in the other, it was cut short and enhanced her exotically pretty face.

Yes, to George she was *exotic*, so very beautiful. Her eyes though, he recalled, were blue and without sparkle. He remembered her hair was soft, and despite her hard life with Lucas Coulter, she always tried her best to smile; she always smelled of vanilla-scented cologne.

But some of his childhood years were blocked from his memory, just too painful to think about.

He *did* remember her funeral. He remembered standing in the heat of a July afternoon, the pressure of sunshine without a breeze. He felt nauseous, standing there looking down at the open grave, watching as the casket was lowered into the ground. Mother ....*My mother is gone.*

He remembered looking at Lucas. How Lucas seemed not at all disturbed by her passing. His face was eroded by bad health and sheer vulgarity. He appeared to be void of emotion; impassive to her illness and probably relieved by her death.

George remembered Lucas held a red rose ... a *rose*, symbolic of love. Love and passion. Soulmates, wives, and mothers. George remembered thinking, *How dare you hold a rose, about to place it on my mother's grave*, onto the mound of dirt covering her like an iron blanket.

You never gave her flowers when she was alive. Why give her one now? I was the one who gave her flowers. I picked wildflowers for her in the summer; I brought her roses on her birthday and Mother's Day. You never gave her a gift. Never a bracelet or a gesture of fondness or appreciation, not even a card.

There was no diamond ring on her finger. George only remembered the wedding band Lucas made her wear. Now he knew why. She didn't love Lucas, but he insisted she pretend.

And of all things, Lucas gave her a cross; it was silver and had small flecks of gold along the border. He remembered thinking, *You bastard. Do NOT put that rose on my mother where she rests eternally, where she is finally at peace.* But Lucas did. He tossed the red rose to the ground, upon the dirt that smothered her bones. Her beautiful resting-face and empty eyes.

After Lucas left, George bent down and picked up the rose. He threw it into the weeds at the side of the road.

George knew even back then that Lucas was responsible for her death.

He remembered how her silky hair fell out in clumps the one and only time she agreed to chemotherapy treatments. She could only handle one series of four treatments because it made her bedridden. She became so weak she couldn't move, couldn't speak. But George held her hand and comforted her. Lucas was always gone. And Reese was too scared to be near her.

All these years had passed, and he resented Dale Washburn, too. Where was Washburn as she lay withering and the cancer, which had started in her chest, ate away at her brain? Where was *my father?*

After leaving Mae at his house, George went to Lucas's and stayed for almost four hours. He sat at the kitchen table, cleaning his pistol. He drank whiskey and waited for Dale Washburn.

He vaguely remembered talking with Lucas— last week or was it yesterday? They were talking about equipment for the logging company or discussing a loan George wanted to ask him for. Something happened, and Lucas got hurt. Lucas mouthed off, as usual.

George remembered one thing Lucas said: *Dale Washburn didn't want her, didn't want you neither. Point that goddamn pistol at him.*

By the time Dale's truck rattled down the plowed driveway, it was almost two thirty in the morning. George heard the churning of tires and Dale's scratchy cough when he stepped out of the truck and up to the front door.

George heard him pause to stomp the snow off his boots, and while he waited, George loaded the gun and steadied it against his knee under the table. "Come on in," he shouted. "Door's open."

Dale pushed on the door and walked into the kitchen. "Found time to plow, I see," he said with a lift to his voice, offering a compliment while he still had the chance.

"Yeah, I've been busy," George admitted. "Found time to plow. Sure."

Dale closed the door behind him. As he looked around the room, his brown eyes flickered and his cheekbones formed crevices, enhancing his age. And the kitchen was way too hot. George had both woodstoves going and the electric heater on as well. Dale went for a handkerchief inside the back pocket of his tan jeans and wiped his face.

George said, "Sit down and have a drink."

"I didn't come to drink," Dale said. "I came because you asked me to meet you."

Dale was a tall wiry man; taller than George but not quite as tall as Jon. He was physically corroded by years of hard work. His outfit was suitable for his occupation: casual clothes but durable at that, although he was particular about personal hygiene. He was immaculate and tidy and smelled of spicy aftershave.

"Did you love my mother?" George asked.

"I wanted her to leave Lucas, but she wouldn't."

George closed his eyes. He remembered her delicate skin and small ears. She didn't belong with a man like Lucas Coulter, or Dale Washburn, either. *She belonged in a palace.*

"I was twelve when she died," George said. "She had cancer."

"I know."

"She was sick for a long time. She went back and forth from the hospital, had chemotherapy once, but it didn't do her any good. It just made her hair fall out. She had beautiful long hair. Then one day she gave up. I know the feeling. I'm there now."

"Maybe you should put the booze aside," Dale suggested. He sat down and slid a leg out against the linoleum. He yawned, not because he was bored with the situation, but because a life riddled with regret had finally gotten the best of him.

George realized he had some of Dale's physical characteristics, mostly the stringent architecture of his face. Carolyn was in George too—in his big expressive eyes. But now George also had a bent nose, broken by Jon Loucher months ago during their confrontation over Mae Lakarri. He also had a gap where one of his front teeth had been.

George lifted his glass in a toast. "What does it matter now?" he asked of the man folded into the chair across the table from him. "If you had told me you were my father after she died, I could have lived with you. If I had lived with you instead of Old Lucas, I might not be so fucked up."

"It's hard to say. I live in a trailer half this size and I don't know much about kids."

"Neither did Lucas. And he didn't know nothing about women either; seems I take after him in that respect. I lost Mae to Jon and Lucas lost my mother to you."

"He never *lost* her," Dale corrected, his voice fractured. "She stayed with him until she died. I gave her my word I wouldn't say anything."

"I remember he slammed her into the dresser in their bedroom. Her chest hit the sharp corner and after that, she got cancer ... here," he pointed to his chest area with his free hand. "I *know* he caused it."

Lucas was drunk and it was late at night. She was waiting up to protect her sons from him. He was a loud, obnoxious drunk. He would see shapes and people that weren't there. He would accuse her of cheating on him. He would tell her she was shiftless and ugly.

George saw the fight. He was only nine years old, and saw it reflected in the shadows of the lamp on the table by the bed. Lucas grabbed her and shook her. *Her bones are going to break,* George thought, *they'll break in two.* Lucas shoved her into the dresser; the corner of it rammed into her chest. George said to himself, *She's dead.*

After Lucas left, George told Reese to help him lift her. She was unconscious, but they lifted her up to the bed where she coughed convulsively. George went into the kitchen and found Lucas sipping whiskey from a smeared glass. He told Lucas, *We have to help her; take her to the hospital,* and Lucas said, *Fine, we'll tell them she fell. You hear me? She fell!*

Dale Washburn said, "Yes," and winced. "It's like I said, she told me to keep quiet. I asked her to leave him. What I can't understand is since you saw Lucas mistreat your mother, why did you do the same thing to Mae?"

George picked at his eye with his free hand and squeezed the handle of the pistol with the other. "What kind of question is that?" he asked. "It's your fault I turned out like this. You're my father and didn't tell me. My mother was the one who had the backbone to finally tell me. I figured you'd come to get me. But you never did."

"I thought it best to leave things alone."

"You thought it best to leave me with an abusive drunkard who took his anger out on women and kids? And then you work for him all these years!"

Dale saw a rifle propped in the corner by the stove. He said, "I've been poor most of my life. Lucas had a business and a good income. He could feed you and put clothes on your back. If your mother told you about me, you could've said something."

"You were afraid of Lucas," George said, point-blank.

"No, I would have shot him same as look at him."

Dale moved to the counter, inspected the glasses in the sink, and rinsed out the cleanest one he could find. "I know you got a gun under the table," he said. "If you're planning on putting a bullet in me, maybe I *will* have a drink."

"Well, good. Get a glass and come back over and sit down." George picked up the bottle and poured Dale a drink. Since Dale had brought up the fact he knew about the gun, George put it on the table in front of him. He was quick on the draw and would use it if necessary. For now, he studied Dale, thinking, *We don't look alike, not really.*

George said again, "So you're my father."

"Yes," Dale said. "And she wouldn't leave him." Dale sat down, swallowed the drink, and placed the glass on the table for another. George poured while Dale talked. "Jon lost his mother when he was a boy too; younger than you were when your mother died, and he managed to keep going."

"Sure, but his father isn't a mean bastard," George said in retaliation to Dale's comparison. "I know Elbert. He's no bastard. Jon didn't watch his father beat his mother, either. And he wasn't beat by Elbert. Like I was by Lucas"

"Yes, there are differences," Dale said blandly.

Dale's grandmother raised *him*. She was no lady. She wasn't gentle by any means, but she never beat him. Slapped him maybe, yelled at him definitely, but she never slugged or punched him.

"I hate like hell that you were abused," Dale said finally. "I should've helped you. *And* your mother."

"Too late," said George. "She's dead and I'm almost."

"There's nothing to do but move on."

"That's fucking brilliant," George yelled. He beat the table with a fist after ramming his glass against it. He lifted his glass in a toast again—to the refrigerator, the oven, the breadbox on the counter. "Why didn't *I* think of that!"

Then he said, "You *still* don't get it!"

He proceeded to pour himself another drink, shook his head, and whispered, "Not too long ago me and Lucas were sitting at this very table discussing cowards and good men. He called me a coward. He ought to know."

"So, where's Lucas now? You shoot him?"

George looked pleased and picked an earlobe. "Sure did. He's out back in the woodshed. Dead as hell."

"Sorry to hear that. I was hoping he was really in Lansing."

"He was going to turn me and Reese in for dumping the chemicals. He couldn't stand for me to make some extra cash. He wanted me tied to him forever, and the only way to get rid of him was to knock him onto his fat ass, dead. He begged me to spare his life. First time he ever spoke to me polite. I had to pay him back for what he did to my mother." George pulled a silver cross from his shirt pocket and tossed it across the table, where it landed next to Dale's hand. "Here, this was hers. You can have it."

Dale raked three fingers through his wavy hair. He picked up the cross, studied it, but gave it back. "What about McMasters? He dead, too? And by the way, are you the one who shot my good friend, Jon?"

"You bet. Lloyd should have stayed in Canada like Lucas told him to do. Lucas said he was hiding at the hunting camp and about to turn himself in, all because Christopher got caught. I told Lloyd to forget about him. But Lloyd said we needed him to alter the levels. And sure, I shot Jon. He tried to take Mae away from me." George lifted his eyes towards the ceiling as his scaly lips sucked in air. "I'm not about to explain all that. It's over. Lloyd's wife's not going to be happy he's dead."

"What's she got to do with it anyway?"

"Nothing. It's just that they got the two kids. Kids, as we just discussed, are very important. What they see and hear."

Dale waited for George to take another sip of whiskey. George's words were already slurred. His eyes were warped. Dale asked, "Where's the body? Out back with Lucas?"

"No. Lloyd's swimming in a fuel truck behind the hunting camp. The chemicals came in handy after all. Probably nothing left of him now but pieces of bone. I had to cut him up some with the saw so he'd fit."

"Hell, that makes you a cold-blooded murderer. I'm not sure I want to call you son under these circumstances."

George leaned back in the chair and laughed. "I'll make you a deal. You don't have to call me son. I don't have to call you dad."

"Why don't you go wash your face and come with me?" Dale stood up, but when George grabbed the pistol and aimed it, he sat back into the chair. "I see, you're going to shoot me too, eliminate everyone who's ever irritated you?"

"We'll talk a little more," George said.

"We'll talk without the gun."

George put the gun back down on the table. He dug around inside the pocket of his jacket and pulled out a photograph. "You can have this picture if you don't want her cross."

Dale picked up the photograph and scanned it closely. He leaned forward against his elbows and blinked to keep his vision focused.

"I got more in the back room," George said. He pushed himself up from the table and slipped the cross into his shirt pocket. "Sit tight a minute. I'll be right back."

When George stood up, he had a flashback of standing at his mother's grave in the cemetery near Trenary and he could see the church at the back of the lot surrounded by aspen and willow trees. He was standing by her grave, placing a single rose—this time white—on the grass that covered her near a patch of forget-me-nots. It was summertime. He saw himself standing at the same spot the evening before he came to Lucas's house for the last time. *Mother*, he said. *I can't do this anymore.* Next, he put twelve pink roses near her headstone, roses he bought at the flower shop on his way to the cemetery.

He was going down the hallway towards the back of the house where he'd found a photo album earlier.

He would ask Dale to tell him everything he remembered about his mother.

But as soon as George left the table, a vehicle pulled into the yard. Then more vehicles approached, until a row of vehicles parked in a line all the way up the driveway. There was only the sound of doors opening and the mournful hum of the refrigerator.

Dale stood up and walked to the window. He pulled the flimsy curtain back and saw two police cars and a Blazer under the spray of yard lights. He opened the front door to four cops, and the man coming towards the house first was Rick Savola, the new skidder operator Lucas hired before he died.

Savola came to the steps and asked, "He's in there?" And although Dale heard the words, he watched Savola's lips form: *He's in there*? As if the words alone prophesized that George wouldn't go to prison.

Savola, or Peterson rather, pulled out a plastic-covered identification card. "DNR," he said. He flipped the case back into his pocket. "We came for George Coulter. If he's here, at least we know he wasn't the one who just torched a skidder at the logging site."

"One of Coulter's skidders?"

"That's right. It happened an hour ago." Peterson motioned for the men behind him to take over. "My name's Peterson. I'm undercover."

"I'll go talk him into coming out," Dale said. "He confessed to murdering Lucas and Lloyd McMasters. Lucas is in a shed and Lloyd's in pieces in a fuel truck."

Before Dale went through the door, he looked over and saw Jon's pickup truck parked up the driveway, but Jon wasn't in the truck and he wasn't standing on the front porch.

Dale walked to the last room at the end of the hallway. The room was cluttered with boxes and mounds of clothing. There was a sewing machine in one corner, card tables, an antique dresser against the north wall, and several pairs of boots, old magazines, lamps, and suitcases shuffled and stacked.

Dale stuck his hands in his pockets. When he turned to the right, he saw George's orange shirt at the exact second George put the end of the gun barrel to his head. Dale stepped forward. "No!"

But the blast from the pistol made the windows vibrate, and George slumped down against the closet door, onto the floor. Half of his head was gone, and so was the area where the bullet hit the closet after ripping through his skull.

Jon found Dale standing in the bedroom near a window. Jon walked over to him and led him out of the room. Reese stumbled past them, followed by Peterson. Reese moved from George's body to the window, shouting, "He can't be dead! No! He can't be!"

The police and Rick Peterson were extremely thorough. In addition, they were used to heinous matters. But Reese, of course, wasn't used to losing his father, his cousin, and his only brother all in one month.

Reese dropped into a gray recliner. Seconds later, Rick Peterson nudged his leg to get his attention. "Reese Coulter?" he asked, flashing his credentials again. "You're under arrest for transporting and disposing illegal chemical wastes. Because of the circumstances and one of your logging sites having just been blown to hell and back, you're going in for questioning after coming with me to the site."

"But what about my *brother*?" Reese asked, tears in his eyes. "Where will—"

"He'll be taken to the morgue."

Peterson helped Reese to his feet. "I wish to God someone would've helped him long ago," Reese said, bawling uncontrollably. "About twenty years *before* now!"

Jon couldn't look at George. Instead, he helped Dale out the door. Although George had almost shot Jon's leg off months ago, Jon knew if not for Elbert, he could be the one dead on the floor.

He bent down, picked up the small silver cross that someone had dropped, and placed it near the hand of Dale Washburn's son.

Chapter 18

Jon limped back and forth across a ten-foot length of flooring between the couch and table in Dale's trailer even though Dale kept telling him, "You can *go* now; I'm fine." But Jon wasn't satisfied that Dale was fine, or that he would ever be *fine* again.

He had followed Dale home after the police questioned him at Lucas's. For the first twenty minutes, Dale sat motionless on the couch, looking around the room as if he didn't recognize it. Now it seemed he was trying to convince Jon that he was all right, that witnessing his son shoot himself was just a diversion from his ho-hum existence. There was nothing to it; he was a strong person and would recover after a short nap.

Jon didn't feel right about leaving him, but he wanted to drive out to the logging site where Peterson and Reese were investigating the charred skidder. Peterson said he was on the trail of the fanatics, the group that had infiltrated the Upper Peninsula, and he had evidence to prove that they had been watching the Coulters' team. They were responsible for the burning skidder, and God only knows what they might do next.

Dale finished his brandy—two flavors together in a concoction he had prepared when they first got to the trailer. He was perspiring, yet the cool morning air suggested rain, and maybe sleet.

Although it was the end of March, warm weather wouldn't come until mid to late May. They might get a brief spell of warmth, but cooler air would be behind it, and back and forth, until maybe, if they were lucky, by July they would get temperatures into the eighties.

For now, it was to-the-bone cold, particularly in Dale's trailer.

Jon offered to build a fire before he left, but Dale told him not to bother. He told him to just turn on the kitchen heater, which was fine with Jon. He didn't want to make a fire in a woodstove that looked risky at best. He imagined flames shooting from the sides, climbing up the walls, singeing the furniture, the rugs, and the moth-eaten curtains.

The kitchen area was only six steps to the left. It consisted of a refrigerator, a Coleman stove, and a square table. Jon crouched sideways and turned the heater button to on. "There," he said to Dale, who had settled himself deeply into the lumpy tweed couch.

Dale closed his eyes, opened them again, and slid his hands between the straps of his suspenders. He brought a hand out and adjusted his pant leg. Jon was anxious to get to the logging site. He decided that George's tragic end was inevitable. They all saw it coming. Jon knew that after killing two men, George would kill himself rather than face life in prison.

Dale said, "Go ahead, do what we talked about. This is your chance to buy the company from Reese. Take the Clara money and do it. Reese won't be able to run the business alone. With Globe One around burning equipment and threatening people, Reese might want to sell. Besides, Peterson said he'll be fined and on probation. The judge might decide he has to do time. He was right there while George siphoned the wastes, right there draining it into barrels and helping to bury it."

Jon knew Dale was right. They needed to get busy and buy Coulter Logging from Reese before he sold it to the wrong person or mismanaged it down to nothing.

"If Coulter Logging is a target for Globe One," Dale said, "we find out who's causing trouble. Someone on the payroll is involved. How else would they know our locations and trucking schedules?"

Jon had always wondered if someone on the crew was involved; now he was certain. He said, "We know it's not Reese or George."

"Right, and we know that Savola character is with the DNR."

"Which leaves us with Tom Foster and Bryan Kinnenun."

"And keep an eye on Melanie McMasters. George mentioned her this morning. He said she'll be mad over Lloyd's death. I think she's behind it all. And by the way, you found Mae tied up at George's, and Reese was looking for him?"

"She's almost eight months along."

Dale was frowning, weary with thought.

"That's what she says," Jon added when he saw Dale's eyebrow lift.

Jon pulled at his earlobe, pacing again. He thumped the floor with his cane. "We'll keep Reese on," he agreed.

"He can be of help. Let's hope the DNR will only make him pay a fine and clean up the chemicals. I talked to Elbert last night. He said the lawyer called. I have to sign some papers and can collect the money now. I'll take Reese with me to the insurance company and bank and put everything into our names."

Jon knew Dale was a strong person, but he would need to keep busy to survive his loss. Jon also knew Dale saved his money in bonds and various accounts. It was obvious he didn't spend money on his home or property. He saved, and he invested.

"The thing is I need to get everything changed over right away," Jon said. "Before we lose contacts. There are jobs pending we need to keep track of."

"The first thing you do is hire back Bill Casey. George fired him."

"Fired Casey?" Jon asked, astounded. "*That* was a mistake."

"George didn't do a damn thing right." Dale turned to the wall and closed his eyes. "Get on out of here and take care of business," he said. "I need a nap. Later I'm going to the undertakers to see about George. And you might keep that in mind when you find yourself thinking about pretending Mae isn't about to have your kid."

Jon wanted to say, *What the hell are you talking about?* But he left the cramped trailer as soon as Dale fell asleep.

He wanted to talk to Reese before going to the attorney's office in Marquette. The problem of Neil Halverson, unfortunately, had slipped his mind. He had already decided he needed to meet Neil first to assess his mental and intellectual capabilities. According to Clara, Neil was not to be considered at all, but Jon knew, iron-clad living will or not, Neil was her only surviving relative, and Jon had heard of blood relatives contesting wills. He knew that an estate could be tied up for months, even years, and to count on Clara's money was foolhardy.

Thankfully, he could work the gas pedal and brakes with his good leg—the right—but nonetheless, being crippled slowed him down, and his cane was always in the way no matter where he put it.

By the time he arrived at the logging site, the fire department had everything under control; however, the skidder in question still simmered. Not only was Peterson walking around the site, taking notes and flashing his credentials, there were fire investigators, two policemen, and a detective named Ron Evans.

"Are you Jon Loucher?" Evans asked as Jon limped towards the skidder.

Evans was of medium height and clean-shaven. Compared to everyone else, he was out of place with his impeccable tidiness. Peterson had mentioned Evans to Jon briefly. Namely that he had told Peterson Jon was part of Coulter Logging, a piece cutter to be exact, and that Jon had been one of George's victims. Jon wasn't dead, of course, but he was clearly maimed.

Evans inspected the dark circles under Jon's eyes and the scratches across the skin on his neck and hands. Jon was otherwise dressed for the weather, although his clothes were of an expensive brand and even his black cap was made of high-quality material. He wore a down jacket, leather boots, top-of-the-line Levi's, and a canvas-type shirt beneath the jacket. Jon didn't have a family to support. He could afford expensive clothes and lavish hobbies. He knew Evans knew this, and he could tell Evans didn't approve.

He said, "Ronald Evans, detective with the Rapid River Police Department."

Jon didn't think a small community like Rapid River had a police department. It seemed more likely that Evans had meant to say Escanaba. Nonetheless, Evans continued, "I'm investigating this fire and would like to ask you a few questions."

"I'd like to ask *you* a question," Jon said. "You're with Peterson? It seems to me people aren't who they say they are. I know Peterson's DNR."

"I'm a detective from Rapid River." Evans put this fact out for the second time. He tampered with his hat and searched the scattered crowd. "What do you know about the environmentalist group? We have reason to believe they torched this skidder."

"I'm sure they did, unless one of *us* is an arsonist."

"That's a possibility," Evans conceded, zooming in on Jon's face. He straightened his tie with one hand and slammed a clipboard against his leg with the other. He looked like he had just stepped away from the dinner table, but whose dinner and which table?

Jon said, "I'm here to talk with Reese Coulter. From now on, we're running the company together."

"Is that right?" Evans asked, picking at the back of his smooth head of hair. He did not like it when facts, significant or inconsequential, slipped past him. "Yet they've been targeted? How do you find that sound?"

"I find *nothing* sound anymore," Jon said. "But if I don't help him, he'll lose the company. I'll find out who's working for Globe One."

Jon could smell Evans's aftershave. He also smelled a honey-scented soap and thought of bears coming out of hibernation. "You think someone in the crew is working for them?" Evans asked, wondering why Jon was slightly smiling.

"Yes," Jon said, the smile gone.

"You can be helpful then. I'll keep in touch."

As Evans was about to turn to find Peterson, Jon poked the back of his leg with his cane. "You might want to wear boots in the woods from now on," he advised, noticing the mud caked on Evan's leather shoes. "Maybe lose the fancy getup." He touched his lip, pretending to pause for memory. "Then again, you're a detective, right?"

"Ask Peterson who I am," Evans said, arrogantly. "I'll catch up with you later."

And there Jon had his answer. Evans was partnered with Rick Peterson, as Peterson had mentioned, probably with the FBI or the EPA.

Shifting gears, Jon found Reese sitting in Peterson's truck. He was drinking a soda and smoking a cigarette. Jon leaned against the door. "What did Peterson say about the chemicals?" he asked. "Did he say anything about arresting you?"

"They're gonna fine me nine or ten grand," Reese said, looking like he might cry. "Guess I'm responsible for paying for the clean up of the barrels too. It was George and Lloyd's plan, now I'm left holding the bag. I told Peterson everything I know, but he doesn't believe me."

"You've got to *make* him believe you," Jon said. "If you were just along for the ride, pay up and forget it. You messed with the woods right along with them. You didn't consider the laws of nature." He saw that Reese was past comprehension at this point, so he composed himself to conclude, "What goes around comes around. That's how it works."

"Lucas was crooked as George," Reese whined. "You worked for him and didn't even know he cheated on price? Didn't know he cut corners and ripped off landowners, claimed gas for trucks for personal use? You're blind, Loucher. And you're guilty too; or maybe just plain stupid, like they was!"

"Okay, I'm blind and stupid," Jon agreed. "But I want to buy Coulter Logging and run it ethically. It's sort of a plan I have: ethics in the timber industry. Forest management, replanting, follow the rules, that sort of thing."

"Holy Christ," Reese whimpered, slobbering. "I need a job to pay these fines!"

"I'll help you run the company," Jon suggested, chewing on a toothpick while thinking. "You can stay on as a piece cutter or whatever you want. What with Peterson interrogating you, you won't have time to run the business. You got to keep the jobs George already contracted out for. We'll go to the bank and insurance company after I talk to my attorney."

"I'll think about it. Right now, I got to take care of funeral arrangements! I never did nothing like that before, picking out caskets. I might just have them both cremated. Their bodies are pretty much mutilated anyway," he lamented, staring at nothing in particular.

"Who would want to come to their funerals? Who has the time?"

"Yes, funerals *can* be expensive," Jon said, although he had never organized one himself. He thought of his mother, and it hit him that he would have to ask Elbert about her funeral and where is she buried? He didn't go to his own mother's funeral. He has never visited her grave. He was five years old when she died, yes, but she *was* his mother. Jon fought back a wave of panic, thinking again, *Where is she buried?*

Reese clicked his tongue against the roof of his mouth. "I got to go close up their houses and get rid of stuff," he said. "I got to get started now!"

"Sure," said Jon. "But don't tamper with evidence. You'll have to talk to Peterson about that. We got to keep the crew moving on the jobs in progress. If you like, you can sign the company over now."

"I need to go see Lloyds' wife," Reese said. "She's probably out of her mind with worry by now."

"Did you mention the fuel truck to Peterson?"

"I did, and he had some cops go check it out. On the way over here, he got a call on the radio, and they found Lloyd in the tank all right! In about fifty different pieces!"

Reese seemed anxious to confess more information. "That Melanie bitch is a vulture. She pushed Lloyd into the chemical thing to begin with. Right after you beat up George for smacking Mae around, Melanie came out to the house to see him. I didn't know they knew each other that good. George said he thought Lloyd was about to run scared. Lucas claimed Melanie was after Lloyd's money. It wouldn't surprise me if he left a life insurance policy behind."

Jon found this new information a lot to consider, and he had no choice but to consider it quickly. He said, “Maybe we should keep this to ourselves.”

Reese flicked the cigarette butt out the open window, past Jon’s shoulder, and watched it sizzle in a puddle. “Peterson won’t believe me anyway,” he said.

Jon wasn’t sure how to go about consoling a person who had just lost his entire family. He started thinking about his mother’s funeral. Was there a funeral, a memorial service? Was she born somewhere other than Upper Michigan? Was she buried at her birthplace?

He obsessed over the matter for ten more minutes as Reese smoked one cigarette after another and chattered on and on about going to see Melanie McMasters.

CHAPTER 19

After the sheriff came to Melanie's house and explained in detail what had happened to Lloyd, she took two sedatives. Her cousin, Ellen, offered to take the boys for a couple of days to give Melanie time to think about what she wanted to do next.

Although she stopped loving Lloyd the day she found out he was having an affair with one of the office workers at the mill, she still felt responsible for his death; after all, she had asked George if he would "take care of" Lloyd, and Lucas too. She was attracted to George, yet Lloyd was responsible for building up her savings account, and she had been the one to talk him into siphoning the dioxins in the first place. In a sense, she had maneuvered both men into doing what she wanted, and it led to murder.

Then there was Tom Foster. Melanie knew she was doing the same thing to him by manipulating him. But George was the person she couldn't get off her mind. He was intensely troubled by his past, and Melanie couldn't recall the exact words he used, but he said something like: "Mae has sad eyes, like my mother's." He then went into a trance. Melanie tried to console him, rub his arm, kiss the side of his face, but there was no response. She knew he was thinking about his mother, or Mae Lakarri. And the very thought of Mae made Melanie shake. She hated Mae that much.

And she hated Lloyd too, ever since the day she found out about the woman at the mill. She was so distraught, she almost shot herself with the .45 Lloyd kept in the closet for protection. All because that woman had the stupidity to call the house, asking for Lloyd. Then Melanie went to the mill one evening. She left her sons alone in the house and drove all the way to the mill and saw them sitting together in Lloyd's truck. She saw Lloyd lean into her, shove his tongue into her mouth; this woman with auburn hair who Melanie had a feeling was only twenty-three, maybe twenty-five years old.

Melanie sat in her car and watched them. She couldn't believe the way Lloyd kissed her, without hesitation; compared to the *labor* he put in to having sex with Melanie. Melanie knew the difference. Lloyd had sex with her; but he *made love* to this woman with the auburn hair.

Melanie wanted to kill them both.

She drove home; didn't say a word to Lloyd about it, ever. She didn't know how long the affair continued, but it worried her that he might ask for a divorce. He never did. Apparently, the affair was lust induced; nothing serious or permanent. After that, she wondered if he really had to work late at the mill, or if he was with that woman. Or maybe he had affairs with several different women. Melanie would never know for sure.

Soon after she found out about the affair, she devised a campaign to badger him into making extra money. She also needed to connect with his cousin, George, and obviously, in order to connect with George, she had to sleep with him.

Before she found out about Lloyd's affair, Melanie had been devoted to him. After the woman called their home and Melanie saw them together, she decided it was imperative to have a relationship with George, and also Tom Foster. Both men were instrumental to her plan of destroying Coulter Logging.

Melanie told Lloyd if he didn't come up with the money to pay for a bigger house, vacations, more clothes and jewelry, she would leave him. Her plan worked. He even enlisted his cousins to help dispose of chemical wastes.

Now Lloyd is dead, she thought. *George is dead, and all I have left is Tom Foster.*

Then around noon Reese Coulter showed up to offer his condolences. Melanie knew Reese didn't like her and blamed her for everything that had gone wrong. Earlier that day, she had taken the sedatives and drank two screwdrivers. Consequently, Reese looked lopsided, standing in the doorway. He talked on and on about his father; how he missed Lloyd, and what in God's name, he asked her, made George go off the deep end? Did she happen to know?

I don't know, she said. She *did* remember asking George if he would eliminate Lucas and Lloyd if need be. Now she wondered if she had pushed George over the edge.

Before he left, Reese told her she could call him if she needed anything. She could count on him, he promised, and she could summon him for funeral arrangements, even money, but Melanie said nothing and watched him drive away.

That night on the local news there were pictures of Lucas's modular home, of George's house, and of the Conrad Paper Mill. It was all tied together, but the details of the eco-terrorism were left out and there was no implication whatsoever that a local logging company was the target.

Brent Christopher was interviewed. He was the weak link, now broken. The allegations were mostly against George and Lloyd, and Melanie assumed that Reese Coulter was probably in the clear. Reese would help the authorities in exchange for lower fines. Reese had been part of the chemical-dumping mayhem, but now he'd tell the prosecutor anything they wanted to know just to get off easier. Reese would go free, and yet his brother, George, had murdered her husband and shoved parts of his body into a fuel tank full of chemicals.

Melanie decided to get dressed and find Tom Foster. He'd know more about the situation. If she had to, she would track him down at home. Never mind confronting the useless hag he was married to. Tom would be the one to help her destroy Reese and anyone else associated with Coulter Logging.

Melanie found Tom at the logging site near Eben working a two hundred-fifty-acre parcel George started part of the crew working on before he died. She parked on the road and watched the logging action.

She watched Tom, the mechanic, drive one of the skidders. She leaned forward and tried to focus Bryan Kinnenun, the man Tom had mentioned might be linked with the terrorists. Bryan stood near the loading deck. He counted the logs and wrote numbers on a pad of paper. There were other men cutting high up on a ridge, but Melanie didn't recognize them and figured they were temporary help.

Once again, Melanie noticed Tom Foster was gangly and emaciated, particularly in the face and legs. He was good with machines, however, and moved swiftly among the thick brush. She watched the skidder churn up the damp ground. She knew that soon the road restrictions would be enforced on back roads such as the one leading to this site, and the crew would deck the logs and move them to the highway for pickup. There would be fines if the trucks were caught moving timber on the back roads during the spring thaw—unless certain people looked the other way, which was sometimes the case.

She waited for Tom to finish loading the back of the skidder with logs. She watched him drive the logs to the deck near the road and unload them, but she got impatient and honked the horn.

Bryan heard the horn blaring and motioned for Tom to cut the engine of the skidder. Tom did, but looked angry until he saw Melanie's car parked on the road. Tom instructed Bryan to take over and pick up the last two piles back in the woods. He hopped down from the cage of the skidder and sauntered to the road. "Mourning your dead husband?" he asked, rolling tobacco around the inside of his cheek with his tongue. The tobacco chewing made it even more difficult to understand him.

He already had a speech impediment and deplorable grammar.

"And your lover, George?" he added, daring to grin.

As Tom walked to her car, he took his hard hat off and put it on the ground beside his boot. Melanie noticed he was bald on top of his head but his hair was long down the sides of his angular face.

Melanie thought, *How dare you handle the death of my husband, father to my sons, as if the tragedy had been expected?* She shook away the blur of alcohol and gripped the steering wheel. "Is that Bryan Kinnenun?"

"Why? Does he look good to you now that you're a grieving widow?"

"He looks good if he can help us destroy this company," she said. "What's going on here? It seems the Coulters are still in business even though two of them are dead."

"Jon was here and told us to move the timber out. Guess he's going to help Reese. Real convenient, I'd say."

"Quite helpful," Melanie agreed. "And interesting."

"I wouldn't be surprised if Jon ends up running the show."

"Keep an eye on him. As soon as I can get the insurance money, we can leave."

"Think they'll be a problem over the money?"

"There better not be. I'm the sole beneficiary. Plus, Lloyd left cash hidden in the bedroom. There are various bank accounts and abundant stock. All you have to do is worry about dumping that pig you're married to and help me relocate. I'll give you twenty thousand for your trouble. You don't even have to stay with us.

Just help us get out of town. Then you can go back to your pig of a wife."

Tom paused and took a breath. To steady his speech as well as his temper, he put his gloved hands against the door of her station wagon. "That *pig* happens to be the mother of my children," he clarified. "I'll leave when I'm good and ready. What more could you want? I said I'd leave her, and I even torched one of Coulter's skidders for you. I think you owe me more than twenty grand for that alone."

"You torched a skidder … for *me*?" She touched her chest to imply she was honored that he would go to such lengths. "It wasn't on the news."

"They're not dumb enough to put it on the news and get people riled up," Tom explained, shuffling about. "It'll shake Reese up though, which was the plan. He'll need Jon to help him. There were cops out at the other logging site; even a cop from Rapid River named Evans. And the new skidder operator Savola—there's something off about him too. Maybe I can find out what's going on from Jon. Like I said, he was just here but didn't say much. He told Reese to move out the timber, and he said Washburn will be back to help, and last of all he mentioned something about the road restrictions."

"Never mind the road restrictions," Melanie said. "I didn't love Lloyd, but I'm not going to let Reese get away with his insane brother murdering him! He's as guilty as George was. Now he's pretending to be an environmentalist, just to save himself! And why is Jon Loucher coming around here giving out orders? Is he planning to buy the company? That would be a huge mistake on his part! Both Jon and Reese could have helped Lloyd. The only person who really tried was Lucas. Lucas helped Lloyd get out of town and even hired a lawyer; but I don't see that the lawyer did much good! I only see that Lucas and Lloyd are dead. Because of George, and because Reese and Jon Loucher didn't try to stop him. I begged George to get help, but he wouldn't listen. Now he's dead!"

"You're getting things twisted around." Tom lowered his voice, even though the crew couldn't hear them among the chaos of machinery and saws. Still, the fact that they were visible made Tom nervous, Melanie could tell. "You got Jon mixed up with Reese and George," he said to her. "He's not one of them."

"He *is* mixed up with them. If it wasn't for him, Mae Lakarri would have gone back to George and he wouldn't have snapped!"

Melanie knew from Tom himself that George went bezerk after Mae left him. Jon humiliated George at the logging site and next thing they know, George kills Lucas and Lloyd and then shoots himself as the grand finale.

Tom stared at Melanie. She could tell he was helpless against her mood swings.

"I can't even have a proper funeral for Lloyd," Melanie went on, starting to cry. "He's all eaten up by chemicals. What will I tell my children? Your father was strangled by some maniac and crammed into a tank of toxic waste?"

"Yeah, well, he *was* a criminal," Tom pointed out, trying to justify Lloyd's death.

"But he didn't deserve to die *that* way!"

Tom held Melanie's hand, hoping to soothe her. "Don't you worry now," he said, defenseless against her tears. "I'll take care of everything."

"Start with Mae Lakarri," Melanie said between sobs. "You're handy with matches. Set her on fire or something!"

Tom lifted Melanie's hand to his lips. Melanie knew he believed she loved him. She knew he believed it with all his heart and soul, and setting fires for her was the least he could do.

CHAPTER 20

One late afternoon during the third week of April, Elbert was watching the news and found out some interesting details about George murdering Lucas and his cousin, Lloyd McMasters, the supervisor at the Conrad Mill. He wasn't surprised that George committed suicide, either; but now he was even more worried about Jon. Jon would want to buy the logging company and help Reese Coulter run it, and such a maneuver would put Jon in the line of fire from the fanatics' point of view.

Certainly, the concept of eco-terrorism intrigued Elbert. He knew all about environmental fanaticism from his years of working in the woods. Basically, there had always been people who didn't understand how the timber industry worked—how the ethical loggers worked—and these people had taken it upon themselves to try and change or regulate the system. They decided cutting down trees, even in a select-cut situation, damaged ecosystems, and they concluded it was due to greed and that the timber industry was solely to blame. Never mind air pollution brought on by factories and automobiles, the dumping of thousands of different types of wastes from other industries, and the simple understanding that this world housed too many people to begin with. They still blamed loggers for cutting down trees.

Then how, wondered Elbert, *do they expect to supply the demand? How are people to have houses, paper, furniture, and other materials made from trees?* There needs to be balance; people like Jon running the show in an environmentally sound manner.

Logging was necessary, but it must be done in a scientific fashion, and therefore replanting, regeneration and forest management techniques are imperative. Acting out of rage and resorting to violence, as some of the environmental protestors were doing is *nothing but insane*, thought Elbert.

On the other hand, disposing of dangerous chemicals in the woods and rivers and contaminating the water and food supply as the corrupt loggers like George Coulter were doing was even more insane.

Elbert knew Jon would plant seedlings, putting back three-fourths of what he had taken. Jon would not tamper with the wetlands. He would be careful with machinery, stay within boundaries, put in proper culverts, and he would adhere to the mandates of soil erosion. He would protect the rivers and streams and he would work the industry honestly and respectfully because, quite simply, he understood the balance of nature.

Furthermore, Elbert reflected, Jon had been through a lot since his mother's absence. After Aubrey died in a car accident, which involved a man she was living with at the time, Jon withdrew into himself. It took Elbert two years to bring him back to the business of living. He made sure Jon finished grade school and high school and took him along when he worked carpentry jobs.

But Jon never asked for details about his mother. He knew she left when he was five and she was killed in a car crash; however, Elbert wasn't sure Jon knew she left with a man. A Jim or Joe something or other. Elbert couldn't recall a name, but if he really concentrated, he remembered the last name was Conley.

Suffice it to say, Elbert wasn't surprised when Aubrey left. She was twelve years younger than he was and only married him because she was out of options. She had been living with one man and then another, and her random love affairs left her without a permanent place to live. Originally from a suburb near Chicago, she lived in Iron Mountain for a while, and moved to Escanaba and onward to the Tennick area. She told Elbert she left home when she was sixteen, and to support herself she worked in restaurants and bars. She explained to him from the beginning that she would never be able to settle down, marry, and so forth. That was not to say she wasn't a dependable person, but marriage material, no, and motherhood, never.

Elbert took the blame for their short courtship and marriage. He had talked her into a relationship even though he knew she was too young and would never comply with the requirements expected of marriage. Elbert admitted he only wanted to help her. He wanted her to have a safe place to live and enough food to eat. After all, she had been living in a run-down motel room near Chatham and working at the bakery full-time. Elbert pitied her, yes, but he was also attracted to her—

her youth, her lithe figure, and the fact that she was a fair-haired, beautiful woman.

He remembered the morning he found her behind the bakery. She was shivering, and he could see that she had been crying. He was going back to his truck from the post office and knew, of course, that Aubrey worked at the bakery from six o'clock in the morning until mid-afternoon. He also knew she worked as a cocktail waitress at the Tennick Tavern at night.

He was drawn down the road behind the grocery store and the bakery and there she was: wearing a white uniform, smoking a cigarette, her face marred by the streaks of her tears.

They talked for a while and decided to meet at the Tennick Tavern later that day. After having dinner, they made a pact to go out on her nights off. Elbert was a confident, good-looking fellow with straight posture. He was always clean and well groomed.

He had light brown skin, suntanned because of working outside in the timber business and carpentry trade. He had the Upper Michigan accent, the swift speed of consonants causing his speech to lower, then lift into a higher pitch. She told him she particularly liked his soft-spoken nature, his dark eyes, and his straight white teeth.

The morning he saw her standing behind the bakery, he asked her why she was crying. She said she couldn't pay the rent on her apartment, so she had to move in with the owner of the bar where she worked at night. Elbert knew him; his name was Rusty Bartlett. A potential problem. A womanizer and a drunkard.

When Elbert took her hand, which was ice-cold due to the early November chill, she smiled at him. She was wearing a thin blue sweater over her uniform. He remembered that he took the cigarette from her because he didn't think she should smoke. He told her she could live with him and that he wanted to marry her. The marriage part, he knew minutes after he suggested it, shouldn't happen. He should just give her money to buy whatever she wanted and needed. But there it was; the words gone. Elbert asked her to marry him even though she said she had never aspired to be anyone's wife.

They went to her apartment building after her shift to pick up her suitcases of clothes and other odds and ends. Another mistake, Elbert could see in retrospect, was that he convinced her to not only quit her job at the Tavern, but also her job at the bakery. Soon after they married, she became distracted and bored. She eventually left, four years and six months after Jon was born. She told Elbert she was going out on a date with a man named Jerry something or other. This Jerry led to a Bob who led to a Mike, and one night she was killed in a car wreck.

He should have just let her live with him, never mind the marriage part. He should have made her prove she was on birth control, realized that since she couldn't afford a place to live, or even food, she didn't have proper medical care, either. When he found out she was pregnant, he was upset, but after the baby was born, she was eager to go out to the bars again, dancing and drinking. He was so preoccupied with the child, he didn't care that she got her job back full-time. Frankly, things were easier without her around.

Eventually, Aubrey left. Elbert hired babysitters to take care of Jon during the day while he went to work. He had to fire two sitters before he found a woman named Anne, whom he liked well enough to keep on. But when Jon started school, she was only needed in the afternoons, and when Jon turned eleven, Elbert decided he was old enough to stay at home by himself.

Elbert was proud of Jon for finishing high school and even happier a year later when he enrolled in a technical school, but two years after, he dropped out to work in the woods. Looking back, Elbert hoped he had taught Jon to not take unnecessary chances. Elbert wanted Jon safe from chaos and harm, and harm for sure was slinking through the woods of Upper Michigan, driving iron spikes into trees and blocking logging trucks from reaching the paper mills, setting skidders on fire, and planting explosive devices inside bulldozers.

Harm was about to knock on Elbert's front door.

Elbert was sitting at the kitchen table reading about George Coulter's suicide when he heard footsteps on the steps of the front porch. Beau lifted his head, growled once, and waited for the knock.

When the knock came, it was as sharp as the snap Elbert gave the newspaper before he folded it and tossed it to the floor with the others. He looked at the clock on the wall by the cabinet; it was three-twenty in the afternoon. He went to the door and peered out to see the squinting face of a stranger. The stranger's left hand was pressed to his forehead, shielding his brow.

He wore a white shirt, black trousers, and a navy-blue jacket. He was tall but slight of stature, and most noticeably, his copper-colored hair was slicked back from the sides of his flushed face. He wore glasses and pushed them up the bridge of his nose.

When Elbert opened the door, the man asked accusingly, "Are you aware there is a dead cat on the road near the end of your driveway?"

Elbert frowned. *My god,* he thought, *not again. Another stray cat gone down!* "I got a dozen stray cats around here," he said. "One dead cat means now I got eleven."

Unlike most people, Elbert couldn't turn away a stray cat or dog. The cats would usually move on, but last fall Elbert noticed eight of them hanging around, and one was pregnant. Although Elbert knew better, he put food out for her, and recently, he noticed she had several younger cats with her. *Problems, always a problem with cats!* Now he would have to worry about finding homes for them.

"Well now," Elbert said to the idea of another dead cat. "Some idiot must have run it over!" He stared at the visitor, thinking, *Who else could it have been but you, a foreigner to these woods?*

The man's lips tightened at the accusation, and also because he had just noticed his pricey leather shoes were covered with mud. He said, "Do you suppose I could come inside? I came to see Jon Loucher. I believe we spoke earlier on the phone."

"The name's Lew-shay," Elbert corrected, thinking he might stall this untimely intruder by coaching him on pronunciation. "It's French Canadian, goes back to the fur-trapping days."

The man pushed through the door, past Elbert, and over to the table where he dropped down a folder. "I just drove all the way from Columbus, Ohio. I need to see Jon Loucher. Is … he …here?" He enunciated the last three words slowly, as if Elbert were hearing impaired.

"Have a seat," Elbert said, "and maybe a glass of tea. I just made it."

But the man didn't budge.

"I know what this is all about," Elbert added. "You're the nephew Clara mentioned, the out of work car salesman with the bad attitude."

"She said I have a bad attitude? Then I probably got it from *her*."

Elbert considered the comment and glanced at the floor. He detested spots and he couldn't stand dirt, silt, or muck of any form in his kitchen. "It irritates me when people track in mud!" he said.

The man tipped his head to exaggerate confusion. His expression itself suggested he had been insulted. "I tracked in mud because your road is nothing but a mudslide," he said. "You should contact the county and get some gravel hauled in here. Or maybe have the road blacktopped!"

"Wait a couple weeks if you want to see mud," Elbert said. "And that's a joke. The County Road Commission doesn't know we exist!"

"They'll know you exist after I get through with them. They're going to get the bill for replacing my muffler, not to mention my exhaust pipe. I almost had to push my car from the highway!"

Elbert went to the window and pulled back the curtains to take a look at the vehicle, stuck past his driveway. "You drove that piece of crap all the way in here?" he asked. "It's April; most side roads in this neck of the woods require four-wheel drive."

"I don't *have* a four-wheel drive. All I want is to find Jon Loucher. I know he works in the woods and lives on Three Cedar Road. Don't bother telling me I got the wrong road. I take it the road is called Three Cedar because of the three big cedar trees near the sign?"

Elbert lined up napkins and silverware on the table. He went to the counter, selected the apple pie instead of the peach. "That's right. Jon lives next door, but he isn't home right now. First off, let me make it clear I won't let you haul Clara's body back to Ohio. She wanted to be buried in the Tennick Cemetery. That's where she is now, and that's where she stays. Do we understand each other so far?"

Neil adjusted the cuffs of his white shirt. He was apparently worried about the creases in his silk trousers and the nicks and stains, not to mention the mud, on his custom-made Italian shoes.

"Who gave you this address?" Elbert asked, pulling a plate from the cupboard.

"My aunt's attorney in Marquette. Who do you think *you* are?" he asked. "You think you can tell me what to do with my own aunt? I'm here to speak with Jon Loucher, per my attorney's advice."

"I'll tell you who I am: Jon's father, Elbert Loucher. I was a good friend of Clara's. She told me you were a two-bit, backstabbing con man, so don't bother fighting the terms of her will. She left everything to my son except for a little piece of land in Ohio. That's what *you* get!"

"How do you know all that for heaven's sake? My aunt was an eccentric bitch, but banish her only living relative? I highly doubt it!"

"She *told* me," Elbert said, plucking his suspenders. "That's how I know!"

"We'll see about that! I'm Neil Halverson, her nephew and only surviving relative. She can stay buried in the Tennick Cemetery; for all I care, you can plant her in your stinking chicken coop. I came for her cash. Then I'll disappear! You and this Jon Loucher character can rest assured I'm not leaving this backwoods shithole until I get it!"

Elbert sliced into the pie, perfect and golden. "You sure got a sharp tongue, bub."

"I also contest wills worth a million dollars." Neil looked over at the pitcher of iced tea. He took off his glasses and cleaned the lenses with a napkin.

He was absolutely refined, very different than what Elbert had expected. Based on Clara's description, Elbert pictured Neil to be a malnourished, feeble individual. But no, he was clean and well-groomed, except for the muddy streaks on his clothes and bug bites here and there across his pale neck, all due to the long drive from Ohio, the walk down Three Cedar Road, and up Elbert's driveway.

Neil shook his head, seemingly so disgusted with the realities of sitting in Elbert's kitchen, he appeared deathly sick. "I hope you have something stronger than tea," he said. "I've had a difficult trip!"

"I might have a bottle of scotch tucked away," Elbert said, thinking it probably wouldn't take much to get Neil blind-drunk.

Neil watched Elbert rummage through the cupboards. "I came a long way and I've been through hell," Neil mumbled, dramatically. "I'll just sit here and wait for your son to get home. I'll wait as long as it takes! How does that suit you?"

"It doesn't," Elbert yelled from the broom closet. "He could be a while."

"Then you'd better bring the bottle and start pouring!"

Elbert returned to the table and put a bottle of scotch and a glass before Neil Halverson. "You go ahead and drink up," he offered. "I sure hope you got lots of insurance. You're going to need it."

"Keep pouring then," Neil said, lifting his glass. "I'm not good at waiting."

• • •

Unfortunately, waiting he did. Jon didn't show up until two the next day. Elbert was outside. He watched Jon drive his truck past Neil's car, into the driveway. Elbert had taken care of the dead cat, which made him even more depressed. He liked cats, and the task had unnerved him.

Elbert, in fact, was worn out by entertaining Neil Halverson most of the night. And he knew Jon wouldn't have the patience to deal with Neil at all. Furthermore, Neil was out to get Jon. He was motivated by his aunt's estate, and he made it clear he would stop at nothing to over turn the terms of her will. Elbert knew Neil wasn't the sort of person one could deal with amiably: he was stubborn and selfish, arrogant and ignorant, and plying him with alcohol had only made the situation worse.

Elbert had been feeding the chickens and sorting through his shed. He put a sack of grain down and rushed over to the steps to cut Jon off. "Don't go in," he said. "Clara's nephew's here. He wants you to drive him to Marquette. He's got a flat tire and he's sitting in my kitchen, drunk."

Jon studied Elbert's face, wondering if he too had had a nip, or maybe several. Also, Elbert didn't have on a jacket, only a shirt and suspenders and faded blue jean. "I can't worry about *him* right now," Jon said. "I came by to take a shower."

Jon wanted to mention the skidder incident. Who else could he confide in but Elbert? But under the circumstances, he kept quiet. He wanted to say, *We are in for a battle. Someone is unstable and dangerous enough to burn equipment and tamper with machinery, never mind the spiking of trees.* He wanted to discuss things with Elbert, but decided it could wait. All Jon really wanted was to get in the shower and go home to take a nap. After the nap, he had planned to go to Marquette and apply for a loan to buy the company from Reese.

But again, Elbert blocked him from entering the house. "Did you hear what I said, son? That Halverson jackass is here to fight Clara's will, or whatever the lawyer called it, which means you're going to have to wrestle him for the money. He claims he can have the will thrown out on grounds that she was mentally incompetent."

Elbert continued to explain that Neil's vehicle was stuck in the driveway. Neil *and* his car were incapacitated. *Don't let him see you here!* But Elbert knew Jon wasn't listening. Jon was too preoccupied with the logging company dilemma; the heating up, to be precise, of the fanatics, the murder, and yes, the suicide. It was all too close to home.

Elbert stepped aside and followed Jon—and his cane—into the kitchen. Once they were inside, there sat Neil Halverson.

Jon studied Neil's expensive, although disheveled clothing first, tie and all. But when he saw the glasses lopsided across Neil's nose, he knew right away that he was indeed blind-drunk.

Neil lifted his glass into a toast and quipped as if recognizing an old friend, "Jon Loucher! The man I came all the way from Columbus, Ohio to see. Here are the facts: My aunt was a lunatic. She was also filthy rich. I'm here for her money, and I'm not leaving until I get every fucking penny of it!" He pounded the table to accent his statement.

Jon ran his fingers through his hair, turned, and shouted as he headed for the bathroom, "Make coffee and sober him up, Elbert!"

"I don't want coffee!" Neil shouted into the heavy air. "You hear me, *goddamnit*. You! Hey, you! I said *no* coffee!"

When Elbert looked at Neil, Neil slid down into the chair. Elbert knew Neil wanted to threaten him; accuse him of kidnapping, tainted liquor, anything to justify his intoxicated behavior; yet at the last minute, Neil was silent.

Even as drunk as he was, there was no mistaking Elbert's frown—a menacing threat—telling him *shut the hell up or a stuck car will be the least of your problems.*

Chapter 21

Neil passed out on Elbert's couch. By the time he woke up, Jon had taken a shower, ate dinner with Elbert, and left for his house next door. In Neil's opinion, Jon had vanished into thin air. He didn't say hello, goodbye, or see you in court. Neil knew from the beginning Jon had no intention of taking him to Marquette to meet with Clara's attorney. He would need to figure out a way to get there on his own, as obviously, his car was still embedded in the road past Elbert's driveway. He needed a tow truck, or at least a winch.

"This is an outrage!" he told Elbert. "Now I'll have to call a cab! I must talk to the attorney this afternoon! For God's sake, doesn't your son realize I could have him arrested for refusing to aid a stranded victim? That's what I am, a victim of all your mud!"

"*My* mud?" Elbert asked, amused. He was sorting through his spice drawer and tossing outdated cans into a trash bag. "It serves you right to sink in mud. You're just another troublemaker we don't need around here."

"I should have gone straight to Marquette," Neil said. "Here I thought I could reason with you people. And *this* is what happens!"

"Let it go," Elbert advised. "No cab's going to come all the way out here."

"How far away is Jon's cabin? I'll walk on back there and talk him into taking me to Marquette."

Elbert shook his head in response to Neil's idea. Jon was next door at his house, but Neil didn't need to know that. "He'll take you tomorrow," Elbert said. "Maybe."

But Neil wouldn't hear of waiting until tomorrow. He knew it was imperative to meet with the attorney as soon as possible. The matter of Clara's will had been eating away at him since the day he found out she had passed away. He didn't know she was living in a nursing home in Marquette, Michigan. He didn't even know she had left Ohio several months prior and moved in with Elbert. Nothing made sense to him. The only thing he was sure of was that he had to overturn her will and collect his inheritance; after all, *he* was her only surviving relative, and more importantly, he needed the money.

Neil said, "Then I'll walk. It can't be that far to the highway. I can make it before dark and hitch a ride the rest of the way."

Elbert finished with the spices and moved on to the silverware drawer. He pulled out slips of paper, pieces of yarn, rubber bands, and string. He said, "If you get there before you freeze to death."

"It's spring," Neil pointed out. "It can't get *that* cold here at night!"

Elbert sighed. When he found several outdated coupons, he tossed them aside with the other odds and ends. "You don't even know what cold is," he said.

"You don't know a thing about it. I'd just give it up if I were you," he added in reference to Clara's will. "She wanted Jon to have it all, so be happy with the property you got."

"It's nothing but weeds and swamp! I'm not letting her bilk me out of the money!" Neil zipped up his jacket and pulled the collar around his chin. "I'm going!"

Elbert stood up and went to his broom closet—not for a bottle this time, but for suitable winter clothing. He returned to Neil, carrying an oversized pair of galoshes and a heavy jacket. "You'll need these," he predicted. "Wear the boots and put on this jacket."

After Neil pulled on the boots and struggled with the jacket, he collected his folder from the kitchen table. Elbert watched him trudge down the driveway towards the road. He had a land-line phone and pressed in Dale's number. He told Dale, "Do me a favor and pick up a fella in a blue jacket with big boots. He just started walking down the road. He's wearing a tie; you can't miss him. He's Clara's nephew. He needs a ride to Marquette and I don't want his death on my conscience. Thanks. I owe you another dinner. What's that? Okay, prime rib it is."

* * *

Elbert's boots helped, but still, Neil struggled with each step. He was not used to physical challenges. The most exercise he got over the past few years was an occasional game of tennis, maybe walking to the post office and the bank. He wasn't used to the woods, or rural areas, of any dimension.

He ignored the sounds at the sides of the road: the cracking of twigs, the muffled crashing and thumping of movement—all somewhere to the left among the trees and weeds. But the long walk gave him the opportunity to think about the will. Clara, his father's only sibling, had left behind a little over a million dollars to some hick living out in the woods of Upper Michigan. *A rude, arrogant, limping hick at that,* thought Neil. Remembering her audacity, her blatant arrogance, he squeezed the folder of papers. *How could she betray him,* he wondered, *the son of her only brother?*

True, Neil was in serious debt and he had counted on her generosity to help him with his financial burden. But excluding him from her estate was beyond belief. Neil's attorney and Clara's, however, had explained to him that she was of sound mind at the time the will had been written, and also when it had been revised to include Jon Loucher as the executor, or new trustee, the only recipient of the bulk of her estate holdings. The will had been notarized and signed by Clara and her attorney in Marquette. The attorney explained that it was actually a living trust versus a straight forward will, which meant there would be no probate court involved. But about two months before she died, right before she went to the nursing home, she had revised the document and appointed Jon Loucher as the executor upon her death. This document, the attorney said, was quite specific, and also costly, to set up and maintain. But again, Clara was adamant as to the property Neil would receive, yet the entire value of her assets—certificate of deposits and bonds and two large savings accounts—were all combined and left to Jon. *And we're talking approximately a million and a half dollars here,* so said the attorney, *give or take.* All for Jon, her newly appointed power of attorney and executor, to manage. No one else was mentioned except Neil, who would receive the parcel of land she owned in Southern Ohio. The attorney told Neil point-blank not to get his hopes up about contesting the terms, but Neil was desperate. His aunt had been the only person he had ever known who could solve his financial problems. All of his other relatives—two other elderly aunts and three cousins on his mother's side—were financially treading water, and there was no one else he could turn to.

Clara, at least, had written to him many times, attempting to establish a bond of some sort. It was no secret that Neil's mother had been self-absorbed and young. And she knew that her brother, Neil's father, traveled a lot and didn't have time for his son. Neil's father basically turned Neil over to his mother's sister, who did her best to raise him, but lacked sufficient monetary means as well. So, when Neil learned of his Aunt Clara's illness and then her death, and that she hadn't bequeathed him any funds, he became hysterical. He felt as if the safety net for his future had been seized by a stranger—and he would *not* allow it.

There was also Neil's ex-wife. His divorce situation had been a nightmare to begin with and had dragged on for two years. His ex-wife, Erin, had been wrong for him, although he didn't realize the full extent until two months after the justice-of-the-peace marriage vows had been exchanged. Erin was now out to destroy him financially, and every other way imaginable. Thank God there were no children.

Neil decided to drive to the Upper Peninsula of Michigan to the backwoods town called Tennick where Clara had supposedly lived with a man named Elbert Loucher and see if he could contact her lawyer and the nursing home where she had died. Surely an eccentric, high-strung woman like Aunt Clara could easily be declared incompetent. Neil knew his rights, by God, and he would contest the will based on the fact that he was a blood relative, no matter who she had named the inheritor and executor in writing.

For now, Neil knew he had to concentrate on getting to Marquette. Marquette was where the legal reversal would happen. He had to find her attorney and speak with him in person, instead of over the phone. Then he had to find the nursing home; perhaps he could find a doctor and nurses who would testify to Clara's unsound mind at the time she revised her will.

But darkness had filtered through the boughs of the pines and balsams. He heard an owl hoot; he heard cars and trucks in the distance. He walked for twenty minutes longer, going onward and onward, it seemed through endless silt and rocks and branches scattered from the rain and recent winds, until the air bit the skin on his face. Until he wanted to fall to the ground.

When he finally found the highway, he couldn't believe there wasn't any traffic. No cars, not even a semi. The three cedars were next to one another in a row by the road-sign, near an area of apple trees, the apples still green.

This remote area, of course, was much different than what he was used to in Ohio. Except for the cedars and apple trees and some tall birch trees, there was nothing he could identify with in the dark. He was grateful there were street lamps here and there along the highway. And, he decided to stop at the first house he came to if he was fortunate enough to find civilization again.

So far, he hadn't noticed a farmhouse, a cabin, or even a public rest area. He had walked for nearly an hour, and now the night was falling fast. All he could do was walk along the highway, with one hand inside his pocket and the other clutching the folder of legal documents, pertinent to his quest.

Adding to the inconvenience and discomfort of the walk, his glasses fogged up from the moist air. His heart beat rapidly. His legs turned numb with the sheer effort of moving. He tried to stay calm, but he kept thinking he could walk for the rest of his life and never see another human being. Then, as if from nowhere, he saw headlights. He moved to the side of the highway, but stood close enough to the center line to be seen. He couldn't be picky about the driver. He knew it wasn't wise to flag down a stranger, especially in this neck of the woods, but he was cold and tired and not so choosy. He waited as a green and white pickup pulled over to the side of the road.

Dale kicked the door open. "Need a lift?" he asked, sounding cranky and friendly at the same time.

"Yes." Even so, Neil was suspicious. "I'm headed for Marquette."

Dale kept the motor running and slid his thumb along the steering wheel. "Climb on in. You really shouldn't be taking a stroll this time of night."

Neil hesitated to climb aboard, but again, he wasn't in the position to be picky, and another vehicle might not come along for hours. Or never. He looked at Dale's pock-marked face and put out a hand. "Neil Halverson," he said, expecting a hand shake.

But as soon as Neil climbed into the passenger's side, Dale shifted the battered truck into drive and swerved onto the highway. He muttered something to the truck as if he needed to coax it to move. He told Neil, "I know who you are. Elbert called me and asked me to pick you up. I work with his son, Jon. I've known 'em both for years."

"Then I guess I'm grateful," Neil said, but he wondered why Elbert hadn't called Dale for help in the first place. "I'll pay you for your trouble."

"No, just sit tight; this old heap's about to stall."

"She can stall after I get to Marquette," Neil said arrogantly. Although even to him, his words rang ungrateful. "Thanks for the ride," he added. "You work with Jon?"

"Yes, and I don't want to hear that some bastard's about to cause him trouble."

"I'm here on business. Like I said, I'll pay you for taking me to Marquette. I have to talk to my aunt's attorney as soon as possible." Neil considered the starlit sky and noticed another set of headlights coming towards them. Once they were almost to Skandia, he said, "Why don't you pull over here at this bar so I can give him a call?"

"I can do that." Dale pulled into the bar called Idle Time. It was one of the popular bars in Skandia, although Dale hadn't been inside it for years. "Make it quick," he said irritably. "And don't plan on socializing."

Neil stepped out of the truck seconds after Dale pulled into the parking lot. He went inside the warm, dark bar and asked the bartender if he could use his phone. He made the call, but was told by the secretary that the attorney, Richard Hanson, had stepped out for a while. She said he would back in the office around nine.

Neil walked out into the parking lot only to find Dale half asleep at the wheel. He nudged Dale's arm. "Okay," he said. "I'm ready to go."

Dale started up the truck and off they went, turning right, and back onto the highway towards Marquette. Even though it was dark out, Neil studied the scenic layout under the highway lights. He noticed that the closer they got to Marquette, hills appeared. The geographical layout turned from flat to somewhat hilly and mountainous. They passed a dairy farm and fields, and finally, there were houses.

After a period of silence, Neil said, "I wouldn't bother your friend about the money, but I owe the IRS about ten grand and my ex-wife fifteen. I'm not an upstart by nature. I'm just broke. I lost my job about a month ago." He stopped there. He didn't want to elaborate, especially since it was clear Dale wasn't interested in his reasons for coming to Michigan—never mind looking up Jon.

Finally, Neil said, "I could end up in prison over it all, and *that* I don't need."

"Maybe Jon will hire you," Dale offered. "We're short of help right now."

While pushing the frame of his glasses up the bridge of his nose, Neil looked at Dale. "Work for you?" he asked, intrigued by the idea. "Doing what?"

"Do you know how to run a saw or drive a skidder?"

"Not really, but I worked at a car dealership. I know enough about mechanics to learn how to operate logging equipment, I suppose."

Neil noticed that Dale kept glancing into the rearview mirror. He wasn't really listening to Neil, either; he was focused on the headlights behind them. "We got trouble," he said in a flat tone. "Someone's been following us for the last five miles."

Neil twisted around in his seat. He saw a truck behind them, but it turned onto a side road. "Someone you know?" he asked, feeling his heartbeat accelerate.

Dale didn't answer; he just drove onward, following the contours of the road. Neil started to think about working for a logging company and decided the idea was idiotic. What did he know about working in the woods? And operating heavy equipment? It was easier to try and overturn Clara's will. He knew not to tell this to Dale—a man he didn't know from Adam, and a friend of Jon's, no less, who could easily be a psychopath.

Dale pulled into a rest area and parked the truck next to an outhouse, leaving the motor running. He stepped out into the paved lot, which was lit up by lamps. He disappeared, leaving Neil to think, *What did he know about Elbert and Jon? What did he know about this man with the green and white* truck?

Dale went inside the outhouse, and five minutes later he reappeared and climbed back into the truck. “Must be something I ate,” he admitted. “I can’t seem to keep anything down lately.”

Dale had been sick to his stomach since the day George shot himself. He was having difficulty coming to terms with the guilt of not helping George years ago when George was a boy, back when he could have made a difference and helped George down a more productive path. Things might have been different if Dale had claimed his paternal rights through the court, despite Carolyn’s protests. Too late now. Dale was left with insomnia, overwhelming guilt, and digestive problems.

Neil became even more nervous as he watched Dale sit perfectly still with one freckled hand folded over the steering wheel. Dale reached into his shirt pocket, brought forth a package of antacids, and popped two tablets into his mouth. Nonetheless, Neil knew he had to encourage Dale to drive him all the way to Marquette. Surely Marquette had decent hotels. Then he’d resume his business in the morning and have a tow truck go out to Three Cedar Road for his car. He couldn’t function without transportation, and who knew what the old man might do with his car. Elbert might try to dismantle critical parts, siphon the rest of the gasoline. One could never tell about these backwoods folks.

Thinking of what all he had to do perked Neil up. “When we get to Marquette,” he said, “I’ll buy you dinner.”

Dale revved the engine. He was about to put the truck into drive when a pickup truck pulled onto the ramp and parked sideways to block the exit.

Neil shoved the folders regarding Clara's will under the seat. "Those people are back," he said to Dale.

Two men stepped out of the truck. They kept the headlights on while walking over to Dale's truck. One of the men opened the door by Neil; the other opened Dale's door. They were dressed in black clothes and their faces were hidden beneath ski masks.

"Move over," the taller one told Dale. He had a .44 and shoved the end of the barrel into Neil's ribs. Neil was so overcome with fear, he couldn't breathe. He moved over when he realized that the other man had a long knife to Dale's throat. Neil couldn't believe what he was seeing, and he concentrated on not vomiting, or worse, passing out.

The man pulled the knife away and slammed the door shut. The man with the pistol told Dale explicitly, "Follow him and no one gets hurt."

CHAPTER 22

The two men wearing the ski masks tied Dale's and Neil's hands behind their backs and moved them through the hollows of a thickly wooded area, fifteen miles west of Marquette. They were told not to speak. And not speaking was difficult for Neil, who was a chatty person to begin with. Dale, on the other hand, was able to control himself easier; it was his nature to be patient. He was nauseated with pain, however, and focused on walking instead of speculating on what these strangers wanted. During the scuffle of getting out of the truck on the road, Dale twisted his left ankle, and Neil thought it was broken by the way Dale grimaced with each step he took.

The poorly postured man with the pistol had warned them both: "Don't talk and don't even think about making a run for it."

If they attempted to run, Neil knew they wouldn't get far in the dark. From the beginning, he tried to memorize the man's voice, so that later on, he could match the voice with a face. Or maybe Dale knew the voice. Maybe he knew one of the men, or both. Nonetheless, it had been a mistake for the man to speak; voices were clues, and so was poor posture.

It didn't take long for Neil to notice that Dale favored his left ankle as they were pushed over fallen branches, up ridges, and through thorny bushes. Dale had deep cuts on his arms and neck, but he didn't complain, not even once. Neil wasn't so steady on his feet. He wasn't athletic, and he certainly wasn't used to hiking around in the woods. He favored pavement and concrete.

The woodland habitat in mid-April was difficult to navigate. The previous winter's snow was melting, leaving sections of ice and pools of water here and there. New plant life was sprouting; tiny green and yellow signs scattered along the forest floor. The winter wind had pushed over saplings and branches that were awkward to step over; the wind had pushed over large trees as well; nutrients for the ground, but a challenge for humans, particularly wounded and bound ones like Dale and Neil. And definitely not easy to do with only a sliver of moonlight and flashlights as guides.

Although Neil had his share of welts and cuts after an hour of being pushed through bumpy roots and sharp weeds, he didn't have broken bones to worry about. He realized at the onset that the kidnappers' plan was to wear them down. Thus, onward they moved for most of the night with no opportunity to escape. But the flashlights did help to light up the deer runways as they walked. The man without a flashlight aimed the pistol the entire time. He aimed at Neil's chest or Dale's head; it didn't matter. Neil decided that aiming at one of them was the same as aiming at both.

The men moved in circles to throw off direction: north, south, east, and west. By the time they stopped to rest, there was no way to determine how far they had walked or from which direction. The man with the pistol shoved Dale into a birch tree. Neil could hear the snap of Dale's bones, probably in his shoulder or arm.

Dale closed his eyes, and when Neil stepped forward to help him, the man with one of the flashlights pulled out a knife and stuck the tip into the bone behind Neil's ear. "*Don't* try it," he said.

"What in God's name do you want?" Neil asked feverishly. The tip of the blade burned through his skin, and a trickle of blood rolled down his neck.

The man pressed himself up against Neil's back and said, "Shut up, or I'll cut your fucking ear off."

When the man holding the pistol kicked Dale in the leg, Neil tried to lunge forward again. But this time, the man who had kept him at bay with the knife pushed him into the trunk of a maple tree. Then the same man grabbed a hold of Neil's thick copper-colored hair, dropping the flashlight so that the beam of light tilted upward from the ground. He slid the blade against Neil's throat. Neil gasped for breath, knowing not to move. With his hands tied behind his back and the blade at his throat, there was nothing he could do but wait. And for the first time in a long time, pray.

The other man with the pistol told Dale to drop to his knees. Dale lowered to the ground, his ankle now swollen twice its size. Neil could tell there was also something wrong with Dale's arm; the elbow was distended. When the man aimed the pistol directly to Dale's forehead, Neil closed his eyes, expecting the worst.

"You're in the wrong business," the man told Dale. "This is a message. We're going to shut you down."

Dale blinked. There was only the dim light of the flashlight to see by, and of course the sliver of moon, but the moonlight had also become a hindrance and cast distorted shadows all around them. The trees provided the illusion that they were standing inside a cave.

Neil was convinced the trees were speaking to him, speaking a cryptic language back and forth and all at once. Whatever the case, there was a conversation going on that Neil did not comprehend. A jumbled speech ricocheting off branches, echoing in and out of brambles and weeds.

Neil strained to hear what the trees were saying. Were the humans speaking *to* the trees, *of* them, or *about* them? Neil wanted to know. But seconds later, there was a startling interruption when the man shouted to Dale, "You have nothing to say?" Dale shook his head no. "Then you both will die out here. Understand me? Tell Jon Loucher *not* to buy Coulter Logging—if you make it out of here alive."

The man's voice was low in an attempt to disguise his identity. This made Neil think that Dale probably *did* know him, if only he could see his face. Neil searched for distinguishable characteristics too, a scar or a clumsy gesture. The only thing visible was the man's bowed posture. Neil would remember that if nothing else.

The man grabbed Dale single-handedly, still aiming the .44 to his head, but because Dale was large-boned, it took extra effort to pull Dale back to his feet.

Once upright, he escorted Dale to a ridge, and without another word, pushed him over it.

Neil's back was to this scene, but he heard the fall. He couldn't help but gasp. He was terrified that Dale might be injured beyond help now, maybe even dead. And the trees kept on talking, warning him, talking all at once, and suddenly the men seemed to talk back, but Neil couldn't understand the fragmented code. He heard bones crack again. He heard branches snap and nocturnal animals milling about, drumming along with the recital of trees.

It was his turn next. He figured this before it happened and still, he wasn't ready. The man with the gun grabbed him from the other man, pushed the end of the gun into his back, and said, "Move it!"

Neil moved it—quickly in fact—more quickly than he ever thought possible, but even with the man pushing him, he tripped on a wedge of granite and somehow got back to his feet and over to the ridge. The man gave him no time for counter-reasoning. When Neil fell however, he managed to untie the ropes around his wrists, which had loosened during the walk through the woods. He fell over the ridge, almost eagerly, because he knew it meant they might leave.

But just as soon as Neil landed, sprawled next to Dale in the damp weeds, the pistol was aimed at them again. There was a loud blast into an aspen tree, a foot away from Neil's head. His heart stopped, and he began to pant; seconds later he couldn't breathe at all.

Then he choked.

"Tell him!" the man said.

There was a crash of branches.

And they were gone.

Dale had landed on his side. His left arm and both of his legs were immersed in icy water. Neil was soaked to the bone as well, but he slid towards Dale on his stomach, across spiked ferns. His shirt had ripped and buttons were missing. His jacket was saturated with mud, and when he tried to move his legs to see if any bones were broken, he realized his trousers were stiff with sap. His head just missed another slab of granite. This territory was rocky in places, he noticed, hilly, and even mountainous.

He crawled over to Dale, but the pain along his ribcage made him sway in and out of consciousness. He thought about Dale lying next to him, suffering with a broken ankle, and now, more than likely, a broken arm. Then he thought about the men, particularly the one with the gun. He wondered if they were still out there, waiting for another chance to shoot at them, next time kill them. *They'll kill you,* said the trees.

Neil muttered, "Help," forcing himself to stay awake. He wanted to sleep and not think about what they needed to do next. He propped himself up to an elbow, and beneath the moonlight, he could see that Dale's ankle was definitely broken. The bone protruded, making his ankle as wide as his knee.

"Can you move?" Neil asked. He wanted to shake him. "Dale!"

"I don't know, maybe in a minute."

"We have to get out of here!"

"Come over and untie me," Dale said. It was clear that he too was having trouble staying awake. His breathing was labored. He was sweaty and smeared with dirt, but Neil had read enough about shock and exposure to know they couldn't go to sleep or they would die.

He untied Dale and examined his ankle. "How did *you* get untied?" Dale asked.

"I pulled on the ropes while we were walking around. Your ankle's broken," Neil diagnosed, with a shaky voice. "I hope you can walk."

"I got to. We need to get back to the highway. I think my arm's broken, too." He tried to lift it but there was no use. "I heard it crack when the fucker tossed me off the ridge. Landed wrong, I guess."

Neil tore a strip of material from his jacket and tied it around Dale's ankle for support. Then he tore off his tie to make a sling for the arm, which was busted beneath the elbow. Dale shifted to find a comfortable position on the ground.

"Do you have any idea who they are?" Neil asked. "Do you *know* them?"

"They're from some eco-terrorist group: a group going around threatening people in the timber industry. Never mind that now. Just help me stand up."

Neil looked aghast but helped Dale stand. Neil had to do most of the work, in an effort to support them both. "Do you know where we are?" he asked.

"West of Marquette somewhere is what I figure."

Neil steadied Dale on his feet by taking a hold of his good arm. He leaned Dale against a tree where they rested. They listened for indications of another invasion.

Neil shook his head, trying to make sense of what had happened to them.

An hour ago, they were driving down Highway 41 towards Marquette, now they were lost in the woods, disoriented.

He was overwhelmed with emotion. "I guess my aunt had a right to leave her money to whoever she wanted to have it!" he said, tears stinging his eyes. It was shame and it was fear; two feelings he wasn't accustomed to. "It was *her* money!"

"Forget that for now!" Dale snapped, unimpressed with Neil's sudden melancholia.

Their very lives depended on Dale's clear thinking and his keen sense of direction. The most important thing for now was that they were both alive. All they had to do was walk towards the highway—*if* they could find the right way *to* the highway.

But Neil was lost in his memory of the trip to Michigan, only two days previously, and how Aunt Clara made a small fortune through personal cunning and persistence and had multiplied her finances throughout the years. She played the stock market and had worked in banking and by the time she retired, she had been the president of a bank in Cleveland.

Meanwhile, Dale braced himself against a tree. It was imperative to keep Neil focused on the task of getting out of the woods to find help. Dale shoved Neil onward. "Quit your blubbering bullshit!" he shouted. "Just walk!"

They continued to struggle onward, and finally, they came to a clearing where Neil paused to look around. "It's almost morning. See the sunrise through the trees?"

Dale was panting and kept touching his chest. *Absent-mindedly,* thought Neil*, like an elderly, worn out man.* Dale nodded when he saw the sunrise emerge from the treetops, filtering out through the buds and leaves. "You'd better sit down," Neil said.

Neil put Dale's hand over his own shoulder and helped him walk over to a deformed cherry tree. "I don't like it," Neil said. "I think there's something wrong with you internally."

Dale took a deep breath and shoved himself away from the tree. "We'd better get going before I pass out!"

They walked for a bit longer, but then they came to another ridge—clearly an obstacle ten times more difficult, with periodic granite slabs thanks to the glacier and volcanic eruptions over three thousand years ago. There were sharp edges to clear, upward, and then back to the lowland.

Neil steadied Dale against a tree and predicted solemnly, "We'll never make that hill."

"We have to," Dale said. "We can't stay here all day."

But Neil was convinced that Dale was bleeding internally. "What about your ribs? Any punctured?"

"Let's go while we still can!"

Neil was amazed Dale could speak, much less move. They descended the hill and almost slipped, but the near-slip caused Neil to avoid panic rather than stop. "Glad Elbert gave me these boots," Neil said, his words caught in the dawn.

Dale nodded, apparently thinking hard as his facial muscles tightened. He said, "Thanks to those bastards, I'm messed up on direction. Listen for cars on the highway."

Neil noticed the ashen shade of Dale's face as he helped him sit down on the ground. Dale closed his eyes. "You'll have to go without me," he said. "Keep walking north." He indicated north with a jerk of his head. "Keep going 'till you find a town."

"That could take hours. I'm not leaving you out here alone!"

Neil hunched down next to Dale. He didn't want to leave, but knew Dale was right; it was the only way. Dale could have a stroke or a heart attack. He could collapse from internal bleeding.

"I don't feel right about leaving you," Neil said. "I don't think I can do it!"

"Do you feel right about dying?" Dale asked him, wheezing.

Neil hesitated before pushing to his feet. He was doing a lot of hesitating. Too much in fact. He'd never had this much trouble making decisions before. Out of habit, he attempted to adjust his glasses and realized they were gone. His glasses probably flipped off his face when the man pushed him down the ridge. Thankfully, he could see well enough to manage.

"I can't believe I lost my glasses and didn't realize it until now!" he told Dale, who sat with his eyes shut. "It might take me a while to get help."

"Keep walking until you bump into someone and hope that person is on our side." Dale said. He stretched his legs out against the cold ground, his back against a tree. He was shivering, and his ankle was numb. "Get going," he yelled. "And bring back coffee!"

Chapter 23

Jon slept until seven thirty the next morning. He had to sleep on the couch again because the bedrooms were not finished. They should be by now, but he hadn't counted on getting shot.

He woke up twice during the night, thinking about Mae. He would have to discuss the baby situation with her. He wanted her to move into his house so he could help her, keep an eye on her.

He made a mental note to hire a carpenter and an electrician. Get things rolling.

He got dressed and walked through the damp grass over to Elbert's house. Now that they were further into spring, the flurries had subsided. But even though the air had warmed up and flowers had bloomed, there was still slush mixed with the dirt, and the grass—just starting to grow and green up—made the ground slick in areas.

Jon took his time walking up to Elbert's front door, careful to step around Beau.

"Beauregard," he said. He liked the sound of it. Plus, the old hound looked like a Beauregard. Strangely distinguished.

He went into the kitchen, letting Beau in first. He became uneasy when he realized that Elbert wasn't at the stove or counter. "Elbert?" he asked the white walls.

No response. What if Neil Halverson had harmed him? After all, they didn't know this Neil character. He could have turned completely irrational, knocked Elbert out and robbed him—or worse. But then Jon noticed the coffee maker was on, which meant Elbert was in the vicinity.

Jon unplugged the coffee maker just as Elbert walked in from the living room. Elbert was dressed in his outside work clothes. He looked at Jon. "Neil left last night," he said. He studied Jon, knowing he wasn't getting enough sleep; or probably very little, if any at all.

Jon shuffled about. He had been caught off guard thinking something horrible had happened to Elbert. "I was worried about you," he confessed.

"You worry too much," Elbert said. "It's a waste of time."

Jon was confused. Hadn't Neil asked him for a ride to Marquette because his vehicle was sunk in the mud past Elbert's driveway? Two flat tires and no spare, proving his negligence. And, didn't Elbert tell him to watch his back?

"I thought he wanted a ride to Marquette," Jon said.

"He didn't want to wait. Dale picked him up."

Jon leaned against his cane. He wasn't in the mood to track down Neil Halverson. He had planned on finding Reese, talk to the attorney and settle Clara's will so he could buy the company. He was through waiting, and now he'd have to rearrange his plans to find Neil Halverson.

"Sit down and have some breakfast," Elbert said. He made his way towards the counter. "The Neil thing can wait."

"There's too much going on," Jon said, summarizing the current situation. "Mae's going to have a baby."

On that note, he walked out the door and back to his truck, leaving his boot prints in the slush and Elbert staring after him.

• • •

Jon drove north along Highway 41 to Marquette and back toward Tennick. There was no sign of Neil Halverson. He stopped at a bar called Idle Hour in Skandia to call Dale, but there was no answer. Although Dale had told Jon he would stay home for a few days and straighten things out in his mind about George's death, it was strange for him to be gone this early. Stranger yet was the fact that Elbert said he gave Neil a ride to Marquette.

Well then, he should be home by now.

Jon bought a cup of coffee to go and left the bar. He wanted to reach Savola—or Peterson rather—but he wasn't sure how to contact him. Perhaps Savola, the DNR undercover investigator, would be at the logging site, still posing as a skidder operator. Of course, he should be. Why change strategy when the Globe One people were in the area, their direct aim on Coulter Logging?

Jon drove out to the Eben site first. His instincts were correct. Reese was there, counting logs and writing numbers down on a clipboard. Peterson was checking over the other skidder. The skidder he had used previously was badly charred, so they had hauled in another to lure in whoever had burned the first one.

Now that Jon knew Peterson's identity, he measured the inaccuracies of his skidder-operating techniques. Jon hadn't paid much attention to Peterson before. He only knew there was something about Peterson that didn't add up. He looked the part all right, with the woodsman garb and the weather-worn face to match, but his physical dexterity was abnormally rigid.

Jon limped over to him. He left the cane behind in the truck and used tree trunks, and even the skidder, for support. He said to Peterson in an aggressive tone, "Dale Washburn's missing. So is a man who was visiting my dad. Any chance you might be able to help me find them?"

Peterson shook some wires, adjusted a lever. He seemed good at pretending to know about machinery and even better at listening between the lines. "How long has Dale been gone?" he asked, his voice low. "Give me a time frame," he added, now whispering.

"I haven't been able to reach him all morning," Jon said. "It's peculiar."

"Don't you think you're jumping the gun to suggest something's happened to him? Maybe he stepped away from things. Went on a trip or something. I would if my son went on a murder spree, then shot himself in front of me."

"Dale doesn't *step* away from things," Jon insisted, wishing he had brought the cane; standing upright wasn't as easy as it used to be. "And he would have called me before leaving town."

"You think I should look for him?"

"Yes, and Neil Halverson, too. He was at my dad's last night, but took off on foot towards Marquette. Dale was supposed to pick him up on 41."

"I'll make some calls." As Jon was about to turn and limp across the wet ground to speak with Reese, Peterson touched his arm to recapture his attention. He said from the side of his mouth, "Here's the short version of what's going to happen. Reese said you are buying the company. That makes you a part of the action. Go talk to Bill Casey and hire him back to drive the logging truck. We're using it as a decoy. Casey will drive, you ride shotgun. Drive around until Globe One tries to take the truck. See those two up on the ridge working the saws?" He indicated the ridge and the two men bent over whining chainsaws. "They're with me."

Jon decided it would be intriguing to assist in an undercover operation. Besides, if he became owner of the company, it would be wise to purge the area of fanatics. "I'll help out, but this problem with Dale and Neil needs to be dealt with first," he said. "I'll talk to Casey and you look for them."

Peterson scowled. "I'll go now," he promised.

• • •

Jon recalled that Bill Casey didn't work on Thursdays, and it was Thursday morning, ten o'clock. He drove fifteen miles west of Trenary to Bill's house. Bill's house was a two-bedroom structure painted white with black trim, situated on twenty acres of land, and crowded with bushes, brush, and scraggly jack pines.

Jon had known Bill for at least ten years. He calculated the exact time: the present year 1994 since January; Jon met Casey in 1984, almost ten years ago, which was as long as they both had worked for Lucas Coulter. Casey contracted out for other logging companies as well, but for Coulter he worked extra hours and made Coulter Logging a priority. Jon thought he heard something about Lucas and Bill going to high school together, but Casey was three years younger than Lucas. He was an excellent truck driver and, considering his ability and esteemed reputation, Jon wasn't surprised that Peterson wanted him to drive the decoy truck. However, Peterson had probably found out Jon and Casey knew each other, and figured Jon would be able to persuade Casey to help them.

Jon heard the garble of a television game show coming from somewhere inside Casey's house. He knocked until an insolent voice said, "Yeah, it's open!"

Jon walked inside and shut the door behind him. The living room felt like a sauna, the air brutally hot. Jon leaned against his cane and tugged at the collar of his jacket. He walked over to the chair where Casey's rotund body was encased. Casey wore boxer shorts and a sleeveless undershirt. He tampered with the remote control, turning the volume down when he saw that the untimely visitor was Jon Loucher.

Casey had a crusty blister on his lower lip. It had been there for years; apparently it wasn't a cold sore or a temporary lesion. Perhaps he just had a habit of biting his lip whenever agitated, as Jon noticed he was doing now.

"Hello, Bill," Jon said. He chose the arm of a threadbare sofa as a seat. "We need a driver. I'd do it, but I about had my leg shot off recently."

"I heard about the accident," Casey acknowledged. He lifted a glass from the folding tray beside him, poked at the ice with a straw, and took a sloppy sip. "I don't like the idea of them idiots pissing with my rig. Because of George Coulter, I know you're a target now."

"I'm buying Coulter Logging from Reese," Jon continued. "I know you and Lucas were friends, but I'd like for you to help us out. We're going to buy our own truck. George planned to when he had Reese fire you. But he had other things on his mind."

"Like murdering people. I heard!" Casey took another sip, set the glass down, and picked up his pipe to pack it with tobacco. "I'm busy right now. I'm working out of Bark River. Got a job starting later today."

"The DNR's working with us undercover," Jon said, wanting the situation to sound interesting enough to get Casey's attention. After all, Casey *was* the best driver in the business. "An investigator from Lansing's posing as a skidder operator. He's got men running saws and he wants you to drive the truck loaded with timber as a decoy to trap the criminals. They've been stopping trucks on the way to the mills and dumping timber where no one can find it."

"The fuckers do that to me," Casey said defiantly, "they'll wish they hadn't tried!"

"We need to catch them at it," Jon said. He watched Casey smoke the pipe. Casey sneered at the TV screen with a fierce glint in his eye. Jon said, "They burned one of our skidders. Things are getting to the point where the DNR agent will do anything for an arrest."

"Maybe they *do* need our help," Casey conceded. "I heard out at Bark River that the DNR's been on them fanatics for months now. Seems to me things ought to wrap up soon. Or could be they don't know what they're doing."

"They need us," Jon agreed.

"I'm feeling poorly these days," Casey said. But Jon noticed he sucked the pipe, and basically rolled his tongue along the stem. Casey added, "It's my heart. I want to keep my schedule light for a while."

Jon said, "Maybe you'd better not do it. How about loaning us your truck until we get one?"

Casey's furry black eyebrow pivoted into an angle. "No one drives that truck but me! You dumbass motherfucker!" he shouted, mesmerized by the audacity of such a suggestion. "Fuck no! Are you out of your mind?"

"We wouldn't want to jeopardize your health," Jon said, trying not to smile, although he truly was concerned about Casey's health.

"I take medication and see my doctor twice a month!" Casey shouted at the obscure figures on the television screen. "I'm careful with my health, goddammit, you fuckers!"

"We'll discuss it with Peterson sometime tomorrow."

"Discuss what, my fucking heart?"

"He might not want you in on the plan if he finds out about it."

Jon knew he had won Casey over when Casey jumped out of his chair, clicked off the television set, searched the cluttered room for his pants, and while doing so, vowed, "Then we just won't tell the motherfucker, will we?"

• • •

Although he shivered from the cold, Neil walked through the weeds for two more hours. Because he had lost his glasses, he could barely see daylight as the sunrays filtered through the trees. He didn't realize it was almost noon. He walked until his legs cramped and he had to sit down on a log to rest and listen for voices or vehicles.

But he heard nothing except the chirp of black capped chickadees and the chatter of squirrels. He studied the tower of trees: a variety of buds on the aspens and maples, but most of the branches blended into a brown and green maze.

There were conifers he could not name.

He stood up to walk again. His vision was blurred by functioning without glasses. He had worn glasses for sixteen years, and only after losing them, did he understand how much he had depended on them. There was a time he had nightmares about losing his glasses. In the dreams, he couldn't find his way—highly symbolic, he knew—but the scenes usually depicted a blurry trail through a city, a fortress of factories and buildings, and bridges. The trees, however, kept him to the ground, not by a physical means, but by the force of their spirits. *They are alive,* he kept thinking, a*live and speaking to me.*

He sat down on the cold ground. He could not identify all of the foliage: various grasses and weeds; green sprouts, everywhere; the scent of leeks, spots of yellow marsh marigolds and tiny, pointed yellow pedals of trout lilies; white buds of trilliums, the off-white of Dutchman's britches. Slash everywhere: fallen branches. The aftermath of winter winds.

As Neil considered scenarios of what could happen to him trapped in the woods, Rick Peterson looked down at him sitting on the ground near a splash of ferns. Peterson asked, "Neil Halverson?"

Neil focused on Peterson, who appeared Christ-like. Except for the ponytail, the jeans, and the faded green jacket. He looked golden, due to the sunlight behind him.

Neil nodded yes. He was about to faint, not to mention partially blind; yet, he sat, stoic. Peterson walked up to him and extended a hand to help him to his feet. He had three fingers on the left hand, Neil noticed.

"DNR," Peterson said. "I've been looking for you and a man named Dale Washburn. You know where he is?"

Neil put his boots flat against the ground and stood up to be eye level with Peterson. He thought he might be dead and face to face with the Son of God, not some son of a bitch with the Department of Natural Resources. Besides, the man didn't look like an official. He looked like most of the people Neil had encountered since arriving in Upper Michigan: mythical or deranged.

Neil said, "Yes, I do."

To Neil, Peterson was physically chaotic. The haphazard design of colors in Peterson's hair—orange, yellow and gray—was perplexing alone. He was thin and anemic looking, although he seemed medically sound. The evidence of good health was in his muscular shoulders and the robust pink of his complexion. He was endowed with wind-carved features. He smelled of soil and smoke. He slapped tiny black flies away while looking into Neil's eyes.

Neil asked for identification. Peterson mumbled something about mothers and bastards and pulled out his ID. He flipped it upright, only a few inches from Neil's face.

"I lost my glasses," Neil said. "But you don't look like a conservation officer to me."

"Undercover," said Peterson, explaining his purposes away. "Where's Washburn?

"I had to leave him a few miles back. He's got a busted arm and ankle. Are you really with the Department of Natural Resources?"

"That's right."

"How did you know where to find us?" Neil asked.

"Jon Loucher asked me to look for you. His father called Dale to pick you up when you left his house. But never mind that for now. What happened out here?"

"Two men kidnapped us from a roadside park. They had been following us down the highway. They brought us out here and threatened us. Shot at us. They muttered some gibberish about Jon not buying a logging company."

"I've been on their trail for a long time. I'll take you and Dale back to town. I can't let the trail get cold. I'm too close."

But the trail got cold anyway. By the time Neil led Peterson back to where he had left Dale sitting against a tree, Dale had passed out from shock.

Peterson knelt down to check Dale's pulse. "Dale Washburn? It's Rick Peterson. Don't try to talk. I'm going back to my truck to call for an ambulance."

Neil stayed with Dale, waiting for Peterson to return. At least a half hour went by until Peterson came back. He brought a thermos of water and gave it to Neil. Then Peterson and Neil attempted to lift Dale. "Be careful of the break," Peterson said. "We'll take him to the road."

They carried Dale for half of a mile through the woods and lowered him to the ground near the road to wait for the ambulance. Neil kept thinking Dale was going to die, and he realized that the idea of Dale dying was more upsetting to him than his own father's death. How could he be so moved by a person he had met only hours before?

Peterson said he had blown his cover by telling Neil the truth, and that he, Neil, would have to keep the information to himself. He explained about the eco-terrorists and Jon helping to arrest them by using a decoy logging truck. In return, Neil told Peterson everything he knew. "One of the men had a .44. They shot at us after throwing us over a ridge. You should check for bullet fragments. The one with the gun had bad posture. The other one didn't talk, but he wore a watch on his left wrist. I saw it when the flashlight shined on his hand."

"That's something to go on," said Peterson. "How do you know Jon?"

"I came here to contest my aunt's will, but now I might ask him for a job."

"I see," said Peterson, although he didn't.

Neil liked the idea of Jon's company posing as bait to get the fanatics. When the paramedics arrived, lifted Dale onto the stretcher, and carried him up a hill to the road, Neil stayed by Dale's side.

As soon as the ambulance drove away, Jon's black pickup truck came to an abrupt stop behind Peterson's Blazer. Jon stepped out of his truck. He wanted answers pronto, and limped up to Peterson, asking, "Dale?"

"He's got some broken bones, but he'll live. Did it work out with Casey?"

"Casey's in," Jon said.

Peterson told Jon about Neil needing a job, but Jon frowned and turned to go back to his truck. "He saved Dale's life," Peterson yelled, a hand bent to his chapped lips. He shrugged at Neil. "Well, whatever. I need you to drive Dale's truck back to Tennick. Here are the keys; his truck is parked up the road."

Neil took the keys from Peterson, but Jon's reaction sent a chill up his spine. He watched Jon climb into his truck and sit there, fumbling with his cane. Finally, Jon pushed the cane to the floor. Neil watched him a minute or two longer before turning to see Peterson disappear into the trees behind him.

Neil ran up to Jon's truck. He slapped both hands against the door. "I was just shot at and left for dead in the woods. And you fucking ignore me?"

"What in the hell do you want from me, Halverson?" Jon asked, his voice shattering the air. He flipped down the sun visor. "What is it, goddammit?"

"I want about twenty-five thousand dollars to pay off my debts to the IRS and my ex-wife, for starters. I'll drop the whole contesting-the-will thing if you'll advance me enough money to get the law off my back. Hire me to work for you!"

Jon started up his truck. "Jesus Christ," he said. "That's *not* going to happen."

He disappeared in a cloud of exhaust smoke.

Neil remembered the Conservation Officer had asked him to drive Dale's truck back to Tennick, and he'd do it as soon as he recovered from Jon's stinging insult. He clenched his hands into fists and turned to the direction where Jon had made his exit.

"You limping backwoods hick!" Neil said, his face flushed with anger. "I'll show *you* a thing or two!"

He listened to his voice bounce off the trees and come back to die at Elbert's boots. There was a rustling of leaves in the distance, and it wasn't Peterson. The noise came from the other direction. Neil started off slowly, then began to sprint, all the way to Dale's truck. He climbed in and locked the door. He waited for the small black and white creature to cross the road. Only then did he drive away, towards Tennick, pushing seventy-five miles per hour.

The last thing he needed was to get sprayed by a skunk.

• • •

During April and May, while Dale recuperated, Jon visited their business contacts. He started with two sawmills, one near Kiva and the other in Gladstone. Then he went to see landowners who had previously contracted with Lucas to get their timber harvested. Jon had always known, of course, that Lucas Coulter bought stumpage to clear-cut mostly, which was fine for thinning out certain species of trees, but obviously, Lucas was in the game for the cash, not to help the landowner manage their timber. Lucas would also sneak truckloads out and not bother showing the owner all the receipts from the mills. He would pay below the going rate, and unless the landowner had done his or her homework and compared Lucas's price with the current rate mills were paying, they were cheated.

When Jon owned Coulter Logging, he would work with the landowner to come up with a viable plan to harvest their timber.

He had talked Bill Casey into driving the decoy truck. He wanted to ride shotgun but decided to wait until his leg was stronger. He wanted to take over soon, because he was concerned about Casey's heart.

Reese volunteered to ride along with Casey; in fact, he insisted, although when Peterson found out about the arrangement, he almost cancelled the plan. "I can't allow civilians to confront dangerous fanatics!" he claimed at the beginning. "I can't and I won't!"

But he did. Jon talked him into it and suggested that Peterson and at least two of his men follow the truck or hide in observation posts along the route. After all, the route was mostly used by logging trucks hauling timber to the two largest mills in the area. Jon had already enlisted Reese's help with driving fuel trucks, bulldozing trails, and making sure the equipment was looked after.

It was Tom Foster's job to see to the mechanical end of the business, but Jon noticed that Tom would disappear throughout the day, and so, he didn't trust him. He told Reese to keep an eye on Tom Foster—and on Bryan Kinnenun.

Reese worked as a piece cutter and was also put in charge of buying two extra trailers for hauling the skidders and bulldozers to the sites and installing new fire extinguishers on all the machines. Jon added more insurance for his workers. The cost was staggering, but he knew that insurance was top priority. They also had to figure maintenance and equipment repairs, operating costs, gasoline and diesel fuel, parts, spending on the truck drivers, costs for buying stumpage, vehicle licenses, and payroll. Then there was the safety gear. Jon updated everything. He made sure the workers had foot and ankle protection, modern hard hats with face and ear guards, and Kevlar safety chaps.

After considering all the paperwork involved, Jon asked Mae's sister, Paula, to help with the books. He had an addition built on his property: a pole barn, 60-by-30 feet, and set it up as an office. The building was the temporary headquarters for the business.

He hired a carpenter to finish the house, even though he could do most of the interior work himself. He hired the carpenter to build a large garage for equipment and another building for the smaller trucks too. He hired an electrician to wire the house. And, he hired a plumber, knowing he had to step up the progress. His primary motivation was that Mae *might* move in with him.

Mae was a problem. He didn't know how to deal with her, particularly now that Paula let it slip about the pregnancy. But, he knew he wanted Mae to move in with him, and for that to happen, he had to finish the house, make sure everything was in order, modernized, hooked up, and completed before even thinking about asking her.

Yet, he barely saw her.

She was still working at the Tennick Credit Union and putting in hours at the insurance company in Marquette. Pregnancy didn't seem to slow her down.

Meanwhile, as he put in twelve to thirteen hours a day with his new company and supervised the finishing touches on his house, Neil Halverson became a horrific pest. He was always within Jon's sight, standing near a bush or leaning against a tree. Jon knew Neil loitered on purpose, wearing his new lumberjack garb; or perhaps what *he* perceived to be lumberjack garb, consisting of a blue and white striped cotton shirt, boots, a down vest, and corduroy pants—a fashion flaw to collect every burr in the county.

To top it off, he'd wear some absurd baseball cap with an even more absurd saying, such as *Kiss Off* or *Dare to Dream*, and his pathetic, broken glasses. Apparently, he didn't have a second pair. He made a big deal out of going back with Peterson to the site of the shooting when Peterson searched for shell casings.

And miraculously, Neil found his broken glasses.

There they were now, slanted upon Neil's white, shiny face, with a piece of masking tape securing one of the stems in place.

Bryan Kinnenun was demonstrating the general maneuvers of Dale's skidder to Neil. Bryan let Neil climb up into the cage, instructed him as to which levers controlled the boom and clam, which one caused the machine to move backward and forward. "You're going to break your neck!" Jon shouted, standing nearby. He attempted to hoist himself up onto one of the huge tires while grasping the door handle.

But he didn't get far. His leg, always his injured leg, stopped most things he tried to do. He jumped back to the ground and winced. His ankle hit the surface too fast and made the nerve endings burn. "Go ahead and ram the damned thing into a tree," he said, dragging his leg, as well as his pride, back to the road. "I hope you kill yourself!"

After Jon left, Bryan taught Neil how to operate the bulldozer.

• • •

The weeks passed, and they were into the second to last week of June. Mae was overdue having the baby. Although Jon regularly asked Paula about Mae's status, all Paula said was the doctor kept assuring Mae that everything was fine.

Jon worried about her, and also the fact that the eco-fanatics hadn't attacked the logging truck. He expressed his concerns to Rick Peterson. "I don't get why they haven't ambushed our truck yet. It's been out day and night."

Peterson glared at him. "I thought I told you no night runs! Now we're going to have to change strategy! I'm sending Evans in for the job. You already met Evans—he's posing as a sheriff."

Jon finished his coffee and crumpled the paper cup in his hand. He recalled that Evans was evasive and too clean to fit the role of detective. Peterson added, "Evans drives the truck starting Friday. That's how it will be."

"I'm going with him," Jon said. "And *that's* how it will be!"

"It's too dangerous! Your job is to watch that Foster fucker!"

"I'm going with Evans," Jon repeated, stuffing the paper cup into his pocket.

True to his word, Peterson had Ron Evans pay Jon a visit the next day at the logging site. Evans acted as if the trip out to see Jon was an inconvenience. He announced, "Peterson sent me."

Jon was sitting on a rock, thinking about ways to improve the company. He lifted a hand to his eyes to shield them from the sun's rays. Then his hand went to the breast pocket of his short-sleeved shirt, brought forth a pair of sunglasses, and he put them on.

Evans stood before Jon in what appeared to be office attire. He was clearly more of a paper-pushing detective than a fieldwork investigator. He was Jon's height, six-foot-one, but unlike Jon, he seemed more concerned with his appearance than collecting pertinent information, especially on days like this when the summer wind threatened to mess up his hair.

"A little windy," Evans noted, trying to see Jon's eyes behind the dark lenses. He elected to scribble on a clipboard, to look official. "I wouldn't want to cut trees down in a wind like this."

"You're not," Jon pointed out.

Evans slapped at an insect that had landed on the back of his neck. "There was another skidder set on fire near Escanaba," he reported. "We have a lead on the two that kidnapped Neil and Dale. Stay close to your crew and don't talk to anyone but Peterson and me."

"You got a yellow jacket near your shoe," Jon whispered back, trying to imitate the secretive tone of Evans's voice. They watched the yellow jacket float away on the wind.

Evans's eyes slid from side to side. "I sure hope there aren't any more of those mothers around. I'm allergic to them! And I already picked four wood ticks off my leg!"

"I'm allergic to people who waste my time," Jon said, his voice bristling. "Peterson told me what he wants to do next."

"Good. Then you know I'm taking over the truck."

"Casey and Reese have it out today," Jon said, which was true; he had talked to them earlier that morning. Casey reported that someone followed them the day before, but he wasn't sure if it had been the fanatics or a group of protestors.

"I'm taking over Friday," Evans said. "You tell Casey and Reese to ease out."

"That's a mistake. You need someone familiar to drive the truck. If they realize someone's driving that isn't in my crew, they'll know it's a set up."

"Who do you suggest? Yourself?" Jon nodded confirmation. "No way," Evans murmured, picking a burr off of his pant leg. "Peterson won't allow it. Neither will I. Besides, I already have an officer lined up to go with me."

Jon heard a swarm of bees somewhere to the right in the brush. He knew that the plan would go up in smoke as soon as the fanatics realized that Casey or one of his crew wasn't aboard. He said, "It's my timber. I'm riding with you."

"You're supposed to cooperate," Evans said, sounding as angry as Jon proved to be. "That was the deal when we lowered the charges against Reese."

"Reese paid the fines and for the clean up of the barrels," Jon reminded him. "He'll be on probation for three years. If you ask me, he's turned out to be a big help."

"A big help indeed. You bought the company from him and then hired him to work for you. I'd almost want to call that hypocritical, especially with all your talk of environmental ethics, Loucher. You can forgive a man who helped dump highly carcinogenic poisonous waste into your beloved woods? You bought him out so he could pay his fines, and you give him a nice paycheck every week besides?"

"You finished?" Jon asked, leaning into the cane.

"No. Mae Lakarri has been providing us with information all along. She seems to know Peterson quite well. I heard they knew each other years ago downstate."

"You'd better mind your own business," Jon recommended. "Maybe concentrate on that yellow jacket's nest near your foot."

Evans stopped thumping the clipboard against his leg and watched the bees fan out into the wind. "Tell that officer you won't need him Friday," Jon said. "I'm riding with you. You should stay put for a while. You've stirred up a nest."

Forty-five minutes later, when Jon was having coffee with Dale, he wondered if Evans was still standing like a statue where he had left him in the woods. If so, he had no business driving logging trucks. He had no business in the woods, period.

CHAPTER 24

Friday seemed a long way off, considering it was only Tuesday and Jon and Bill Casey were about to meet up with the protestors. They were driving down the usual route about a mile from the Bissmer Mill. Spring break up was long over and the weight restrictions had been lifted, but they were cautious around the corners, because the surface was spongy in spots and June was ending with a lot of rain.

In the distance, Jon saw a lineup of people with signs and knew that they were to come face to face with the protestors he had heard about over the radio from his colleagues. It wasn't Globe One; it was a smaller group that misunderstood the basic methods of harvesting timber. Apparently, they had nothing better to do on this sunny afternoon than block Bill Casey's truck as it headed for the mill.

Casey said, "Oh, look what we got here!" and shifted his stout body in the seat behind the steering wheel. He rolled down his window. "Look at this, hey? We got ourselves some punks with cardboard signs."

Jon peered out the windshield for a better view. "Try to drive on through."

"And kill a few in the process?" Casey scrunched up his nose. "I don't want to get my tires all bloody!"

The Bissmer Paper Mill was another bid Jon won since taking over the company. They had taken the route back and forth for several days, hoping to snag Globe One, but not wanting to attract the protestors. Apparently, they were getting the protestors instead. Peterson's men hadn't been following the truck for the last couple of days. He had them watching the logging crew, surrounding the paper mills, and patrolling the area north of Marquette.

Casey stopped the truck and leaned out the window for a better look. He waited for one member of the group, a bushy-haired man of about thirty, to walk up to the rig. He said, "You folks are blocking the way."

"We're protesting the fact that you're cutting down every tree in sight for profit," the man informed them in a high-pitched voice. His knuckles were red, braced tightly around the handle of a sign. "Some people don't agree with cutting down large stands of trees. Some people want to protect our natural resources. It's our opinion, based on scientific research, that loggers like you are destroying delicate ecosystems. We want logging restricted more than it presently is, and we thought this might be a good time to bring it to your attention."

"Well, this isn't a good time," Casey informed him. He shifted again and the motion itself expanded his bulging frame. He searched the dashboard for some chewing tobacco and proceeded to stuff his cheek with a wad of it. He chewed and spoke: "Not a good time at all. I got a load here to get through to the mill. So, move aside."

"I don't think so," the bushy-haired man said. Every time he moved, the sunrays caught the watch on his left wrist and caused a sparkle. "We want you to consider the options." He pulled some pamphlets from his back pocket. "Perhaps you'd like to read up on how the ecosystems work? Study how one level affects the other, and so forth."

"Perhaps you'd like them papers shoved up your ass," Casey suggested. "And so forth!" he shouted boisterously. He snatched the papers, tossed them sideways, and watched them flutter in the breeze.

"Now listen up," Casey advised audaciously. "Maybe you'll learn something. Paper, like them pamphlets, is made from trees. See the logs in the back of this truck? They go to the paper mill where me and my friend are taking them now. But I had to slow my truck down and take time to educate you people. I'm going to say it one more time: get the *fuck* out of my way!"

The man was sunburned on his face and exposed arms. He shook his head and grit his teeth. "You just made a big mistake," he told Casey. "I don't like it when people treat my information on the ecosystem with disrespect." He glanced over at the side of the road where the white papers had scattered like shot doves.

Casey reached for the door handle and kicked the door open with one boot out into the air. "Get out of the way, you scrawny punk! *Who's* making the mistake? I'll wrap that sign around your fucking neck!"

Jon grabbed Casey's arm. "Hold on!" he said.

Casey's face turned red and perspiration gathered at his curly hairline. His stomach rippled with each breath he took, but he controlled himself enough to say, "I hate idiots who don't know what they're talking about. Yuppie-type fucking rich brats who don't got nothing better to do! What we ought to do is climb on out of here and tie them up to the trees. Or tie them up onto the logs in back and cart the whole bunch of them to the mill!"

Jon was considering the most effective way to appease Casey. "The Globe One people are around here too," he said, trying to stay composed. "This get-together was planned to distract us."

Casey settled back behind the wheel and pulled the door shut. Thus, the bushy-haired man went back to his group. There were about twenty of them. They all looked clean-cut and dissatisfied. They also looked healthy, well fed, and lacking for nothing in this life.

"Goddamned punks!" Casey insisted, talking and chewing tobacco both. "They don't want trees cut? What do they think their fancy houses is made of? Or their goddamned pamphlets? What would they wipe their prissy asses with without trees cut! The idiots don't know what they're talkin' about!"

Jon said, "They're breaking up; heading back to the cars behind the trees."

Casey shifted the gears of the logging truck and inched the rig forward. The group had filtered over to the right side of the road and disappeared into the tree line. Some of them had already climbed into their cars.

"See," Jon said. "They broke up. I'll bet the Globe One bunch is somewhere close by. Note the expensive watch on the guy with the big hair. That watch looked to be solid gold. His dad's probably the president of Bissmer."

As they continued along the bumpy road, Casey drove with expert precision. He chewed tobacco, chomping a syrupy wad around inside his mouth. He glanced out the rearview mirror now and then, and they didn't get too far before a truck barreled down the road behind them. "Look at this!" he said. "Some idiot's trying to mess with us. I'll show him who knows every inch of this road!"

"Settle down," Jon said. "Let him pass."

"He isn't wanting to pass. Look at that! He's about two feet away from the back of the pup. He slows down and then speeds up, the little motherfucker. When he gets that close again, I'm hittin' the brakes. We'll smash up his front bumper some!"

"Don't do it," Jon advised. He sat forward in the seat, the excitement proving to be more than he had bargained for. "It's probably one of the protestors. Just drive along normal. He'll get tired of it and pass."

"He'll get tired all right! I'll hit the brakes if he does that again. Look at the fucker! Now there's two trucks. Look at this, two pickup trucks riding my ass! I won't allow it!" His complexion turned a disturbing hue of violet. He grabbed the steering wheel so tightly, the veins in his arms popped out. "The fuckers!" he said again. "I'll show 'em! I could drive this route with my eyes shut!"

"Oh boy," Jon muttered.

"That looks like Kinneun's truck, goddammit!"

At the mention of Bryan Kinnenun, Jon looked in the side mirror. "It can't be, unless he's clowning around."

"He'll be a clown all right. When I'm through with him, he'll *look* like a fucking clown! Hey now, check this out, both trucks think they're going to split up and each take a side of me. They think they're gonna pass on my sides! Hold on now! I'm gonna veer to the right up here near this field and slow 'em down a bit."

"Call for help on the radio," Jon suggested. "Call for help, Casey!'

Casey picked up the microphone to his CB radio and clicked the button. But the line was dead. "Well, shit!" he said. "Someone's fucked with my radio! You warned me them idiots was nearby! I know that's Kinnenun back there. I heard all about what Lucas done to his dad years back; they had some argument about cutting too close to a wet land. Bryan's dad threatened to turn Lucas in, so Lucas fired him right in front of the crew. He went crazy after that. He flung hisself off a cliff by Lake Superior. I'll bet Bryan's mixed up with them loony fanatics!"

"I doubt it," Jon said. "He's worked for Lucas a long time. He even came to Lucas's wake. I don't think he'd want revenge for what Lucas did to his father."

"Could be I'm wrong," Casey conceded. "Watch this move now. We're coming to the field, so hold on!"

But when he came to the turn before the field, Casey misjudged the angle of the curve and missed it entirely. Due to the truck moving at a high rate of speed, his chest cramped and a current of pain shot through his back and down his arm. When he removed his hand from the wheel to push against his chest, his shoulder buckled. His arms convulsed, until he slumped forward.

Jon grabbed the wheel. He moved almost into Casey's lap, but at least he was able to keep the truck from crashing into a wall of balsams. He hit the brake with his boot, using all of his strength to press down, and he used the hand brake as well. Finally, the truck skidded into the field and rolled forward, hissing and bellowing as it came to a stop inside a crater-like hole. The hole wasn't big enough to make them topple over, but it was big enough to slow them down.

The truck came to a stop. Jon turned the key in the ignition, leaned his head back, and closed his eyes. After catching his breath, he moved off of Casey. He checked Casey's pulse. He loosened the buttons on Casey's shirt and unbuckled his belt. "I'll get help," he said when he realized Casey couldn't speak. "Don't try to move."

Jon stepped out of the cab of the rig. He searched the trees for indications that the drivers of the trucks might still be around. But the only sound was the creaking of truck parts, and so, he started walking down the road.

He walked all the way to the Bissmer Mill, explained what had happened, and called for an ambulance. A man from the mill drove him back to Casey, who was still unconscious. Jon waited a half hour for an ambulance to come and take Casey away. After Casey was gone, he waited for a wrecker to pull Casey's truck out of the ragged hole.

He climbed into the driver's seat of the logging truck and drove the logs to the mill. Next, he headed for Tennick. Although it was almost dark, he had to find Dale as soon as possible. He wanted to tell Dale who Bill Casey claimed to have seen in the truck that ran them off the road.

• • •

Jon poked at the ground with his cane as he walked around. He couldn't get Casey off his mind. And his leg was so stiff and sore he was considering going to the doctor to tell him that he had lied, his leg wasn't better at all; it felt worst, from his knee up to his thigh. Thinking of his physical regression on this breezy June night, he shifted away from his fears and focused on surveying the logging site.

Seconds later, he realized a skidder was still moving in the distance, picking up logs. He walked over to the loading deck. He heard the clang of the boom and the clamp of the clam, and under the floodlights, he could see the dark outline of a person. *It has to be Bryan Kinnenun.*

But as he walked further, he realized that the operator was Neil Halverson. Neil was actually working the skidder. Up and down he worked the boom, picked up a log and moved it into the bed of the skidder. There he stacked it, carefully, on top of the others.

Jon leaned against a tree to watch, thinking, *What an odd character. But persistent. I do give him that.*

It had been weeks now and no more talk from Neil about contesting Clara's will. Neil meant it when he said he would drop the matter, but obviously, he wasn't going back to Ohio. Jon knew it was time to deal with him directly. So far, they hadn't been able to speak civilly to one another, and yes, Neil *could* work the skidder, but Dale was the one who drove the machinery, and he'd be back to work soon.

Jon walked to the area where Neil was operating the boom from side to side. Jon ducked as Neil swung the clam a little too far to the left. He ducked again when the clam came around for a second time. "Hey," he shouted. "Shut it down. I want to talk to you!"

Neil cupped a gloved hand to his hard hat to suggest he couldn't hear over the racket. In fact, apparently, he had studied the appropriate wardrobe of the other crew members and bought the right type of hard hat, complete with ear guards. Jon shook his head. "Shut it off!" he shouted again.

When Neil turned off the ignition, the machine shuddered to a halt. "I told you I could learn how to drive one of these things," he said triumphantly.

Jon watched Neil adjust his glasses, the pair with the masking tape on the stem. As he studied Neil, he put an elbow against one of the dirty tires, thinking that Neil certainly knew how to make use of damaged possessions, even one as important as eye gear. "You're still wearing those broken glasses," he noted.

"I can't find my other pair," Neil said. "I must have left them in Ohio."

"And I suppose you don't have money to buy new ones."

"I don't have two cents," Neil admitted, sounding euphoric. "But I did manage to buy some clothes with what was left on one of my credit cards."

"Maybe I could lend you a few thousand."

Neil rested an elbow against the wheel and sighed dramatically. "Oh, I plan to work for it. I've always worked."

Jon knew Neil had been living with Dale in Dale's trailer, but he didn't say anything. He had been too caught up in his problems with Mae to worry about where Neil lived. As long as he wasn't sponging off of Elbert, Jon didn't care.

"You already owe me two months' pay," Neil persisted, his expression firm. "I've been training with Bryan Kinnenun, and technically, I've been helping the DNR investigator. I know all about the eco-terrorists. Well, obviously, since I was attacked by two of them, I have as much interest in catching them as you do. I've also been taking notes. Do you know Bryan leaves every day at two o'clock?"

Jon rubbed the back of his neck. He wasn't wearing a hat, and he swatted at a cloud of black flies that were in abundance during late spring and early summer. He decided to ask, "Where are you living?"

"In my car."

He almost sounded proud.

Jon stared into the hazy evening; it could be true, but no. He knew for a fact that Neil was living with Dale. "Come to think of it, your car isn't stuck past Elbert's driveway anymore."

"I pried it out weeks ago. I could only afford the towing costs. Having no money means I eat berries and squirrels. Although yesterday I bought a candy bar."

Jon pulled his wallet out of his back pocket. Normally he didn't carry a lot of cash with him, but he had four twenties and a ten. "Can't have you eating squirrels," he said. "Here's part of your pay for the last two days." He noticed Neil hesitated to take the money. "We'll see how it works out," he added, sensing Neil's dislike of charity. "And if you want, you can live in my cabin behind Elbert's. It's not much, but it's better than sleeping in a car." *Or in Dale's cramped trailer,* he thought.

Neil shoved the bills into his shirt pocket. Jon was about to get into the specifics of Neil's finances and ask him which part of Ohio he was from, but they heard Reese's truck rumble down the road and stopped.

From the driver's side window, Reese said, "Casey isn't doing well. It *was* a heart attack, Jon. Like you thought."

Jon remembered all too well the conversation he and Casey recently had about Casey's heart condition. "But he's alive?"

"It's touch and go," Reese said. He elected to stay at the hospital with Casey. And he had other news for Jon as well. "Casey swears he saw Bryan Kinnenun driving the truck."

Jon was too busy keeping the truck from crashing to notice who was driving the truck behind them. He turned to Neil. "Didn't you say Bryan left early that day?"

"Yes, he leaves every day at two o'clock," Neil confirmed, watching Reese, who was breathing heavily and looking like he too might have a heart attack. "Right after some guy came here to talk to him," Neil continued. "He parked up at the corner. I was on break and followed Bryan. The other guy was slouched down in the car. He had strange, puffed-out hair."

"Big curly hair?" Reese asked. He put his hands out near his head to explain just how big he meant. Neil nodded yes. "I seen him today," Reese told Jon. "He's one of the protestors that stopped me and Casey on the road to the mill last week."

Jon recalled the group of protestors he and Casey ran into the day of the wreck, but he couldn't describe them individually. "I think it's time we have a talk with Bryan," he said. He was already hobbling towards his truck.

Neil adjusted his glasses and jumped from the skidder. "Wait up," he said, keeping in step with Jon. "I'm coming too, and *I'm* driving!"

Jon was too upset and in too much pain to argue. He said, "If Casey dies, someone answers for it. And it looks like that'll be Bryan Kinnenun."

• • •

Neil was confused. He couldn't believe that Bryan Kinnenun was involved. Bryan taught Neil how to use the equipment and, besides, he didn't seem like the hostile type. He seemed friendly and helpful, although maybe a bit too quiet.

But Jon told Neil that Bryan was probably one of the two who kidnapped him and Dale. "Just keep going down this road until I tell you where to turn," Jon said as they drove through Tennick.

"The guy with the big hair," Neil said. "Do you have any idea who he is?"

"No. It seems I don't know anyone anymore." Even with the present drama in full swing, Jon couldn't help but brood over Mae. The thought of Globe One, and Neil driving his truck—somewhat erratically, he noticed—couldn't distract him. The realization that Bryan Kinnenun was probably a traitor didn't even come close to making him forget about Mae.

What has it all been for, Jon wondered. *Why bother moving forward by building my own company, and finish my house, if I'll always be alone?*

Neil took a sharp turn seconds before Jon told him to. "If Casey dies," Jon said, "*I'm* to blame. I knew about his heart condition and talked him into driving anyway."

Neil drove Jon's truck haphazardly but at least they were headed towards Tennick and not away from it. "After I talk to Bryan, maybe we'll go look for Peterson," Jon said. "I'm tired of people not showing up where they're supposed to be. Turn left here at the light."

Neil turned left at the light, but Bryan's truck wasn't parked in front of the cabin he rented; in fact, his truck wasn't anywhere near the cabin or in the parking lot of the grocery store beside it. "Try the bar," Jon said. "Turn around here at the stop sign and go down Main Street. Hold it!" Neil stopped the truck, causing people on the street to turn and stare, including Mae, who had just left the grocery store. Jon opened the door and stepped out. He hobbled straight over to Mae.

She turned to look at him. "What's wrong?" she asked him. "Are you dying?"

"Probably," Jon said, not caring who overheard him. "Why are you out this late at night?" he asked. "Why aren't you resting or something?"

"Resting or something? It looks to me like *you* should be the one resting. Why are you having so much trouble walking? Have you seen your doctor lately?"

"You're the one who needs a doctor," Jon pointed out, nodding towards her stomach. "Why haven't you had this baby yet?"

Mae blew a curl of hair from her eyes. "Too many questions!" she said, annoyed. "I haven't had the baby because it's not time for the baby to be born!"

She glanced over at Neil sitting in the driver's side of Jon's truck. "Are you in so much pain you can't drive?" she asked. "You need Neil to drive you around?"

"I want you to move in with me *now,*" he said. "Tonight."

"I don't think so!" She smirked at his urgency, then changed the subject. "What are you two up to?"

Obviously, Jon wasn't going to tell her about the plan. She walked on, but Jon held her back by putting the tip of his cane in front of her. He said, "I heard you've been working with Rick Peterson. And you've known him for years. Why didn't you tell me?"

"Because I knew you wouldn't like it if you found out I was helping him. Anyway, I already told you I was watching George. But I'm not helping anymore. Or haven't you heard? He's dead!"

"I have all the interior work done in the house. You can have your own room."

"It's more comfortable for me at Paula's. I have everything I need there. But I tell you what, I'll come by tomorrow night. Meantime, I wish you'd go back to your doctor. You can hardly stand up." She could hardly stand up herself. She was losing her balance, trying to hold the grocery bag and find a comfortable position against a lamppost. "I'll try to come over tomorrow night. If I don't get these groceries back to Paula, she'll come looking for me."

Jon watched Mae walk away and climb into her jeep. She pushed the bag over on the seat, put the key into the ignition, and started up the vehicle. He watched her adjust the mirror, check the street, and she was about to pull out when Jon tapped on the window.

"*What* is it?" she asked, after rolling down the window.

"Take my spare set of keys," he said. "To the house, and if I'm not there, just go in and look around. I think you'll like it so far."

Mae took the keys. "All right. I'll try to come by tomorrow night, but I'm not making any promises."

She rolled the window back up and steered into the street. She turned left, towards her sister's farm. Jon couldn't stop thinking about how pretty she was and how shiny her hair looked. He was so preoccupied with watching her drive off into the night and thinking about her hair and lips that he didn't see Tom Foster standing five yards away in the shadows of the doorway of the bar. Neil beeped the horn, bringing Jon out of his trance. Jon was encouraged by what Mae had said, but his hopes for the future—the pictures in his mind of the two of them and their baby living in the new house—made him blind to the fact that Tom Foster had walked right past him.

Because Neil had parked Jon's truck at an angle while waiting for Jon to talk to Mae, he didn't see Tom Foster, either.

Neil motioned for Jon to hurry back to the truck; he even kicked the door open. "Let's go," he shouted.

Jon climbed into the truck. He was relieved that Mae might consider moving in with him, but worried about her going into labor.

Jon knew he had to focus on finding Bryan Kinnenun. If Kinnenun came up with the right answers, he could be eliminated from their list of suspects. "Go to the end of this street," he told Neil. "Turn right. We'll try the White Pine."

Neil took a hairpin turn onto the highway, towards White Pine Tavern. Not only was Bryan's truck there, thirty other pickup trucks were there as well, and Jon counted at least fifteen cars, all parked along the highway.

After Neil parked, Jon grabbed his cane and climbed out of the truck. Neil ran after Jon, who amazingly, was already through the door. Jon detested the loud music blasting from a corner jukebox; he wished he was wearing ear protection, the kind he wore while cutting down trees. Only when Jon pushed his way through the crowd did Neil head towards the bar to search the other direction.

Jon listened for Bryan's voice, but the voices all blended together. No words were decipherable. Jon wanted to go outside for fresh air. He couldn't remember the last time he felt this claustrophobic.

He racked his memory for information on Bryan Kinnenun's father. How long had Bryan's dad worked for Lucas? Was he still working for Lucas by the time Jon was hired? Jon was in his twenties when he first met Lucas Coulter; was Bryan's dad working for the

Coulters at the time? Bryan Kinnenun's dad was a troublemaker, that much Jon *did* remember. He was always stirring up a conflict. Jon recalled a discussion over contaminating wetlands, and it wasn't the only issue Lucas had cheated on, not by a long shot.

With this in mind, Jon moved faster; in fact, he made it all the way to the door. He would do what Neil had suggested in the first place: wait outside. He bumped into several people as he walked through the smoky room, and he was almost to the door when he saw Bryan.

Neil saw Bryan at the same time, and they all three ended up outside the bar.

Bryan stopped in his tracks. He was wearing the same outfit Neil had seen him in earlier at work, everything in shades of brown: from his hat—a light tan—to his brown and white shirt and tight pants. His hair was brown too, and so were his eyes.

Bryan said, "Jon, haven't seen you out on the town in a long time." He put a finger to his lips to show that he was thinking things over. "But you've been busy taking over Lucas Coulter's business."

"I didn't take it over," Jon corrected. "I bought it."

Jon thought about the bear claw Bryan had given him, probably as a distraction. Jon had stashed it somewhere in his cabin. God only knows where.

When Bryan slid a boot sideways as if he intended to leave, Jon pressed his cane against Bryan's chest. He said, "Bill Casey's had a heart attack. Someone ran his truck off the road the other day."

"Is that right?" Bryan inquired. "I wouldn't know anything about it."

"He knows," Neil shouted, stepping under the lamplight. "Casey saw him!"

"Casey didn't see me because I wasn't there," Bryan told Jon, not Neil. He had a curved backbone, clearly.

Jon knew to be careful. He didn't have proper evidence to confirm Bryan was a criminal; and furthermore, he had always liked him. Of everyone in the crew, at least Bryan was prompt and quiet.

And he never made trouble ... until now.

Bryan leaned against the wall. "Believe me, Jon," he said. "I had nothing to do with it. Casey was a friend of my father's."

When Neil lunged forward, Jon put out a hand to stop him. He told Bryan in a steady voice, "Casey saw *you.*"

Bryan opened his eyes. "It wasn't me, Jon. I swear on my mother's grave."

Jon nodded to Neil, signaling he was finished talking, for now. He turned to leave and didn't see Bryan's smile. But Neil Halverson did.

Chapter 25

Tom Foster walked up to Melanie's station wagon and leaned against the door. He was out of breath. He is on the verge of a mental breakdown, she decided. *He just isn't strong enough to see this through.* Besides, he was a filthy mess. His blond hair hung from his skull and his bangs were matted, somewhat crossed over his forehead. He acted as if he had awakened from a bad dream.

Melanie waited for him to catch his breath. Her elbow rested against the open window. She was angry that she had to wait twenty minutes for him to show up. He told her to park away from the street lamp so no one would see her.

"Where have you been?" she asked in a hoarse whisper. She had just finished smoking a cigarette. She was wearing a sweater and jeans and hadn't brushed her hair for two days. Her nerves were ragged, and her hands trembled. She persisted. "Answer me!"

"Guess who I just s-s-saw?" he asked, stuttering in his anxiety.

"I don't have time for guessing games," she said. "Spit it out!"

"Jon Loucher was just here, looking for Bryan. The logging truck was run off the road today. Casey, the driver, had a heart attack. I *know* it was Bryan and some hotshot with the Globe One folks that done it to Casey."

"Go on. What happened?"

"C-casey's in the hospital. I just now s-seen Jon and his sidekick, Halverson, talking to Kinnenun, asking him about running Casey off the road. Kinnenun denied it, course. I think Jon believed him, because he and Halverson turned and walked off, like things was settled."

"Big deal, he's a good liar. You wanted to meet me for this? I had to drop my kids off at my cousin's again, and by the way, she's starting to ask a lot of questions. So, I'll say it one more time. I want to leave *now*." She proceeded to cry. "I can't … stand thinking … about Lloyd! I have to … get out of this town!"

Tom touched the back of her head. "Let's not talk here," he said. "My truck's parked on the next street. I'll get a room at that place outside Rumley."

"You mean the Carriage something?" she asked, wiping her eyes with a tissue.

"Sure. You meet me there. We can't talk out here in the street."

Actually, the motel was called The Lantern, Melanie noticed as she sat in her car in the parking lot and stared at the blinking sign. She waited ten minutes, although Tom was already there. His truck was parked at the side of the building. *Here I go again,* she thought, *about to screw another loser.* She had considered suicide for the first two weeks after Lloyd's death, but realized she couldn't leave her sons with the legacy of suicide. She also realized that someone had to manage Lloyd's money. He had two bank accounts, invested in property, and had acquired ample stock. There was also the six-hundred-thousand-dollar insurance policy.

As always, the thought of Lloyd's money motivated her; now all she had to do was get herself together and reel Tom Foster in for the final act. Tom assumed tonight would be a night of sex, she realized, and it *would* be if necessary to get him to set fire to Jon's house, or maybe Reese Coulter's house. She wasn't going to leave town without an act of vengeance.

She noticed there was only one other vehicle in the parking lot, a truck with mud flaps and extra lights. She didn't see anyone in the vehicle and assumed it was unoccupied.

She stepped out of the station wagon when Tom opened the door to room number eight. Unlike Lloyd, Tom stank, and was covered with scabs. He stood in the doorway with that idiotic grin, revealing shards of teeth streaked with tobacco. His hands were scratched up as well; such was the life of a mechanic, he explained to her. Always smelling of grease and oil.

A haunting image of Lloyd in pieces—bloody, veins and intestines ripped apart, along with the hum of the chainsaw—made her dizzy. She heard Lloyd call for help. Heard him beg and scream. She could see George standing over him with the chainsaw *murdering the father of my children.*

And because of her children—and Lloyd's money—she couldn't end her life. She took the glass of vodka

Tom held out for her and sipped. "I stopped by the store for a bottle," Tom said.

She sat down on the corner of the bed. *I'll have to get him to do what I want—again. It's always the same with these men.*

"Tom, I can't quit thinking about Lloyd," she said. And it was true.

Tom took a big gulp. "Oh, now darlin'," he said. "Let's not think about all that depressing shit, hey?"

"I want to leave tomorrow!" Melanie said for the fifth time this week.

Tom leaned against the table that held the television set. "Guess what?" He watched her on the bed. Her jeans were tight, and her hair flowed around her shoulders. He touched her hip. "I seen Jon Loucher talking to Mae," he said solemnly. "She's pregnant."

Melanie recalled the two times she told Lloyd she was pregnant. He was happy back then. *I can't, I can't.* She took a deep breath. She knew Lloyd was somewhere in the room. She could feel him listening, and watching.

But Tom went on: "She's gonna have the kid any time now. And well, everyone knows it's Jon's. First, we thought it was George's, but no, it's Jon's."

"Keep going," Melanie said, watching Lloyd in the shadows.

"They was talking about Mae moving in with him. He wants her at his house. You know, the one he's been building on Three Cedar Road?"

"Don't you get it?" Tom prodded, childlike, excited. "*L-listen* to what I'm saying!"

"Yes, I know. Because they're in love," she said. "I used to be in love!" Lloyd was hiding from her; that much she knew. He hid behind the green and yellow striped drapes, watching her and paying close attention to how she reacted to Tom.

Tom emptied his glass to pour more into it. "I know you was in love with George Coulter," he said. "Not Lloyd and not me. But that d-d-damned Coulter!"

Melanie realized Tom had taken a wrong turn, and she needed to steer him back to the subject of Jon and Mae. She had to get his mind off the fact that she didn't love him and never would. "Back to Jon Loucher. So, you overheard him talking to Mae. Does he know who's working for the Globe people yet?"

Tom looked at the television stand where movement caught his attention; but then, just as quickly, he looked back at Melanie. "Dale Washburn and Halverson were kidnapped and threatened by two of them people. We don't know who done it yet. Jon thinks it was Kinnenun."

"And was it?" She suspected Tom knew more than he was saying. He fidgeted, making her believe he was holding out on her. "Kinnenun?"

Tom said, "To tell you the truth, I don't know. I seen a detective everywhere I go lately. Lucas thought he was a skidder operator. I hope he didn't follow me here."

"Will he tell your wife?" Melanie said, flirtatiously. She leaned sideways to put the empty glass on the nightstand. She beckoned him over to the bed while unzipping her blue jeans and kicking out of them. "Come here," she said.

Tom studied her long legs. He couldn't take his eyes off her hands, now pulling the sweater over her head, making the strands of her hair snap with static. Melanie helped him off with his shirt; she worked on his pants next, which were sweaty and difficult to peel off his legs. "You know," she began, "if Mae moved into his house, wouldn't it be terrible if someone torched it and God forbid, she was inside at the time?"

Tom was breathing hard as she worked her hand up the inside of his leg. "I knew you'd say that. But I couldn't hurt a woman about to have a baby."

"Oh, she won't die; maybe just faint. Aren't you going to leave to be with me?" She rubbed gently and watched his eyelids flutter.

She stopped rubbing him when he closed his eyes. Obviously, he didn't want to listen to her anymore. "I want you to burn down his house," she said.

Tom pushed her hand back, but she wouldn't comply. "He's not the one who murdered Lloyd," Tom stressed.

"I told you before. Because of him, George went over the edge. I don't want any of those people profiting from papermills. It's that simple!"

"George was crazy to begin with," Tom whispered as she massaged him. He couldn't hear her anymore; his lust was far too strong.

"Jon Loucher pushed him over the edge! So did Mae. And so did that moron Reese Coulter. Reese knew George was walking the line and he did nothing to stop it!"

Tom put a finger to his lips. "Shh now, honey! Now, *now*!"

"I can't stop thinking about George murdering him and cutting him up with a chainsaw. My children have to live with that, you know!"

"Oh now, now," Tom muttered again, as if *now* was the only word he had left to calm her. "I'll help you anyway I can."

Melanie didn't slide her naked body beneath the sheets. She knew Tom had to see her naked because she was well endowed. She had been told so over and over, by Lloyd and George Coulter, and other men, too. Tom couldn't take his eyes off her. "You listen to me," she said, taking his hand and placing it on one of her breasts. "You'll do it. You'll burn down his house Friday before we leave."

She watched him closely. "We'll leave for a couple of days and come back for my boys. I already have it worked out with my cousin to take them for the weekend. I told her I might be moving. I was thinking maybe Wisconsin. You'll have to tell your wife."

"She hates me anyway," Tom said of his wife. "It won't matter to her."

"Yes, just give her enough child support and she'll be fine about it." Tom looked upset when she said child support, but Melanie stroked him again. "Don't worry about the money. You won't believe how rich Lloyd was."

Tom said, "You'll have to get rid of the old man. He'll be a problem."

"What old man?"

"Jon's dad, Elbert. He lives next door. If I find the right time to torch Jon's house, you'll have to come up with a plan to get him out of the way. And another thing: I heard Mae tell Jon she'd drop by his place. We'll do it when she's there by herself; maybe while Jon's out doing the logging truck thing. They're trying to snag the Globe One bunch with a decoy truck. They're doing it Friday night."

"You get it done," she said. "I'll take care of the old man."

Melanie took his hand and pressed it between her legs. She slid downward, licking his skin as she went; knowing she had him exactly where she wanted him.

When he fell asleep five minutes later, it took all of her energy to get dressed and sneak out the door to the parking lot. She got into her car and started it up. She was too exhausted, and disgusted by her memories of Tom Foster naked in bed to see the truck that had been parked near the motel when she arrived. She didn't see Rick Peterson smoking and watching; and five minutes after she left, he left too.

CHAPTER 26

Jon knew that because of the ankle and knee injuries Dale sustained during the kidnapping, he was still having trouble walking. Dale had taken a leave of absence, and then one day, he called Jon and said he was ready to come back to work.

Jon was in his new office, sitting at his desk with his feet propped up. He wondered where Paula put his magazines. *And where are my files?* She was a meticulous person. Maybe he should check her alphabetized file cabinet—he might find what he wanted there—but what about paper clips to twist while thinking?

He thought about how Bryan Kinnenun claimed innocence the other night at the bar. Too bad Bryan slipped up and mention he could "swear on this mother's grave." Jon checked around. Bryan had two sisters, both with good jobs; one sister in real estate, the other a nurse. The rest of the family had moved on—except for his mother. She wasn't dead; she was eighty-nine and living in Munising. Jon abhorred this lie, particularly since he didn't know where his own mother was buried.

Again, he decided he would ask Elbert: Where's my mother's grave? Is she buried in Michigan, or was her body taken back to the Chicago where she was born, and if so, exactly where in Chicago?

Furthermore, Jon couldn't help but think about Neil Halverson's motivations. First, Neil comes to town to contest Clara's will, then he's kidnapped due to unavoidable circumstances; he helps Dale out of the woods, which leads to his participation in helping catch the criminals; thus, along the way, Neil changes his mind about the will. Now Jon employs Neil and ends up giving him ten thousand dollars towards paying off his debts, and in return, Neil proclaims a newfound loyalty to Jon.

Fortunately, as it turned out, Neil knew a lot about mechanics, and since Tom Foster was asking too many questions, Neil was elected to take Tom's place if it came time to fire him. Even so, Jon wanted Tom to over-hear certain information, if only to study his reactions.

On this particular morning, Neil was late. Jon told him to sleep in because he knew that the next two days would be rough. Thinking of rough, Jon heard someone coming. A person with a sluggish gait. He knew it had to be Dale with his walking stick. Even this long after the broken ankle, Dale still needed assistance when walking. Unlike Jon's aluminum cane, which had a rubber base on the tip for traction purposes, Dale's walking stick was made of hickory. It was bent and without a tip, therefore, it made a loud thumping noise.

As Dale entered the polebarn office, a temporary structure for their business, he looked the same, except for the stick. Jon noticed that for some reason he wore a better quality shirt. His graying hair had grown out, and splayed downward over the collar of his green shirt. He was wearing baggy Levi's and suspenders, and Jon noticed there was a slipper on the injured foot and a boot on the other.

Dale hobbled over to the chair directly in front of Jon's desk and sat down. "Fancy looking desk," he observed, moving a hand over its smooth surface.

"Paula's been working on the books and sometimes Mae helps her," Jon said in reply. "I can't have them working out of a drafty, unfinished house."

Dale seemed to perk up at the mention of Mae. "I should stroll on over and see what Elbert's cooking up today. Maybe he baked a pie."

Hoping to find a cigar, Jon opened a desk drawer but only found pencils. He told Dale as Dale envisioned Elbert's pies, "I'm waiting for Peterson. I called him on the radio and told him to meet me here. We've got to make final plans for tomorrow night. Reese and I will drive the decoy truck and he'll have to live with it."

Dale pressed an eyelid with an index finger. "I heard about Casey. I can't believe he's dead."

"Dead?" Jon shouted before slipping into a reflective daze. "Dead," he said again, in wonder.

"Yes. His brother called me this morning. He said Casey died during the night. He also said Casey knew he was on borrowed time, so don't blame yourself!"

Jon stood up and walked over to the window. "I don't have time for blame," he said, "but I *did* know about his heart." He slammed the palm of his hand against the wall, making the file cabinet rattle. "We're getting the sons of bitches tomorrow night—with or without Peterson!"

Dale had taken to plucking his lower lip when Jon started to pace. He said, "It seems to me that Peterson and his so-called army should have wrapped things up long ago. Neil and me were threatened. Casey's dead. What's next?"

Jon put a hand against the windowsill and looked outside at the trees, the deep-blue sky. "Everything points to someone in our crew," he said. "We're going to find out who's working with Globe One tomorrow night."

Jon watched Peterson's Blazer careen through the lane among the maples and cedars, all the way to the yard behind the house. Jon limped over to the door and held it open before Peterson made it half way across the parking area. But Peterson didn't get past Jon before Neil did. Neil came from around the corner, carrying a thermos of coffee, a container of sugar, and a bottle of cream. "Elbert sent these," he said with a superior air. "He'll have cinnamon rolls in a half hour."

Neil put the coffee and condiments down on Jon's desk and proceeded to blend in with the woodwork. Jon motioned for Peterson to hurry. Once inside the office, Peterson's body filled up three-fourths of the doorway. He was tall and burly. He was also dressed in layers.

"You cold, Peterson?" Dale asked as he accepted a cup of coffee from Neil. "You're all buttoned up. Expecting a blizzard?"

"No, but I'm protected with a bullet-proof vest. Are you?" Peterson asked. "You think you *really* know what you're doing?"

When he glared at Jon, Jon fired back, "I'm riding with Reese in the truck. We'll put Evans in the back with the logs— to suit you."

Peterson tugged at the bill of his black cap. He was too warm already from the heat of the day and the vest didn't help. "That might work, hiding Evans in the back, but I'm not comfortable with you and Reese involved."

"Well, dammit!" Jon yelled, making Neil flinch and almost spill his coffee. "We've been involved from the start. Have you forgotten the kidnapping?" Jon pointed to Dale's leg. "He's been laid off." Next, he pointed to Neil, who was dressed smartly, as usual. "And he's been traumatized for life!"

"I've already made some arrests," Peterson said. "Globe One is statewide. The people around here are just messengers."

"Messengers with guns," Neil added. He offered a cup of coffee to Peterson, but Peterson declined.

"We've arrested three people near Marquette," Peterson said. "So, your man's either Bryan Kinnenun or Tom Foster. But, the big shot's from Oregon. He used to work for a well-known paper mill and turned environmentalist when he realized illegal procedures were being conducted excessively. He became an extreme fanatic and formed groups across the United States."

"The guy with the big hair, I'll bet," Neil said.

"He's just part of it," said Peterson, and continued, "I do agree we need to wrap this up. But some things can't be rushed. Last night, I followed Melanie to a motel where she met Tom Foster."

Apparently, he expected some indication of surprise. But Jon sat quietly, waiting for more. Peterson said, "They have something going. I know she collected six hundred-thousand dollars in life insurance money on Lloyd. I know she leaves her sons with a cousin named Ellen Conroy who lives in Chatham. She cashed in bonds, withdrew her savings accounts. It looks like she's about to leave town. And I say with Foster."

"Foster's married with kids," Jon said. "I doubt he'd up and leave."

"Do you know Melanie McMasters?" Peterson asked without resisting sarcasm.

"No, but she can't be *that* persuasive."

"She was persuasive enough with George Coulter and Foster too while married to Lloyd. At Lloyd's funeral, I don't remember tears. You'd think it might shake a woman up if her husband was found in bits and pieces, floating in a fuel tank."

"Lots of married folks don't like each other," Dale pointed out. He appeared to savor the coffee and stared thoughtfully at the rising steam.

"True," Peterson admitted, "but Lloyd's death was uncommonly gruesome. And believe me, I *know* gruesome. The thing is, a man like Lloyd must have been pressured to risk everything. He had to have known he'd get caught. It seems a little odd that he just happened to latch onto Brent Christopher, knowing Christopher was corrupt. Let's say he knew far more than he should and did his homework besides. Melanie, on the other hand, is a gold digger. She's managed to use a few men to do her dirty work. It must be the reason she's with Foster now. He's not exactly Mr. Romantic."

"And Reese Coulter," Peterson added to the list. "In her confused mind, maybe she blames Reese for what happened to Lloyd." Peterson looked as if he thrived on psychological travesties. His eyes were bright and his lips tight.

Jon said, "Stick to who's a threat against us and who's not. I don't give a shit who's sleeping with who."

Jon remembered what Ron Evans said about Peterson knowing Mae; primarily that they had met down state years before. When Peterson left, Jon decided he would walk out with him and find out how *well* he knew Mae.

For now, Jon wanted to get the plan down for tomorrow night. He said, "So someone watches Foster. But I think Bryan Kinnenun's with Globe One."

"Not sure yet," Peterson confided. "Kinnenun has motive because of what Lucas did to his dad. I think Melanie McMaster's responsible for orchestrating the whole deal. I'm trying to link her with Big Hair, as you call him." That part, he directed towards Neil. "His name is Steve Whitman, by the way."

Jon said, "I say Kinnenun's the one. You say Tom and Melanie McMasters. But I still don't see why she'd want to go after Reese. All the more reason for Reese to drive the truck. I ride with him. We put Evans in the back. We'll dig out a place among the logs and you can have some of your men follow us."

"Are you through?" Peterson asked in a sarcastic tone. "I like it. We'll do it. But there's one problem. If you want Reese to ride with you tomorrow night, you'd better go over to his house and talk to him. Tomorrow night at dusk, we stick Evans in among the logs. We meet at the Eben site. One of you go over to Ellen Conroy's house; it's a gray house outside Chatham. Ask her if she knows where Tom Foster is and find out her reaction to Melanie. Who's up for the job?"

Neil stepped forward. "I'll do it."

As if Peterson controlled the entire nationwide DNR, along with the FBI and any other group of authority, he touched the brim of his cap, turned, and walked towards the metal door.

They had their orders: they were to meet the next night at dusk.

Jon followed Peterson out the door. He had to know what Peterson's relationship was—or had been—with Mae. "I've been meaning to ask you something," Jon said, but stopped there. How could he be apprehensive about Rick Peterson, or any other man in her life? She never mentioned commitment.

Peterson saved Jon the trouble by saying, "Mae and I are friends."

And because of the way he said it, and by looking Jon directly in the eye, Jon believed him. Jon watched him leave and then turned to follow Dale over to Elbert's house.

CHAPTER 27

Neil had to ask around town to find out where Ellen lived. As it turned out, she lived in a two-story gray house next to the laundromat, a reminder to Neil that he needed to do some laundry. He had been staying with Dale and moved behind Elbert's into Jon's cabin as soon as Jon offered it to him, but the cabin was rather primitive with the absence of plumbing and electricity.

Neil wanted to find a house of his own, but for now, he had to focus on this woman, Ellen, Melanie McMaster's cousin. Ellen didn't know Neil and obviously Neil didn't know her—or even Melanie for that matter—but he had to bring up the subject of Tom Foster to Ellen and find out if the name rang a bell.

Neil noticed the swing set in the back yard and heard children laughing and playing. He knew that the children—two young boys—were Melanie's. The scene was familiar: a mother leaving her children with a relative or stranger. Neil's mother did the same thing, far too many times. She had only been twenty years old when Neil was born, and she had other interests besides rallying the patience necessary to take care of a baby. So, like Dale Washburn, Neil was practically raised by his grandmother. Neil's was attentive and soft-spoken, however, compared to Dale's gruff, mannish, cigar-smoking grandmother.

Neil walked into the backyard. He was surprised to discover how young Melanie's children were, probably two and three. They played in the sandbox and wore suitable outfits and hats to protect their eyes and skin from the hot sun.

Neil leaned against the gate. He decided to pose as one of Melanie's boyfriends. "You know Melanie McMasters?" he asked, unable to come up with a better opening.

"She's my cousin," the woman, presumably Ellen, said.

"She applied for a job at my store," Neil said, making things up just to get the woman to keep talking. "Where is she?"

Ellen stood up from the corner seat of the sandbox and brushed off her square hips. She wore stretch pants and a sheer white blouse. Her hair was black and fuzzy with silver threaded throughout. She had to be in her mid to late forties, and in Neil's opinion, she didn't seem too bright. Her eyes, a glazed blue, shifted, as if she knew more than she was willing to say. She wore heavy eyeliner and mascara and a reddish tone of blush; everything about her was false and brassy.

"I didn't know Melanie had a job," she said, her feet crammed into cheap tan sandals. "She said she wants to relocate."

"Oh, that's great!" Neil said, feigning inconvenience over Melanie's absence. "She told me she'd start working this morning, and now you tell me she plans to move? I'd like to know where. And I'd like to know why!"

But the act didn't pan out. He tried to catch her off guard, assuming she would be easy game, but apparently, she wasn't as stupid as she looked. "I couldn't tell you," she said in an icy voice. She indicated the children playing in the sandbox with a nod. "She don't seem to care about her kids anymore."

Neil asked the big question. "Is she leaving with that man who was with her when she applied? The mechanic?"

"Yes, Tom Foster," Ellen said, filling in the blanks willingly. Her eyeliner, Neil noticed, started to blur as it melted in the heat. "I hear his wife's suing him for divorce. Everyone knows he's involved with Melanie."

"You think they'll leave town together?"

"Maybe they already did," she said, irritably. "And if Melanie don't come after these babies in five days, I'm calling social services. I can't keep them forever!"

While Neil tried to find out what Ellen Conroy knew about Melanie's future plans, Jon had problems with Reese. Reese wouldn't wake up, even after Jon pounded on the front door. Jon went to the back of the house and climbed in through an unlocked window. Reese had moved into George's house right after George was buried. He was too lazy to clean it out and put it on the market for sale.

Jon had forgotten about Mae going to see *his* house. All he could think about was getting Reese sobered up before tomorrow night. He knew Reese was crucial to the plan.

The kitchen table was covered with sticky dishes, and the floor was littered with paper bags, boxes of trash, suitcases, and stacks of knickknacks and kitchenware. There were piles of clothes on the counter; shoes of all sizes, boots as well. The stench of rotted meat and soured sweat and beer was almost unbearable. *Reminiscence of Lucas's* was Jon's first thought.

Jon pushed a box of chicken bones across the floor with the toe of his boot and followed the steady beat of music to the living room, where he found Reese curled up on the floor next to the couch. "Wake up," he yelled, poking Reese with his cane. "We're taking the truck out tomorrow to get the bastards who killed Casey."

Reese turned on the floor until his nose pressed against the couch; it was clear he couldn't open his eyes. "Get up," Jon said. "We've got work to do!"

Jon hated to roust Reese from his delirium, but they were running out of time. Jon wasn't about to coddle him. Reese opened his puffy eyes. He pushed his swollen face with bloated fists and nodded, struggling to speak. Jon leaned on the cane and waited while Reese propped himself up against the couch. "What do you want, Loucher?" he cried through clenched teeth. "What!"

"We're going to drive the decoy truck along the route tomorrow night," Jon informed him. "You and me in the front and Evans in the back."

"I can't," Reese said, spraying spit. "I can't do it!"

"You'll do it," Jon said, "even if I have to drag you out there and tie you behind the wheel. *You* have to drive."

Reese's beard had grown in thick and his hair was gritty. "You don't understand," he pleaded. "Casey's dead. My dad's dead. Even George is dead as hell! I don't care anymore. I don't care about decoy trucks!"

Jon walked towards the kitchen. "I'll make coffee."

"No! Get out of my house, you goddamned pain in the ass!" Reese shouted, although his words landed flat on the floor with the rest of the debris. He muttered a series of vulgar replies. Jon went to the kitchen and banged cupboard doors open and shut, searching for the coffee and filters. Eventually, Reese pushed himself up off the floor and began the arduous climb up the stairs to the shower.

• • •

Mae stood on the front porch of Jon's house, looking through her bag for the key to the front door. The fact that she couldn't find the key added to her misgivings about driving out to Three Cedar Road to see Jon's new house. First of all, Jon's truck wasn't parked in the driveway, or even over at Elbert's place. Second, it was dark, and she didn't have a flashlight. Jon hadn't thought to turn the porch lights on for her, and he hadn't installed one of those dusk to dawn lamps, either.

She couldn't believe he had forgotten they were to meet. *Had he not pestered me for days about moving in with him?* she wondered. *Was I dreaming that he gave me a key?*

She found the key and opened the door, picked up her suitcase, and went into the kitchen. She hit the light switch and was pleased to see that the electricity had been hooked up—just as he had promised her. The plumbing, too, was in working order.

She studied the room. He had bought a long wooden—she guessed oak—kitchen table with six matching chairs. The counters were flawless, and so were the cupboards, which were made of cherry. She looked at the sink, perfect also with the shiny brass faucet and fixtures, tall cabinets below, a microwave mounted above, and a cylinder light up at the top. The sink reminded her of the night she came to him with the news about George and Reese dumping the chemicals. Jon was putting in this very sink, or repairing it. She couldn't remember.

She imagined blue and yellow curtains in the windows; the colors would look good with the dark walls. She also imagined flowers. She could see framed pictures, decorative vases, paintings, carpeting here and there; and that was just the beginning.

She wished Jon would show up so she could discuss her ideas with him. Maybe she would move in a few weeks. But first, she needed time to get used to the idea of motherhood. She thought about calling Elbert but decided not to; it was late, and he might be resting. At least the phone was hooked up and ready to go should she need to call Paula. She considered driving back to the farm but decided to wait until the next evening. If Jon didn't show up by then, she'd leave.

She liked the spacious layout of the house, the kitchen counters and deep cupboards. She walked down the hallway past a pantry with steep hickory shelves, two side by side, and a washer and dryer already installed and ready to go. Impressed, she walked towards the bedrooms. The master bedroom was finished, or close enough to it. There was a dresser and a rocking chair; a king-sized bed too— a four-poster with a mahogany frame—a blue and white bedspread over the mattress, and four fat pillows. Mae knew Elbert's mother had made the rugs and bedspread. Elbert had showed Mae many varieties of both items with the same patterns and designs.

Mae opened the top drawer of the dresser to find a stack of papers; they looked like invoices, receipts, tax forms, and so on. On top of the stack was a Christmas card. She opened it, even though she recognized it as the card she sent Jon last Christmas. She smiled at the realization that he kept her card all this time.

She wanted to look at the rest of the house, study the bathroom and the laundry facilities some more, see what he had done with the den and other three bedrooms, but she decided to lie down on the bed for an hour or so. Before she stretched out on the bed, she opened both windows and listened to the night sounds—birds, frogs, and crickets for the most part. She went to the bed to lie down. She watched the breeze lift the dark blue and white cotton curtains until she became drowsy

She thought about the day she had met Jon. He came into the Tennick Credit Union to deposit his check. After he left, she couldn't get him off her mind. She did some investigating and found out he worked as a piececutter for Coulter Logging, the company owned by her current boyfriend's father. Jon kept returning, always to Mae's window. Finally, one day he asked her to meet him after work for coffee. They met for coffee, had dinner a couple of times at the Tennick Bar, but when he found out that she was seeing George Coulter, he lost interest in her. But they did have that night back at his cabin. That night. He knew all about what happened *that* night, thanks to Paula.

The phone rang, startling her out of her thoughts. The phone was over on the table near the door. She got off the bed and walked to the table, pausing to catch her breath before grabbing the receiver. She said hello, but no one answered. She went back to bed and fell asleep, thinking someone had dialed the wrong number.

• • •

Tom Foster hung up the phone and turned to Melanie. "She's there," he said. "Let's hope she stays put."

"Do it now," Melanie said. She had been packing all day and now she was pulling things out of the refrigerator and dumping molded food down the drain of the sink. "I want it done!"

Tom watched her from his chair at the table. He had withdrawn most of his savings; now all he had left to do was pack clothes. He said, "I can't do it right now. Jon might be there. I lifted this new phone number from a paper on his desk."

Melanie wiped down the counter with a dishrag. She detested Tom, the very idea and smell of him, but for now she would use him to the fullest extent. He was crazy enough to start a fire and create a diversion to put Mae Lakarri out of commission.

Melanie moved around the kitchen, wearing bikini underwear and a bra, doing last minute chores. She told Tom as she cleaned, "We should leave now and get a motel room. I told Ellen I was leaving this morning."

"I don't think so," Tom said, picking at the ovals of candle wax that had dripped onto the tablecloth. "I still have to go home and get some clothes. I told Janice I was leaving town to clear my head."

"Let's go to that motel *now*, okay?" Melanie suggested, without even listening to him. "Tomorrow I'll take care of Jon's dad, you take care of his house, and we'll leave at night."

As Melanie searched the room to see if she forgot anything important, they both froze to silence at the sound of an approaching car. Melanie turned on the outside light; she lifted the end of the gauzy red curtain to look out the window. "It's Ellen," she said. "I told her we'd be gone today."

"I'd better hide," Tom howled, jumping to his feet. He sized up the route to the back door and ran into the pantry instead. Melanie wanted to follow him, but knew Ellen had already seen her car. Melanie slipped into a robe and opened the side door that led to a stone path out to the driveway. She smiled when she saw that Ellen had both the boys in the car with her. "I'm so glad you dropped by," she lied, hoping she sounded pleased to see them. "I decided to wait until tonight to leave. Let me see the boys!"

Melanie leaned inside the car to give each boy a kiss. They seemed happy to see her, but it didn't stop them from fussing. Melanie noticed that their hands were covered with chocolate. At that exact moment, she decided she would leave them behind.

"I told you a thousand times," Melanie said, attempting to scold with motherly concern, "don't give them chocolate. It wires them up!"

Ellen kept both hands braced around the steering wheel. She was visibly flustered, pink around the eyes. She said haughtily, "I thought you were leaving this morning. I decided to drop by, thinking maybe you lied to me."

"What do you mean, lied to you? What are you getting at, Ellen?"

Ellen shifted behind the wheel; she was dressed in yellow cotton, with her flesh squeezing out of the seams. Her face was a mask of scorn. "A man came by the house this morning and said you were supposed to start working at his store. He asked me where you were."

Melanie stopped rubbing her youngest son's chin. "A man about a job?" she asked, thinking over the possibilities. "I don't know who *that* could be."

"He knows *you*. He knows Tom Foster, too."

Melanie pulled out of the car window and looked at Ellen as if Ellen were making things up. "Well, that's a lie! I don't know a Tom Foster. What did the man look like?"

"He was good-lookin'—clean cut, mid-thirties. He asked about you and Tom Foster as a couple. I told him I don't know nothing about it. And when he asked if you were planning to leave town, I denied it. You aren't going to leave these precious angels with me, are you?" Her eyes welled up with tears. "*Are* you, Melanie?"

"No! For God's sake! Whoever this man is, I don't know him. I don't know any clean-cut, good-looking men, believe me; not since Lloyd! He's just trying to make trouble. I swear to you, the last thing I need is a job. I've got more money than I know what to do with." She tugged at Ellen's flabby arm. "I told you my plan: I'm going to Wisconsin to visit a girlfriend. We were best friends when I lived there with my parents. She's going to help me relocate. I can't live here anymore!"

Now it was Melanie's turn to cry. She brought tears to her eyes and tipped backwards with dramatic flair. "Oh, I'm sorry," Ellen said, caressing Melanie's shoulder. "I know you're upset about Lloyd. I understand why you want to make a new start. Who wouldn't?"

Melanie continued the crying act. She put her hands over her eyes, but hoped she wouldn't have to conjure up more tears in order to keep Ellen convinced of her despair. "I don't know a man named Tom Foster," she insisted, "or this other man who claims I applied for a job. If it's more money you want, I'll get it for you!"

Ellen glanced into the rearview mirror at the children in the back seat. They were whimpering now, and obviously, it would be best not to start a scene in front of them. She asked Melanie, "You'll be back next week?"

"Yes," Melanie assured her—for what she hoped would be the last time. "I wouldn't leave my sons."

"Call me if you need me," was the last thing Ellen said to her.

From beneath the glow of the porch light, Melanie watched Ellen's car drive away. Ellen waited until Melanie went back inside the house and turned to the left of the yard, where she spotted Tom Foster's truck. He had parked it out of sight, but not far enough behind the shed.

"You liar," Ellen said under her breath. "I knew it. I'm calling the law this time, and you won't make it out of Tennick."

• • •

Soon after Ellen left, Melanie talked Tom Foster into going back to the motel. They rented the same room as the previous night, with the memories of Lloyd still lingering among the drapes and furniture. Melanie had arranged to drive out to Three Cedar Road the next afternoon and take care of Elbert. She'd knock Elbert out, or maybe kill him. There's no way she could allow him to become an obstacle. She explained to Tom as they got into bed, "If he has a barn, I'll hide in there and bash him over the head with a two-by-four."

"That's nice," Tom mumbled as he slid both hands under her blouse and tried to kiss her on the neck. "You're such a sweetheart."

"I could smash his head in with a baseball bat," she said, biting her nail while contemplating.

"Just a *sweetheart*," Tom said again. He started licking her ear, her shoulder, her neck. "I like it. We ought to leave now," he said, his voice strained. "Why make it harder by sticking around to burn down someone's house?"

"You want money; then do what I say!" Melanie couldn't control herself. "You want sex—burn what I want burned. Or I'll tell them you set that skidder on fire!"

Melanie thought Tom was going to hit her. He lifted his fist above her face and held it there—longer than he should have—but apparently decided better of it. "You're *crazy*," he said again. "A crazy hell-cat! Looney bitch! I should have known you'd turn on me!"

"Just burn Jon's house and make sure she's in it. That's all I want from you! Then we'll leave, and you'll get whatever you want!"

"I'll get whatever I want *now*," he said, licking her again. "And later on, too! Fires don't come cheap. I could end up behind bars thanks to this fucking whim of yours!"

"George is dead. The father of my children was brutally murdered! I'd hardly call that a whim, you bastard!"

Tom laughed and pressed a hand against her mouth. His eyes clouded up as if he were overcome with a vile infection. His scorched skin highlighted the sawdust in his eyebrows and hair. "The father of your children," he mimicked in a high voice. "Like you wasted a minute of your time mourning *him*?"

Melanie watched Tom's eyes as his hand went between her legs and she felt his dirty fingernails scrape her. He had her pinned down and pushed into her so hard. She wanted him dead.

CHAPTER 28

Jon got home the next evening around six o'clock and found Mae's jeep in the yard. Only then did he remember they were to meet the night before. He had Reese with him and parked his truck near the office pole barn. He had decided to come home to change his clothes before they headed over to meet Evans and Peterson.

"Stay here until I get back," Jon told Reese as he stepped out of the truck.

Mae was sitting at the kitchen table. She was sewing a square of red material to a square of blue. She wore a checkered blouse and white shorts. Her hair, tucked into a twist at the back of her head, is what he noticed first.

Her hair was styled differently every time he saw her.

She said, "I've been waiting for you." And bent her head over the material, determined to finish what she had started an hour ago.

Jon didn't know what to tell her. Finding her here was more than he had hoped for; it meant that she trusted him. "Reese is waiting in the truck," he said. "We're going after them tonight."

Mae stitched a few more inches of the material together before putting down her work. "I'll wait here for you," she said.

But she didn't say for how long.

• • •

After Jon changed clothes and told Mae goodbye, he drove over to Elbert's and parked in the driveway at the gate. He asked Reese to wait and leave the motor running. Elbert was in the kitchen, hammering nails into a cabinet beneath the sink where he stored household cleaning items. He was positioned awkwardly at the waist, with one hand braced against the wooden side and the other pounding away with the hammer.

Jon waited for Elbert's gray head to emerge from the cabinet. Elbert had been looking for something; he selected a bag of pasta. "What now?" he asked impatiently. "Neil said something about a timber heist."

"We hope to get them tonight," Jon said. "Bryan Kinnenun's one of them."

Elbert's torso contorted this way and that until he stood upright. "Too bad. Although I never met the rascal."

"Mae's next door. Will you keep an eye on her?"

"Yes. She could have the baby any time now. But you know that, I'm sure!"

"She can have it *after* tonight, Elbert," Jon said. Elbert knew that when Jon was irritated or his conscience intruded, he would call him "Elbert," and if

Jon were at ease, he'd call him "Dad." It had been this way since Jon was eight.

"I want to ask you something," Jon said, changing the subject. "I want to know where my mother is buried. I want to know if she had a funeral."

Elbert put the box of pasta down on the counter and picked up a glass of water to take a sip before speaking again. "I had to respect her sister's wishes and send her remains back to Illinois."

Jon looked out the window at a hummingbird fluttering near a spruce tree, hunting for flowers. "Makes it difficult for me to visit her grave if she's in Illinois," he said. "I suppose she was cremated since she was damaged in the car wreck."

"How did you know she died in a wreck?" asked Elbert. "I never told you that."

"I heard you talking about it to someone. I forget who."

"I had to send her home."

Jon looked Elbert in the eye. "*This* is her home."

"She wasn't happy here," Elbert said, his eyes focused on the tablecloth. "It's best if you don't dwell on it. It's complicated."

"So, she had a sister? I have an aunt maybe and never knew it?"

"The sister, Marie, was older than your mother. She came to visit a couple times after Aubrey died. But then she died too, later, when you were about eleven."

"And my grandparents?"

"Aubrey left home when she was sixteen. Marie said they never heard from her again and didn't know what happened to her until I contacted them when she died. Aubrey told me she had an older sister, and their father died when they were young. The mother died about three years after Aubrey did."

Jon pushed himself up from the table. He had heard enough. He collected his cane and moved towards the door. "Mae's at my house," he repeated. "I'd appreciate it if you'd keep an eye on her. If you can do *that*," he added, thinking how Elbert didn't protect his own wife, Jon's mother.

"You got it!" Elbert said, expecting Jon's anger and ignoring the sarcasm. He lifted out of the chair and headed for the stove to stir a pot of spaghetti sauce. "You'd better get going. You're so *sure* the baby will wait for *you* to be ready!" Elbert turned the burner off under the sauce because Jon was about to, and lowered the wooden spoon down on the counter with a bold smack. "I got a chicken coop to fix," he said, wiping his brow. "I'm going outside."

Jon followed Elbert out the door and down the front steps. It was time to leave and meet with the crew waiting at the logging site, but he wanted to be sure Elbert would look in on Mae.

Jon didn't feel right about insinuating Elbert had been negligent towards his mother. He knew fully well that one person could not make another be a certain way. "So, you'll look in on her in a couple of hours?" he asked of Elbert's rigid back. "You'll go over there?"

"You bet!" Elbert said. He tried to put the subject of Aubrey out of his conscious mind for so long now, the thought of her burning in a car wreck shook him to the core. What was worse was that he sent her ashes back to the Chicago area, when he had wanted to bury them near him, and near her son, in the Tennick Cemetery, or even his yard. His guilt over trapping her in a marriage she didn't want had overshadowed his judgment at the time. He had to let her go, back to her hometown.

All he could do now was focus on the moment. He concentrated on the tools he would need for mending the chicken coop; it was almost nightfall and the chickens would want to roost. He checked his overalls for screws and nails. After walking a few yards towards the barn, he turned to Jon and said, "Be careful, Son."

• • •

Elbert wasn't planning on fixing the chicken coop. After all, he had made several attempts to repair the door and sides during the past few months and decided it was time to build a new one. Nothing lasts forever. He sat down on a stump and shook his head at the heap of two-by-fours. He turned to a group of hens pecking in the dirt for bugs and scattered feed. "In the kettle you go, hey!"

He studied the birch trees surrounding his yard. He noticed the purple and white lupines were in bloom; they thrived in the field beyond the barn. He watched the wild daisies bend, right and left in the breeze. He saw groups of black-eyed Susan as well, and clover dotting his recently mowed yard. The birds—finches and sparrows, and even the hummingbirds—were not in abundance as in previous years; probably due to the over population of cats. However, Elbert rarely saw the cats in his yard. There was only a gray tabby and a tan and white that he fed and somewhat pampered; maybe the others had moved on.

Thinking of Mae's condition brought back memories of Jon's mother. There wasn't much to reminisce over. She was so young, in her early twenties, and they were only together for five years. He cared for her a great deal, more than he had cared for any other woman, ever, in his life. But yes, he had talked her into marrying him, although he knew she didn't love him.

Why do some people force emotion? Attempt to dream up passion? He didn't know the answer and never would. After the fiasco with the bakery owner, Aubrey didn't have anywhere to go. End of story. Or so it should have been. As Elbert had just explained to Jon, she was miserable living in the woods, on Three Cedar Road. She was trapped, she claimed; too secluded and lonely, and one day, she left with that Conley fellow. Elbert, not one to waste time with theatrics or dwell in the aftermath of regret, knew that people couldn't be restrained. If Aubrey wanted to leave, he couldn't stop her.

Elbert loved her, he truly did, but he couldn't make her his prisoner, smother her, or harm her in any way. He couldn't direct her heart. If she stayed—sad and angry—Jon would associate her sadness with himself, thinking she was miserable because of him. Elbert decided to single-handedly take on the responsibility of parenthood.

And now Elbert would become a grandfather. He knew Jon and Mae loved each other, but they weren't good at expressing it. The situation would probably get worse before it got better. Elbert knew this for a fact, just as he had known Jon's mother would leave. He also knew Mae would go into labor that very night.

After the recent conversation with Jon, Elbert was able to solve the mystery of Jon's fear of fire: his constant checking of oven burners, his need for fire extinguishers and smoke detectors in every room, his scowling at the mere sight of a lit match. Now Elbert understood. Jon had overheard Elbert telling someone about Aubrey partially burning in a car wreck and the image had haunted him throughout his childhood, his adolescence, and now into adulthood.

Elbert moved back to the present by studying the trees around him. A persistent breeze caused the flat needles of the cedars—the healing, purification, and protection tree—to tremble, and the flowering tips of the lupines and daisies and dandelions to sway nearly all the way down to the earth. Yes, like Jon, Elbert needed to be surrounded by flowers and trees. He needed to hear the whisper of the maple and aspen leaves, feel a soothing wind on the back of his neck. How odd that after such a warm summer day, the evening turned overcast and threatened rain. The sky was a bluish-purple, and fluffy cumulus clouds had expanded and started to form gray and wispy segments, almost spinning with motion.

Elbert was about to go see Mae when Beau barked somewhere behind him. He stood up quickly, because Beau never barked unless something was wrong.

Elbert listened closely to gauge the location of Beau's bark. He thought it came from behind the shed, or maybe *inside* the barn. Elbert approached the door of the barn, which strangely enough, had been left open. He might have left the door open, but it was his habit to keep it closed. He looked into the shadows, the cool dark corners, and the old red pickup truck, his prized possession. Some day soon he would take it for a spin.

Beau was lying down in a corner. He looked up at Elbert and whimpered again. Then Beau stood up and ran out of the barn, as fast as his old legs could carry him, barely making the corner.

As Elbert was about to turn and go back outside, there was a quick, if not mighty, thump across the back of his head. He lifted a hand by reflex and felt dizzy as his eyesight blurred. He fell to his knees, then onto his side. He lay on the scratchy straw, willing himself to keep his eyes open long enough to see her turn and run out the barn door. Last of all, he heard Beau yelp in the distance.

• • •

Melanie had to park up the road past Elbert's house so that no one would see her car. She ran from the barn, all the way down the driveway. She hoped Mae didn't see her from the house next door; she also hoped there wouldn't be any traffic going by when she stepped out to the gravel road towards her car. Luckily, there were no vehicles and the evening sky became a yellowish - gray gloaming with red and orange colors fusing and fading behind the field.

Sneaking behind the old man's house and hiding in the barn was a complicated ordeal. Then that damned dog came along and she wanted to beat it over the head with the baseball bat. But she realized that the dog would be helpful. He would bark, Elbert would hear him, and wander on back to the barn. Unfortunately, she had to hit the old man rather hard; it might not have been a very smart move to throw the baseball bat in the weeds, but she didn't want to take it with her.

She opened the car door, although her hands were still shaking, and after taking deep breaths, she slid into the front seat. As she explained to Tom earlier, all she had to do was walk back to the old man's barn, wait for him to come inside, and thump him over the head. She hoped she had hit him hard enough to keep him unconscious until Tom had enough time to set the house on fire.

She turned the key in the ignition and drove at a moderate pace. The next step was to get past Jon's house without Mae seeing her car. That shouldn't be too difficult; Jon's house was behind a fortress of trees and set back in from the road. One would have to be standing on the front porch, possibly with binoculars in hand, to see who was driving by and the color and model of the vehicle.

Melanie had been past Jon's house many times before, mostly when she was first acquainted with the chemical dumping scam between Lloyd, George, and Reese. She had scouted the area, thinking someone might be watching Jon or that the authorities assumed Jon was involved because he worked for Lucas Coulter.

After successfully passing Jon's house, she drove down the road, looking for Tom. He was to wait until he saw her drive past; then he was to move onto Jon's property to deliver his part of the plan. As she approached the highway, she knew she should have passed Tom by now. It was nine-fifteen. They calculated that by nine o'clock she should be finished with Elbert.

Finally, when she turned towards the highway she saw Tom's truck—the brown one he didn't drive too often. The truck came from the right and signaled as it turned onto Three Cedar Road. She waited for him to turn and she nodded as he passed her. The nod meant Elbert was out of the picture.

Melanie exhaled and relaxed; things were going to go her way, after all. Tom would burn down the house, and no one would ever know why because she was leaving town. Poor Tom, he really thought she was going to stick around and wait for him to torch Jon's house. She had put it all in motion. The back of her car was packed. She was on her way, not to Wisconsin, but to Minnesota, and no one would ever find her. Ellen would *have* to take her children. They would be better off with her anyway.

Melanie reached for her cigarettes, found them inside her purse between two envelopes of cash. In about an hour, Tom would have set fire to Jon's house and no doubt, he'd get caught. To be on the safe side, she decided to report the fire to the police. They would nab Tom; it would be his word against hers. Besides, she had warned Tom that if he ever made trouble for her, she would tell the police he had been the one to put one of the Coulter's skidders in flames. All they had to do was check his record, and they'd discover that he had been arrested for burglary when he was a teenager.

Melanie drove along for another quarter of a mile before she saw a flashing red light in her rearview mirror. She tried to concentrate on her driving, but knew she had to pull over to the side of the road. Her vehicle might have a burned-out headlight, or could be her turn signal didn't work.

She pulled over and touched up her hair. "Officer," she said, sounding out of breath, when a young cop of about thirty stepped up to the window. "Was I speeding or something? I'm not used to driving at night." She smiled, although he was stone-faced.

He asked, "Melanie McMasters?"

"Yes." But all she could think about was Tom Foster on Three Cedar Road, holding a lit match to a bed of dry weeds.

"You'll have to come back to Tennick for questioning," he informed her in a businesslike manner. He kept an eye on the cigarette between her fingers.

"But why? What for?" Her voice collapsed, and her heart wouldn't stop pounding. Certainly Tom hadn't torched the house this fast, and most assuredly, Elbert hadn't seen her. Not when she was so careful to hit him from behind.

"For charges of child abuse," he said. "Abandonment and neglect. We have a witness who says you left your children."

It took Melanie a few seconds to understand what he had said. Once his words registered, her hands shook out of control and the cigarette fell to the floor between her feet. "You'd better pick that up," he said. "You don't want to burn yourself."

"Ellen," she said out loud. But it was Lloyd she blamed; it was Lloyd she couldn't stop seeing everywhere she went. He betrayed her with that other woman. He loved that other woman more and dared to leave Melanie sick and shattered in the dirt.

CHAPTER 29

Reese was able to stay alert at the beginning of the ten-mile route towards Bissmer Paper Mill. He checked the rearview mirror often. They had carved out a space among the logs for Ron Evans. Rick Peterson had to be ready to radio and instruct the officers riding on parallel roads near the trucking route. Ron Evans was dressed in dark colors, as was Peterson, and the two men he brought with him to the logging site. They had black smeared on their faces. They were armed and wore bulletproof vests.

Jon wanted to carry a shotgun with him in the front of the truck under the seat, but Peterson flat out said no. He warned Jon that if he carried a firearm anyway, the entire plan was off, so Jon agreed he would leave all firearms behind. But Reese didn't, so Reese hid a .38 behind the seat.

They drove the entire route twice before Jon suggested that it probably would be a good idea to check on Evans. Reese pulled over to the side of the road, diesel fumes spewing and hydraulic brakes hissing. "Stay here," Jon told Reese as he climbed down from the passenger's side of the truck and slouched along the shadows with a flashlight and the ever-present cane.

Reese leaned his head back and closed his eyes, listening to the crickets in the weeds and the frogs in the swampy marsh through his open window. They had the CB radio on low so they could listen to the other truckers and pick up information about logging traffic and so forth. But they couldn't communicate with Peterson and his men. He said it would be too risky.

Jon limped back to the bed of the truck. "Everything all right?" he whispered to Evans.

"Yes," Evans said hastily. "But I got poked in the head by a branch on that last turn. Tell him to slow down!"

Jon pushed at a tire with the side of his good foot and walked back to the front of the truck. Reese was messing with the radio but turned it off when Jon appeared. Jon climbed back into the cab of the truck. "Evans says to slow down."

At the advisement to slow down, Reese consulted his wristwatch. "It's ten twenty already and nothing. Let's call it quits."

Peterson had instructed them to turn back if they weren't stopped by Globe One by midnight. They couldn't very well spend the entire night driving up and down the ten-mile trek of this particular logging road. Globe One could be watching, or maybe not. They might decide to hijack the timber another night.

"I don't like it," Reese said dejectedly. "I'm not repeating this back and forth shit, not even one more time!"

Jon said, "Shut up. Drink some coffee."

Neil and Dale were to spread the word that the truck would go out as bait. Jon reflected on the fact that

Dale was spending a lot of time with Neil, almost as if he was trying to replace George. Nonetheless, they made sure Bryan Kinnenun was privy to the plan, as well as Tom Foster, whom they saw briefly at the logging site. Tom Foster checked the equipment over, collected his paycheck, and said he had a long weekend planned with his wife.

Jon climbed back into the truck. He thought about Tom Foster as the truck bumped along the gravel road. He had decided that Bryan Kinnenun was probably involved and had been from the start, but he would be completely surprised if Tom Foster had anything to do with it. Tom didn't seem bright enough, or ambitious enough, to get caught up in a venture this complicated. An affair with Melanie McMasters, yes, but anything more dangerous than cheating on his wife? Jon figured it was unlikely.

Jon asked Reese if he thought Neil and Dale were behind them.

"It's hard to say," Reese mumbled, barely able to stay awake. He looked sick. He was peaked and perspiring. He was also belching a lot. "I seen Neil roll his eyes when Peterson told him to stay clear of the truck," he added, and belched again.

They drove along the bumpy road in silence until Reese asked, "Did you hear that? Something hit my door. There it is again."

"I heard it that time," Jon said, turning.

Reese grasped the steering wheel even tighter. There was a line up of bodies ahead of them on the road, and it was difficult to determine if the obstruction was behind a cluster of flashlights or a small fire. "Christ! *Look* at that!"

"Slow down," Jon said.

Jon noticed that Reese had pressed himself tightly against the worn upholstering and the veins in his wrist and hands pushed outward.

Yet Jon was calm. He was anxious to proceed and get the matter over with. He unzipped his jacket, asking Reese for the gun. Reese reached behind him and pulled out the pistol. He pushed it across the seat towards Jon. When two of the men came forward, Jon picked up the .38 and stuck it inside his belt at his back. He could make out two bodies in the headlights of the truck but didn't recognize either one of them. They wore black paint on their faces and were dressed in gray and green. The men were all the way up to the window on Jon's side of the truck when seven more figures appeared ahead on the road. They all stood in a line, and they were armed with rifles.

"Let's hope Evans is awake," Reese whispered. "Please be awake."

But Jon startled Reese when he leaned sideways against the opened window and yelled, "What the hell is this?" Quickly afterward, he became tongue-tied at the spectacle of bodies and the quality of firearms. He lowered his hand to his belt, thinking he might as well have a squirt gun against the arsenal before him. "Looks like we're finally about to have a conversation with these bastards," he told Reese nervously. Although he was mentally ready.

Jon knew to play this hand carefully. If they suspected he was afraid of them; the confrontation would be over before it started. "What in the hell do you think you're doing?" he inquired again, this time shouting. When Reese muttered *my God* and squirmed in his seat, Jon nudged him in the leg to silence him. "Move out of our way," Jon said, his voice strong.

"Step out of the truck," the tall one said.

Jon looked him square in the eye. "I doubt it." He was mad enough now to be arrogant, and worried enough to pull the arrogance off. But then the tall man lifted his rifle and aimed it for Jon's forehead. "Out!" he repeated.

Jon opened the door and stepped out, barely landing steadily because he had left the cane inside the truck. He knew if they saw him crippled up, another disadvantage would be against them. Now his injury was undeniable. He favored the good leg and leaned back against the truck, thinking, *Any minute now Evans will jump out of the back and spotlights will fill the woods, courtesy of Rick Peterson and his undercover officers. We're not alone. Not alone.*

That was the plan anyway.

The man aimed the rifle at Reese's forehead. "Out of the truck, Jack!" he ordered.

Reese lowered himself onto the ground and was promptly escorted around the front of the truck by one of the armed men until he stood beside Jon. *Whatever you do*, Jon thought of Reese, *don't look back at Evans.*

As if his thoughts were broadcasted through a speaker, the tall man walked the length of the logging truck to the back end, where he aimed his rifle. "Out of the truck!" he yelled. "Hold your weapon high!"

There was the scraping of tree branches, a commotion of feet hitting the ground, and a litany of obscenities before Ron Evans appeared next to Jon, the rifle now aimed at his back. They took Evans's rifle and searched him. *Genius,* thought Jon. Sheer genius how they had painstakingly carved out a box-like area with a chainsaw—after loading the timber onto the truck and chaining it down tightly—with a square hole for Evans to hide inside, camouflaged by the timber itself.

All very brilliant, but it didn't hide Evans completely. "Are you FBI?" the other man asked—not the tall one, but the one with the big hair.

"That's right," Evans said. "Shoot me and you go to prison for life."

"Shoot you and we get silence too," Big Hair said.

At that precise moment, Jon noticed that the big-haired man Neil had mentioned earlier was in the group. He knew they were now face to face with one of the Globe One leaders who had posed as a protestor the day Jon and Casey were bullied off this very road.

Evans said, "Be smart and put down the rifles."

The wrong thing to say, thought Jon. Somewhere to the right, a rifle was fired, and by the time Jon and Evans were able to make sense of what had happened, they noticed that Reese had fallen to the ground. He had been shot in the foot. Reese twisted in the dirt and gravel, screaming incoherently.

When Jon stepped forward to help him, he was stopped by the end of Big Hair's rifle. He said, "Move again, you die." There was no arguing with a 30.06, but when Jon looked over and saw Reese lying in a pool of blood, for the first time since the Globe One situation started, Jon felt helpless. The tall man motioned for another figure in the shadows to move towards Reese. The figure slumped forward, walked up to Reese, and pointed the rifle at Reese's temple. "Pay back," he said.

And that was all Jon needed to hear to identify Bryan Kinnenun standing over Reese, thinking about murdering him in cold blood.

Reese doubled up against the ground, panting hard. Jon knew he had to attempt a diversion or Bryan would shoot Reese. He didn't understand why the Globe One group would allow a cold-blooded murder to unfold, instigated by Bryan, who had joined their cause only to seek revenge against the Coulters. Globe One wanted the timber, to steal it and discard it in order to symbolize their views on environmental maintenance. And they were willing to let Bryan Kinnenun carry out a deadly act of revenge.

Three of the men surrounding the truck proceeded to shoot out the tires. When there was silence again, the tall man told Jon to put his hands on his head and drop to his knees. He told Evans to do the same. Jon and Evans lowered to their knees. Evans wasn't crippled like Jon, but even so, he had trouble functioning.

Nonetheless, Jon kept his attention on Bryan, who kept a steady aim on Reese's chest. Bryan wore the same smeared makeup as the others, but now Jon knew who he was and why he was here. He felt the anger radiate from Bryan's bent spine, like vapors curled among the trees, as if Bryan wanted all to hear: *It's an unforgivable thing—what you did to my father.*

"Roll the logs off the truck into the ditch," ordered the man with the big hair. Obviously, he was the leader, although the taller one had been more talkative up to this point. Four of the men ran to the back of the truck and proceeded to release the lever that loosened the chains securing the logs to the sides of the bed. The clanking movement distracted the man with the all the hair, and the tall one as well. They watched the procedure of log tossing, as if it were a ritual to appease their beliefs.

Jon moved his hand from his head to reach for the pistol tucked inside his belt at the instant Bryan Kinnenun pulled back the trigger of the rifle. Jon aimed the pistol for Bryan's shoulder; next came an explosion of activity. Bryan bolted, and the rifle fired, shooting for Reese's arm, and with that move, Jon nicked Bryan in the shoulder to stop him from firing again. The half-mile area—from one tree line to the other, from the back of the logging truck to the front—became illuminated with floodlights.

The order for everyone to halt came loud and clear. Evans collapsed onto the ground and somehow lifted back up to his feet. Bryan Kinnenun turned to the woods, but one of Peterson's armed men cut him off before he made it ten yards. Peterson strolled up to the middle of the group, as each of his men, dressed in undercover attire, had a rifle pointed at a Globe One member.

Peterson took the .38 from Jon's hand and tucked it inside his own belt. He instructed one of his men to take care of Reese and the rest of them to handcuff the Globe One individuals.

Jon said, "You took your sweet time!"

But it was Ron Evans, the meticulous FBI agent, who came forth to reprimand Peterson. "We all could have been killed, you idiot!" he declared to the barrel of Peterson's rifle, held steady towards the man with the big hair.

Peterson glared hard at the man with all the hair, elusive for so long now; he just couldn't look away. The man had been among the protestors who had stopped Casey and Jon. He had been one of the two—and the other, with the slumped posture, had been Kinnenun—who had kidnapped Dale and Neil. He was the leader of the overall Globe One group, and tonight, he made the mistake of wearing the gold watch, the same watch Neil had detected the night of the kidnapping.

In answer to Evan's remark, Peterson shouted, "I got the man I want right here!"

For what the remark was worth, Jon thought, the fanatics are in custody. Maybe he could run the new business now without worrying about an ambush, an accident, a murder. After the chaos ended, Jon realized Reese's arm was grazed by a bullet. He would consider it fate that Reese was only wounded in the foot and arm. The wounds were minor; he would recover, and Byran Kinnenun had been stopped from committing cold-blooded murder.

After all, seeing his family fall apart when he was a young boy, thought Jon of Bryan, *should have been more than enough to deal with.*

•••

Elbert opened his eyes to the wooden interior of the barn, but the walls and corners were filled with shadows, and he wished he had a flashlight. Then he remembered the lantern he kept near the front door. He grabbed a pitchfork, stuck it into the straw beneath him, and pushed upward to his feet. His head pounded as he moved. There was a bump on the back of his head, but no blood. He steadied himself upright and hobbled out the door. Right before he passed out, he saw a woman run from the barn. She was of average height, with long dark hair pulled back into a braid. She reminded Elbert of someone, but he couldn't recall who, and then he drifted off into unconsciousness. Once outside in the cool night air, he saw that the dusk to dawn light was on above his front door and followed it. Beau was waiting in the path.

"You warned me," he told Beau. The dog followed closely as Elbert headed for his house. "I'm sure glad you're okay."

Beau lay down near the front steps. Elbert was about to climb up the steps when he heard a car engine, or maybe it was a truck. He wasn't certain. The rumbling sound of the engine came from the direction of Jon's house, and then Elbert remembered Mae was over there, and he also remembered her condition. Something told him not to shout out to her, but to walk towards Jon's property for an inspection. First, he decided to go inside the house for a flashlight. He reached across the kitchen table and located one without turning on a light. He didn't want to draw attention to himself, and, before he went back outside, he traded the pitchfork for a double-barrel twelve-gauge shotgun.

Elbert walked down the driveway and cut across a narrow path along a stand of balsam which separated Jon's property line from his own. He suddenly felt quite alert, and happy that whoever had hit him was off aim and only grazed his skull.

The porch light of Jon's house was on, which meant there was no need for the flashlight, but he kept it tucked inside the pocket of his overalls. He heard a shuffling sound from the side of the house near the back porch. He took his time moving in the grass near the driveway, not wanting to take chances by crunching gravel beneath his boots. He noticed that not only was the kitchen light on; so was a light in the far-right bedroom. Mae's jeep was in the driveway. He heard a frantic conversation, but only one voice.

He walked up to the shed, where he saw a man bent over a lantern. The man held a lit match in his fingers and appeared ready to place it to a gasoline-drenched torch. Elbert felt a fierce tug in his chest, thinking that Jon's worst fear had surfaced. Someone was about to burn down his house. And Mae was inside the house, ready to go into labor with Jon's child.

Elbert lifted the shotgun to the side of his cheek and said, "Blow it out!"

Tom jumped at the intrusion, almost dropping the match. "G-g-goddammit!" he yelled, more startled than anything else. "I started up my truck and was about to l-l-leave!"

Elbert approached Tom until the two round holes of the shotgun were approximately a foot away from Tom's nose.

Tom, clearly shaken, made a feeble attempt at humor. "I was about to leave but decided to have me a little cookout," he said, and blew out the match.

"You're cooked all right," Elbert reiterated. "Reach into that shed and hand me a rope."

Tom did as he was told. Elbert's shotgun was proof that Tom didn't have control over anything, anymore, and more than likely, Melanie would have to carry on without him. Obviously, he wouldn't be residing in Wisconsin with her; he'd be doing time in prison.

Elbert cradled the shotgun in the crook of his arm and took the rope. "Turn around," he ordered, and Tom quickly complied.

Elbert leaned the shotgun against the wall of the porch. He used the rope to tie Tom's hands behind his back and looked around inside Jon's shed until he found another one. He was about to tell Tom to walk over to the stairs so he could tie him to a post on the porch when he heard Mae say from the front steps, "Elbert? Is that you? I need to go to the hospital." She was wearing a blue robe and her hair was shaggy around her face.

"Sure," Elbert said. "Give me a minute and we'll be on our way."

Elbert escorted Tom to the porch and up the steps while Mae went back inside for her bag of necessities. Elbert shoved Tom into a chair, the very chair Jon kept on the front porch in case he needed to sit among the trees to think. He proceeded to tie Tom to the chair, tugging on the rope as hard as possible, and oddly enough, Tom didn't complain until Elbert yanked with all his might. This is when Tom became hysterical. "M-melanie McMasters is behind it all!" he screamed, jerking around spasmodically. "S-s-she told me to set fire to Jon's house because of what happened to her husband and her lover, George Coulter! S-s-she paid me to do it and I sat here for three hours, thinking about it!"

Elbert said, "Sure, you did," and brought his handkerchief out of his back pocket to gag Tom's mouth. "Three hours of thinking and you *still* made the wrong decision."

Tired of listening to the groan of the engine, Elbert went to Tom's truck and turned it off. When Mae came back to the porch with her items, he said soothingly, "I got to go get my truck. I'll just be a minute."

Finally, an excuse to use the truck. He knew the time would come. It was the same truck he had driven Jon's mother in to the hospital the night she went into labor. A good thing he kept it filled with gasoline and maintained it well.

He returned to Mae in less than ten minutes. The truck chugged up the driveway, stopping next to Mae. Elbert pushed the door open for her. She was an agile, athletic person and climbed easily into the passenger's side.

"I'm having twins," she told Elbert after putting the bag down at her feet and situating herself beside him. "I couldn't tell Jon. I just couldn't!"

Elbert was pleased he had been right. The fact of twins had been a clear premonition; he had dreamed four times in a row that Mae and Jon were going to have twins. He dug around inside his pocket with one hand and steered with the other. "I know," he said. "Here, have a cigar."

Although Elbert had vowed to quit smoking years ago, he had bought and stashed seven cigars the day after Jon told him Mae was going to have a baby. Elbert knew the baby was Jon's. He just knew. With that thought alone and Mae sitting bravely beside him, he had to take a ragged cloth from between the seat cushions and wipe his damp brow again. His handkerchief, as he recalled, was stuffed inside Tom Foster's mouth.

Elbert had to do a lot of shifting and coaxing of gears, but they moved along Three Cedar Road without too much delay. When Mae started to moan, Elbert tried to comfort her by assuring her that they would get to the hospital in time. But suddenly, she doubled over in pain. She didn't yell or scream, yet it was clear that she was having severe contractions.

Elbert turned left onto the highway. "Hurry," Mae said, "we're not going to make it in time!" And she started to rattle on: "I love Jon, but I couldn't tell him I was having twins. Who wants that, two babies, not one but *two babies*, crying in the night? Two babies to take care of! He won't want *that*!"

"He'll want it," Elbert promised. "Having two at once saves time!" When Mae started to cry, Elbert pushed on the accelerator with his big boot. He knew that the only thing he could do for her now was get to the hospital as soon as possible.

Somehow, Jon would know to meet them there.

• • •

Jon and Peterson had driven Reese to the emergency room of the hospital. Peterson left to deal with the results of the Globe One heist and Jon was elected to stay with Reese. Jon was exhausted from trying to convince Reese that one, he was going to live, and two, it was a flesh wound in the arm and only one bone was splintered in the foot. Three: *Okay, we'll be your family, or at least we'll try.*

Ever since arriving at the emergency room, Reese droned on and on about dying, about his father and brother, and cousin, Lloyd. *Dead,* he screamed. *Dead because of the goddamned chemical dumping, all because of the money involved. Money, it's always about money!* He rambled on about death: the how and why of it; the act of murder in general; the subject of cancer; dementia, and finally, the sheer hideousness of a life cut short. For at least fifteen minutes, Jon listened patiently.

Finally, Jon stood up and turned to the door, relieved to escape Reese, and his hot, suffocating cubicle.

By the time Elbert's truck pulled up to the curb, Jon was sliding quarters into a soda machine in the hallway. Not too far from where Jon stood, Elbert ran into the emergency room entrance, supporting Mae in his arms. "My daughter's in labor!" he told the nurses at the desk. There was a commotion of activity, voices colliding into one another, colors flashing, and before too long, Mae was taken away, leaving Elbert to go back to the desk to use a phone.

After talking with Mae's sister, Paula, and calling the sheriff to report where he had left Tom Foster tied up and gagged, Elbert walked the hallway again, right past Reese's room and back to the soda machine where he bumped into Jon, who was staring like a blind person until he realized, *well, that's Elbert, my father.*

Jon looked at Elbert and shook his head, thinking how that pregnant woman he just saw looked a lot like Mae. "Dad?" he asked.

"Good," Elbert said, taking a deep breath. "You're here."

Jon forgot to push the selection button and turned. "Yes, I'm here," he said. "Reese got shot in the foot and arm. We caught the Globe One ..." But he couldn't finish. He waited for Elbert to explain his presence.

"They rushed Mae off to the delivery room," Elbert said. "I called her sister to let her know."

Jon sat down on the bench next to the vending machines. The excitement of the Globe One heist and now this news was enough to take him down.

But Elbert, understanding Jon's confusion, put a hand on his shoulder. "Mae loves you," he said. "She *told* me. Now you go tell her the same."

"I'll try," Jon said.

"You'll *try*? No, no! Son! You'll go *do* it!" Elbert reached into this pocket and pulled out a cigar. He had two more saved in the glove compartment of the truck: one for Dale and one for Neil.

Jon studied the cigar. Leave it to Elbert to think of handing out cigars. Leave it to Elbert to remind him that it was time to *get with it.* Jon put the cigar into his shirt pocket and wiped his damp palm against the front of his shirt. "She came to see the house," he said. "I still can't believe it."

Elbert's attention shifted from Jon's leg up to eyes similar to his own. "You can walk without your cane now."

Jon didn't realize he had left the cane in the truck. He had been walking on his own, for how long? Since helping Reese get to the hospital? He was in a hurry, that was it. And all he could think about was getting Reese settled and going home to Mae. Clearly, the absence of the cane was something significant to think about. Later.

Right now, he needed to focus on what Elbert was saying.

As if to pause Elbert's speech, a nurse came over with news. "Your daughter's fine." Then she smiled at Elbert. "And so are your granddaughters. Someone is the father of twins."

"That's him," Elbert said, patting Jon on the back. "My son. He's right here!"

Jon watched a flutter of legs and arms disappear around the corner. "She said *twins*. What the—"

Elbert leaned in closely. "Don't worry, I'll teach them how to cook and you'll never go hungry. Now go see Mae, but first buy her roses at the gift shop downstairs. Go on!"

Jon was grubby from the timber heist ordeal, but he didn't have time to worry about his appearance. He had to face Mae and give her the diamond ring he bought before his accident. But the ring was back at his house on Three Cedar Road, hidden in a cup. He thought about leaving the hospital and going back to his house to get it, but Elbert was watching him, closely. Elbert knew Jon better than anyone. If Jon left now, he would not come back. Find the elevator and go downstairs to the giftshop or head for the door marked *Exit*? Jon stood up.

And decided, *Buy her roses, for now.*

Made in the USA
Columbia, SC
18 May 2019